Cross Your Heart and Hope to Die

Other Books in the
Blackbird Sisters Mystery Series

How to Murder a Millionaire

Dead Girls Don't Wear Diamonds

Some Like It Lethal

"Slay Belles"
in Mystery Anthology *Drop-Dead Blonde*

Cross
Your Heart
and Hope
to Die

A Blackbird Sisters Mystery

Nancy Martin

 NEW AMERICAN LIBRARY

New American Library
Published by New American Library, a division of
Penguin Group (USA) Inc., 375 Hudson Street,
New York, New York 10014, USA
Penguin Group (Canada), 10 Alcorn Avenue, Toronto,
Ontario M4V 3B2, Canada (a division of Pearson Penguin Canada Inc.)
Penguin Books Ltd., 80 Strand, London WC2R 0RL, England
Penguin Ireland, 25 St. Stephen's Green, Dublin 2,
Ireland (a division of Penguin Books Ltd.)
Penguin Group (Australia), 250 Camberwell Road, Camberwell, Victoria 3124,
Australia (a division of Pearson Australia Group Pty. Ltd.)
Penguin Books India Pvt. Ltd., 11 Community Centre, Panchsheel Park,
New Delhi - 110 017, India
Penguin Group (NZ), cnr Airborne and Rosedale Roads, Albany,
Auckland 1310, New Zealand (a division of Pearson New Zealand Ltd.)
Penguin Books (South Africa) (Pty.) Ltd., 24 Sturdee Avenue,
Rosebank, Johannesburg 2196, South Africa

Penguin Books Ltd., Registered Offices:
80 Strand, London WC2R 0RL, England

First published by New American Library,
a division of Penguin Group (USA) Inc.

NEW AMERICAN LIBRARY and logo are trademarks of Penguin Group (USA) Inc.

ISBN 0-451-21395-5
Printed in the United States of America

In fond memory
of
Bernard Lefkowitz

Acknowledgments

The Renaissance Hotel in Pittsburgh is one of the most delightful hotels you'll ever enjoy. Barbara McMahon and her top-notch staff will make you feel welcome and pampered. I couldn't have finished this book without them all.

It was my friend Lisa Curry who came up with a brilliant title. And at the last hour Sandy Stephens dashed to my rescue, along with Meryl Neiman.

The other members of the Mary Roberts Rinehart chapter of Sisters in Crime have all offered support and lunches out. Thank you, Gina Sestak, Joyce Tremel, Kristine Coblitz, Cyn Crise, Becky Mertz, Mary Alice Gorman, Cynnie Pearson, Judith Evans Thomas, Jan Yanko, Judy Burnett Schneider and Mike Crawmer. See you in Deep Creek!

The real Monte Bogatz is a perfectly nice person, no kidding. Thanks for the use of your name, Monte! Hope your friends and family aren't horrified. The real Sue Mandell and her generous husband Steven Steinbock deserve many thanks for their contribution to RICA. Surprise, Sue!

As always, deepest heartfelt appreciation to Ramona Long and Sarah Martin—my first readers. And if I haven't mentioned them lately, Ellen Edwards and Meg Ruley are the best team in the biz. Thanks, girls.

And Lyle Lovett? You inspired me, honey.

Chapter One

I was still in bed recovering from Christmas, when the phone rang.

On the other end of the line, I heard the roar of a chain saw. No, on second thought it was the voice of my boss, Kitty Keough.

"Get your coat, Sweet Knees," she squawked. "And get your ass into the city right away. I need you to cover a fashion show that starts in less than an hour."

"Kitty," I said, "I could use a little more warning when it comes to assignments."

"Oh, barf," she shouted in the same dulcet tones as before. "Are you whining? Because nobody's going to kiss your tiara in the newspaper business, honey. You want to stay at home and count silver spoons? Or you want to get paid this week?"

I could hear the blare of traffic in the background and figured she was phoning from a taxi that careened through the snowy streets of Philadelphia, speeding Kitty to a high-society party that somehow outrivaled the assignment she was tossing over her shoulder to me. No doubt her brassy blond hair was blowing in the wind and she was whipping her driver with the moth-eaten feather boa she carried to formal events in the misguided belief that it lent glamour to her appearance. "Quit playing footsie with the Mafia Prince and get your butt in gear."

"He's not—" I stopped myself from giving her further ammo to use against me and reached for a pen. "All right, give me the details."

Which is why I threw a fur coat over my nightgown, slipped on a pair of Chanel boots and headed out for an evening that promised to be legendary. It was go, or lose my job.

And oh, baby, I needed the job.

I applied lipstick and three coats of mascara while my sister drove into Philadelphia. Michael had other business to tend, so I'd called Libby to go with me. On the way, she told me about her new business venture.

"Donald Trump says a successful entrepreneur has to be passionate about what she does," she informed me as she fearlessly drove her minivan through the snow.

"What does that mean?"

"So I found my passion. My greatest wish is to electrify the romantic relationships of everyone I know."

"Electrify? Sounds like you're selling vibrators."

"At Potions and Passions, we call them intimacy aids."

I nearly scratched my cornea with the mascara wand. "You're kidding, right?"

"Adult products are a booming business! I'm an official Potions and Passions consultant now. I get my first shipment of sex toys this week. Except we're supposed to say erotic enhancements." With a charmingly demented smile, she asked, "Don't you want to know what the buzz is about?"

While she laughed, full of delight and adventure, I said, "Libby, why couldn't you pay off your Christmas debt by going to work as a telemarketer or something? You could sell lawn mowers to bedouins!"

"I'm not passionate about lawn mowers. I am passionate about sex."

Cross Your Heart and Hope to Die

For Libby, the path to self-fulfillment was a long, winding highway with many roadside attractions. Still a few years shy of forty, she already had five children, each one a life-affirming holy terror. She visited the graves of two husbands and at least one "very dear friend." Before her children were born, Libby had been a rising painter, not to mention a founding member of the local erotic yoga society. But nowadays she was always flinging herself into diversionary pit stops that sometimes made me long to strangle her.

"Anyway," she said, "I need to make a living. I hate being penniless, don't you?"

Poverty was new to both my sisters and me. Groomed for debutante balls and advantageous marriages, we had been badly burned when our parents lit a match to the Blackbird family fortune. They spent our trust funds faster than drunken lottery winners could buy a fleet of Cadillacs, then ran off to South America to practice the nuances of the tango.

Mama and Daddy left me to cope with Blackbird Farm—a difficult challenge in itself with its crumbling roof and ancient plumbing. But the $2 million debt of back taxes really threw me for a loop. Maybe it's an old-fashioned notion, but I couldn't let the family legacy be bulldozed to make room for a Wal-Mart, so I sold everything I could to start a tax repayment plan, and then I ventured gamely into the world of employment for the first time in my life.

Okay, so I hadn't been reduced to eating out of Dumpsters, but my lifestyle went from frocks and rocks to macaroni and cheese in a hurry. I had to get a job. My blue-blooded ancestors were probably rolling over in the Blackbird mausoleum, but now when Kitty Keough, the society columnist for the *Philadelphia Intelligencer*, called, I came running.

"Why can't Kitty go to this big-deal fashion show herself?" Libby asked. "It's just her kind of thing, right? Famous people sucking up and free goody bags, too? Why send her assistant instead?"

"I don't know. She didn't say. It's probably part of her plot to get me fired. But I have to go, don't I?" I tucked the mascara back in Libby's handbag and checked my watch. "And it starts in ten minutes."

"We'll get there," Libby promised, flooring the accelerator of her minivan. Snow blasted the windshield, but my sister showed no fear. Expertly, she dodged potholes and checked her cell phone for messages from prospective customers. "Meanwhile, we can plan your Potions and Passions party."

"My what?"

"A home-based presentation to help today's woman satisfy her innermost desires and express her feminine freedoms. See? This is the company bracelet." She waved a stainless-steel band under my nose.

"That's a funny-looking bracelet, Lib."

"It's a little plain, I'll admit. And tight. But I wear it proudly. I'm going to be the best damn Potions and Passions consultant ever."

I was still looking at the bracelet. "Is it meant to go around a wrist?"

"Where else would it go? We have an extensive product line of sensual candles, stimulating gels, educational items and, of course, our patent-pending ErotaLotion. Which has a divine texture, and even heats your skin. Can you smell the fragrance?"

"That's you?" I asked, thinking she had forgotten a gallon of Christmas eggnog in the back of the minivan.

"If you host a party in your home, I can give you a ten percent discount on the first hundred dollars you spend. And the parties are fun. We play games with the products."

"Sounds like Tupperware for porn stars."

"Exactly! And doesn't everyone secretly want to be a porn star?"

"Uh—"

"We'll talk to some of your friends about hosting Potions and Passions parties, too. My calendar is wide-open."

"Lib, my friends aren't exactly your core customer group."

"That's where the party comes in. I can teach them! I'm a born instructor when it comes to sex. It'll be great. Hang on," she cried. "Here's our exit!"

She yanked the minivan across two lanes of heavy traffic and scooted down the exit ramp to the blare of horns behind us. "Oh, rats," she said. "I meant to bring you some photos I took at Christmas. They turned out really well."

As exasperating as my sister could be, she always melted my heart with acts of kindness interspersed with her usual lunacy. Underneath her ditsy exterior thrummed a heart of purest gold.

The snow lightened as we abandoned her minivan with a parking valet. Then Libby led the way to the door, her coat wide-open to reveal a leopard-print sweater with a neckline that plunged all the way to Panama. I said a quick prayer for my dignity and followed.

A splashy fashion show wasn't my usual beat. In my job I usually covered B-list events—quiet garden club luncheons, civic awards banquets, the occasional reception where Old Money philanthropists gave money to worthy but unfashionable causes. Kitty tended to nab the high-profile parties for herself.

So I followed my sister through the mob of the fashionably thin, wondering why Kitty gave up a red-carpet night to me.

"Keep in mind," Kitty had lectured me early in our working relationship, "I'm the boss and you're my assistant. You do what I say, or you can go back to drinking tea with the Kelly family."

I chose not to tell her that the Kellys weren't big tea drinkers, knowing that my insider knowledge really lit Kitty's fire. Instead, I did whatever she ordered me to do.

For such a special fashion show, people had gussied up in their fanciest finery, and the resulting clothes could sprain an eyeball. Local Philadelphia TV stations filmed artsy tarts dressed in chic tatters as well as the dowagers in their winter tweeds and Hermès scarves. After their fifteen seconds of fame, everyone pressed past the cameras toward the entrance of a formerly grungy warehouse that had been dolled up for the occasion.

"Are those the gift bags?" Libby shouted over the noise and music. She pointed to a scrum of well-dressed hunter-gatherers, all yelping like hyenas as they snatched goodies from a frightened assistant.

"You could lose an arm in that mob," I said, properly prudent.

"You're too dainty to use your elbows, I suppose. I'll see what I can do."

"Godspeed."

While Libby dashed off to grab the giveaway treats, I noted the warehouse had been lit up brighter than a Broadway premiere. Jewelry glittered, smiles sparkled. Rock-and-roll music thundered. And Kitty was going to be furious when she found out what she'd missed.

Most dramatic of all, video images spun around us—on the walls, ceiling and bodies of the guests. Everywhere, we saw dancing pictures, moving, vibrating, undulating. Around me, people reacted to the images eerily reflected on themselves. A woman flinched at a rush of spiders that swept over her. A genteel man laughed as nude girls danced on the face of his companion. A tangle of naked limbs washed across a threesome of shocked ladies. The place was ground zero for Philadelphia's artistic and social elite.

A huge logo had been painted on the rear wall. The designer's name.

Brinker.

Everywhere, the logo flashed at us. And with the logo smirked

Brinker's face—steely-eyed, lantern-jawed and sneery-lipped. For a man on the edge of fame and fortune, he looked contemptuously down on the people who had come to buy his designs. By tomorrow, the whole world was going to know his name, but his photograph conveyed how pleased he was to inflict a torturous new fashion on womankind.

Brinker Holt, fashion phenomenon.

Brinker Holt, son of a bitch.

At the end of the velvet rope, a thug in full biker regalia guarded the guest list. Reptilian tattoos crawled around his thick neck and down his muscled arms. But despite his air of menace, he wore the new ubiquitous badge of authority at fashion events, an electronic headset.

The bruiser took my press pass and made a show of glowering at it as if I were smuggling explosive shoes into an airport. "Just a minute," he growled at me, then pulled his microphone close and spoke into it.

"Problem?" a voice asked from behind me as I waited for the gatekeeper's verdict.

I turned around and found myself staring at Richard D'eath.

"You're Nora Blackbird, right?"

We had been introduced only once or twice, and he'd given me the brush-off as soon as he learned I wasn't a journalism school grad. "It's nice to know I'm memorable," I said dryly. "Hello, Richard."

Okay, I'll admit Richard D'eath was good-looking. Handsome, even, if I were completely honest. But it was his reputation as an unstoppable New York newspaperman—bolstered by years of waging war on gangbangers, corrupt union leaders and at least one politician who tried to have him killed—that really made him drop-dead delectable. He was a defender of the innocent and downtrodden, the kind of man you half expect to run into a phone booth to don his cape now and then.

Lately, though, Richard had been sidelined from his superhero crusade by injuries suffered in a dark New York alley while chasing down . . . well, not a story but a cab. Which ran over him and left him barely mobile. After eight months of treatment at the hands of a renowned Philadelphia specialist, Richard was still hobbling around with a cane, although he looked frustrated enough to break it over one knee and hurl the shattered pieces into a blazing fire.

He wasn't exactly Mr. Congeniality.

Richard leaned on the cane in front of me. "Are you here to breach the fortress of fashion?"

I heard the disdain in his voice, but endeavored to sound as pleasant as I could manage. "I left my sword at home."

"Too bad. Even you might need to protect yourself in this crowd."

The leading newspaper in Philadelphia had jumped at the chance to hire Richard for the short term while he recovered from his surgeries. I'd heard he took the job to keep busy while he healed—at first writing from a bed and finally using a cane to do the legwork—making it clear that as soon as he could go back to his old life in a real city, he'd be history. He quickly found his niche exposing criminals and local politicians gone bad, but I heard he still hankered for the more exciting action of his old life. In the meantime, he couldn't be bothered to mingle with amateurs.

"You have a pass to get into this thing?" he asked, his attention already wandering to the hectic scene around us.

"Yes, I do."

"Can you get me inside? My press pass isn't good enough. I guess nobody wants any real reporters here."

"Why, Richard. Do you hang out at the local Victoria's Secret, too?"

His gaze snapped back to me. "I'm not here to ogle supermodels. I'm working."

"When did you decide to leave the stratosphere and wade around the Style section?"

He gave an impatient sigh. "I just want to get inside. Can you do it?"

Libby returned to us at that moment, flush with the triumph of hand-to-hand combat. "Gift bags, and they're loaded with goodies!" she cried. "Oh, look! Hooray!"

With a delighted yelp, she came up with the prize—a pink plastic silicone figure eight.

"What in the world . . . ?"

The three of us stared at the contraption that Libby dangled from her forefinger.

"What the hell is it?" Richard asked.

"You don't know?" I said. "It's the reason everybody's here. It's the Brinker Bra."

"The what?"

Libby said, "I don't get it. This isn't a bra. Where are the straps? The hooks? And I definitely need a bigger size."

"Jesus," said Richard. "That's what this show is for? Underwear?"

"The Tempest in a C-cup," I said, recalling the press release. "A revolutionary design made of a new silicone material engineered to cling to human skin. The figure-eight shape provides support for the female body. No need for straps or uncomfortable wires. One size molds to fit all and makes every woman perfect. It's going to revolutionize lingerie."

Libby continued to look confused. "It looks like a child's toy. Like a miniature, twisted-up hula hoop. How is this thing a bra?"

"Panty hose seemed weird at first, and now we never think of using garters."

"Speak for yourself," said my sister. "At Potions and Passions, we believe—"

"Libby, I'd like you to meet Richard D'eath."

Until that moment, my sister's usually superb testosterone radar had failed her. And when Libby finally became aware of Richard, she was struck dumb by his male physique, never mind the cane. Her gaze grew large and lustrous as she drank in his long-legged handsomeness. Within a heartbeat she regained herself and managed to communicate her willingness to give Richard a lap dance on the spot.

"Hello," Richard said, impervious to my sister's seductive bosom. Then to me, "Is this how you aristocrats spend your free time? Going to underwear shows?"

"As a matter of fact, I'm working, too."

"The intrepid society columnist always chases the most important stories, I suppose."

Libby's eyes had begun to narrow. "Nora's not the columnist. That's Kitty Keough's job, although most of us feel the best thing Kitty could do is drop dead and let Nora take over."

"Libby," I said.

"Well, it's absolutely true." She faced Richard with her jaw jutting as stubbornly as her breasts. "My sister does a wonderful job at the *Intelligencer,* so you can climb down off your high horse, mister."

Richard didn't bother to respond. "Look," he said to me, "if you can't get me into this thing, I'll find somebody who can."

I hated that he could be so dismissive of my sister, and the fact that he looked so damn heroic made it even worse.

"I might be able to get you into the fashion show," I conceded. "But you're going to have to tell me why. I won't aid and abet some kind of fetish."

"Forget it. I'll find another way in. I just thought you might want to do something right for a change."

"For a change?" Libby demanded. "Since when do you get off

insulting my sister? Nora is here to support a charity event. Breast cancer awareness is—"

"Charity event? This is a PR extravaganza, pure and simple. They'll use any excuse to promote their product, even a disease."

I said, "Do you want to go inside with us—yes or no?"

He wanted to say no, but obviously his nose for news was twitching. "Yes."

So I turned to the biker, who was still muttering into his headset. I plucked my press card from his hand and leaned close to whisper, "Keith, dear, I love the tattoos, but your mom is going to have a seizure when she sees them."

Keith Rudnick, a part-time actor and full-time waiter at my favorite lunching spot, broke character and winked at me. "They're temporary, darling, and she helped pick them out," he whispered back. "Now, look, we've been ordered not to allow Kitty Keough inside. Straight from Brinker—no Kitty."

"How weird."

"Yeah, he hates her guts. But you're not on the nix list, so I'm trying to get you a seat close to the action. If we'd known you were coming, we'd have front-row center waiting. But at this late hour—"

"I don't need special treatment, Keith. Anywhere's fine."

"But you look so divine, we want to show you off. And I presume Mr. Hunkalicious is with you?"

"Hunkiness is only skin-deep, Keith. Can you seat all three of us? Not necessarily together." I didn't feel the need to see the show with Richard.

"Only in the second row," Keith said. "I'm *so* sorry."

"It's perfect. I owe you a favor of your choosing."

He hesitated, then began to look like a kid who'd just found one more present under the Christmas tree. "Let me borrow your

Lagerfeld wrap for the Gay Pride parade? The one with the koi motif?"

"It's yours."

"Three seats coming right up!" Going butch again, he summoned one of his similarly costumed colleagues. Ten seconds later we were through the curtains and into the bedlam of the Brinker Bra fashion show.

Chapter Two

*T*his," Richard muttered beside me, "is crazy."

The Brinker Bra had made headlines even before its official launch into retail stores. With no underwires, cups, straps or any of the traditional corseting elements, the bra created the now famous "push and plunge" form desired by every woman between the ages of twelve and two hundred. It was a work of genius, touted by architects, engineers and fashionistas alike. The fashion world had come to Brinker's doorstep to see its official unveiling.

In hot pursuit of our usher, Libby called over her shoulder, "C'mon! The show's going to start any minute!"

We were bombarded by the combined music and noise of several hundred people jammed into the space. To reach the center of the tightly packed second row, we first climbed over the laps of three bejeweled women who looked seriously displeased about getting stuck in the dreaded second row. Next came a lineup of young aristocrats who all clutched their programs and chattered like kids at the circus. Richard struggled to climb over their perfect knees. I dared not ask if I could help him. I doubt I could have made myself heard over the music anyway.

We squashed into our seats—second row, but dead center—and found ourselves surrounded by exotically dressed bodies in rows of gilt folding chairs, all facing the runway in a theater-in-the-round configuration. Milling behind us like lions ready to devour the Christians was a pride of roaring photographers.

As Richard sat down, his cane thunked the back of the head of the man sitting in front of him.

The man leaped up, clutching his head, and spun around. "What the hell are— Why, Nora!" His voice was too musical. "It's Nora Blackbird!"

It was all I could do not to call him by his teenage nickname.

"Hemmings," I said, although *Hemorrhoid* danced on the tip of my tongue.

Hemmings Pierce, immaculately groomed, wore the current uniform of the urban male narcissist—tight pants riding low on his hips, Prada shirt unbuttoned enough to reveal a hint of waxed, moisturized chest, narrow shoes with stainless-steel buckles. His hair was carefully mussed and his manicure was perfection. I knew him as my college roommate's pain-in-the-butt kid brother who had a horror of germs. Although he was all grown up now, he still had a sly, darting look in his eyes, as if plotting to catch a glimpse of me in the shower.

"How long has it been, Nora? You look beautiful."

I held my coat tightly closed and leaned down for him to give me two air kisses. "Hello, Hemmings," I said. "It's been ages."

"Since my sister's wedding, I think. Oh, dear, you have a thread!"

"A what?"

He reached into his pocket and withdrew a tiny pocketknife, which he flipped open to a scissors attachment. "Allow me," he said, and pounced on one of the oversize buttons. Between thumb and forefinger, he nipped a tiny thread that had been hanging from the button, then snipped it off with a single cut with the miniscissors. "There! Perfect. Don't you look amazing now? Where did you get this fabulous coat?"

"I . . . It was my grandmother's."

"I remember her. She kept a diary of her clothing so she'd never be seen twice in exactly the same ensemble. I use the same method myself. What a gal!"

For being called a "gal," my grandmother would have whapped him upside the head with a Burberry umbrella and left him in the exhaust of her departing silver Bentley.

"I didn't realize you knew my grandmother, Hem."

"Of course I did!" Even over the roar of music, he sounded false.

My job required a wardrobe of party-suitable clothing, which, unfortunately, I could no longer afford to buy for myself. So I mixed my old clothes with pieces raided from the closet of Grandmama Blackbird, who had in her lifetime amassed one of the world's finest collections of couture and matching accessories. She had gone to Paris and Milan twice annually for fifty years, so I possessed an astonishing selection of beautiful things to wear as long as I didn't move too strenuously and took care to reinforce the seams. In haste tonight, I had dug out Grandmama's chinchilla swing coat, dyed Schiaparelli pink and sporting three large black Bakelite buttons down the front. It covered my nightie quite modestly, thank heavens. I only hoped the antifur advocates weren't on the prowl tonight.

Hemorrhoid folded up his pocketknife with military precision and tucked it back into his pocket. "Have you met my nephew, Orlando?"

If he hadn't spoken the child's name, I never would have recognized the boy sitting beside him. Hemorrhoid goosed him to stand and face me, and the child complied sullenly. He'd gained forty pounds and grown several inches since I'd seen him last—perhaps two years ago, before his mother died.

"Why, yes. Hello, Orlando. Last I saw you, it was your birthday."

The boy stopped glaring at his handheld computer game only long enough to send a surly glance up at me. "Who are you?"

"Nora Blackbird. I was your mother's friend."

"I don't have birthday parties anymore. They're for kids."

Hemorrhoid put his hands on Orlando's shoulders and tried to straighten his posture. "Be polite to Miss Blackbird, now."

"Why?"

"Because she can write good things about you in the paper."

Hem tried to grab the game from the child's hand, but Orlando evaded him with a practiced maneuver.

During our junior year in college, my dear friend and Philadelphia heiress Oriana Pierce had married Randall Lamb, an aptly named sheep farmer whose family owned a textile conglomerate and half of New Zealand. Theirs was the most spectacular wedding I'd ever attended. The very young bride and her starry-eyed groom stood on a glorious promontory overlooking the Pacific and spoke poetry to each other as if the rest of us were hundreds of miles away. We all drank a champagne toast and threw our glasses into the rocky sea. Afterward the happy couple took off in a helicopter that flew them to the Lamb yacht for a three-week honeymoon cruise.

I'd never seen anyone so ecstatic to share the news of her pregnancy when I met her in New York a few months later. To celebrate, I'd taken Oriana to Le Cirque for lunch—very chic for a couple of young women. Oriana dropped a buttered roll on Henry Kissinger's shoe, but he graciously accepted her giggling apologies and sent a bottle of wine to our table.

But on a scuba diving trip to the Great Barrier Reef several years later, both Oriana and Randall disappeared, presumably drowned. They were never found, and now here was Orlando, a pale lump of an angry ten-year-old stuck with his anal-retentive uncle.

Orlando's hair had been cut to look just like Hemorrhoid's, and his clothing was clearly chosen by a stylist trying to give the kid a persona that didn't fit. Wool pants looked far too adult on his doughy frame, and the silk shirt, worn Mick Jagger style over a T-shirt, read GIVE BLOOD. PLAY RUGBY.

But I couldn't imagine Hemorrhoid allowing the boy to play any game more strenuous than checkers—and that only if the game pieces were disinfected first.

Hemorrhoid straightened Orlando's rumpled shirt collar. Orlando held still for the fussing, but his face was shuttered.

Unable to decipher how he was feeling, I said cheerily, "How have you been, Orlando? I understand you go to school in New Zealand now."

"We're on break," he snapped.

"Of course. I didn't mean—"

"This is Orlando's first fashion show," Hemorrhoid intervened. "I thought he ought to start learning something about the family trade before he takes over the company in a few years, don't you agree?"

"I thought Lamb Limited was textiles."

"At the moment, yes." Hem twinkled with a secret. "But who can guess about the future in this age of diversification?"

"I see."

"I hear you're scribbling great things for the *Intelligencer* now."

"Why, thank you—"

"Why don't you mention my name in your next piece? I've changed it, you know. I'm calling myself Hemmings Lamb now, just to make things easier to raise my wonderful nephew. I think my sister would approve, don't you?"

I thought I could hear Oriana screaming from her grave.

Hemorrhoid was too busy scanning the crowd for more useful networking contacts to notice my reaction. "Well, enjoy the show. Catch you afterward!"

He sat down, and I saw him sharpen the crease in his trousers with his fingers.

I sat down, too, wedging myself into the seat between Richard, who had overheard every word, and Libby, who was still busily foraging through her gift bag.

More to himself than to me, Richard said, "This is worse than Pamplona."

I resisted the urge to remark about running with bullshit. "Your first fashion show?" I asked instead, conscious that we were hip-to-hip and entwining elbows for lack of space.

Richard bumped my chin with his cane, then stowed it between his knees without apology. "I suppose you feel at home here."

"You might be surprised."

"Don't bother denying it. You even knew the secret handshake to get in. These people are your kind."

"These people?" I repeated. "My kind?"

"You know what I mean. Hoity-toity." He indicated Hemorrhoid with a nod. "The ones who care about Rolexes and fancy labels on their clothes."

"And nothing approaching brains or social conscience, Mr. Gandhi?"

"Come on. You don't believe that breast cancer smoke screen, do you? You weren't born yesterday."

"Thanks," I said tartly.

He shrugged. "People talk in newsrooms. You're not brainless."

"Here," I said, thrusting a program at Richard in hopes of shutting him up. "Read about Brinker Holt."

He took the program and looked at the cover photo. The designer of the Brinker Bra sat astride a motorcycle with his trademark camera in hand. Three startlingly endowed models swooned around him. "You know this Brinker guy?"

"As a matter of fact, I do."

"What's his story?"

"You mean his latest incarnation?"

"He has incarnations?"

I wanted to shut myself up, but I couldn't. "Brinker is always reinventing himself in an effort to be famous. For a while, he owned a comedy club. Upchuckles."

"How Noël Coward."

"His comedy act was just as sophisticated. He showed videos of people while he ridiculed them. Like *Candid Camera,* only less high-brow. About a year ago the club burned down. I like to think it was a random act of human kindness by an arsonist with good taste. Anyway, now he's a lingerie designer."

Richard pointed at the photo. "He hardly looks like the fashion type."

"Fashion isn't pretty girls in lace anymore. A successful designer needs a shtick, a concept, an identity. Brinker has always thought of himself in marketing concepts, so maybe he has a shot."

"How long have you known him?"

I hesitated. "Our families associated."

Richard turned a wry look on me. "Associated where? The polo grounds?"

"A bathing club," I said coldly.

"So you sipped mint juleps in a hot tub with this guy?"

"It was a swim club, a private pool. And lemonade, actually. I could use some now. It's hot in here." I fanned myself with my program.

"So take your coat off."

I refrained from stripping down to my nightgown and found myself thinking of the Holt family instead. Their money came from a gear needed in all movie cameras, and they lived the high life thanks to an old patent. Brinker's father wore bow ties and could get drunk by sniffing a cork. Mrs. Holt smoked Virginia Slims, loved ballroom dancing and spent so much time on cruise ships that they eventually sold their Main Line estate and bought a suite of rooms on a condominium ship that sailed around the world with an orchestra that never quit and a cocktail bar that never closed. Before they set sail, they kicked Brinker off the estate and out of their lives for assorted transgressions. In retaliation, he set fire to his Porsche and became a comedian, starting with home movies of his parents.

Richard tapped the picture again. "Looks like Brinker is trying to forget his aristocratic roots. The motorcycle, the scruffy beard. He's gone blue-collar on you."

"On me? We're barely acquainted."

"He likes bikes, though?"

"I have no idea. Why?"

Richard shrugged. "I like to know things about people. It may be a way to get close later."

At that moment, the two of us were as close as two people could get without discussing condoms. And I suddenly became aware that Richard D'eath smelled good. The heat of his leg against mine felt alarmingly intimate, too.

I pulled away quickly, and he pretended not to notice. Thank heaven the roar of motorcycles exploded in the air. The crowd around us shouted and applauded as the lights went down. Then a Harley burst out from behind the black curtains and thundered onto the runway, controlled by a young woman almost entirely naked. Immediately behind her came a steady stream of equally stunning girls, all precariously balanced on high-heeled biker boots, wearing thong underwear and sporting the plastic harness that was the Brinker Bra.

The crowd leaped to its feet and screamed orgasmically.

Beside me, Richard D'eath cursed.

The runway filled with strutting models, each one a perfect Amazon. A pair of long-legged twins paused in front of us, both with pouty faces and poker-straight white-blond hair down to their elbows. Their space age-y Brinker Bras looked like they might pop off at any moment.

Behind us, the photographers shouted for the crowd to sit down so they could shoot their photos.

In my ear, Libby shrieked, "I'm going straight home to book a bikini wax!"

I barely heard her. Although the action on the stage was riveting, a different drama was taking place in the row in front of us. Orlando Lamb had been glued to his seat until the model on the motorcycle suddenly ripped off her traditional bra and exposed the Brinker Bra beneath. She threw the old bra into the air . . . and it landed directly in Orlando's lap. The boy leaped up, beet red and crying with embarrassment as he threw the bra away from himself.

"I won't do it!" His shout was barely audible over the thundering noise. "I hate girls! This is gross!"

Hemorrhoid tried to subdue his nephew. I couldn't hear his words, but I saw his face as he reached to grasp the boy's shoulders.

"No!" Orlando wrestled for his freedom, and his shirt tore. "I won't! You can't make me!"

The annoyance on Hemorrhoid's face twisted into rage. Before I realized what I was doing, I stood up to intervene.

"Hem," I said. But the noise was too loud around us.

From behind me, Richard caught my arm.

Hemorrhoid grabbed Orlando's torn shirt.

"Hemmings!"

At the sound of my voice, Hemorrhoid loosened his grip and the child wrenched free. Orlando ran past the runway, ducked through the security team and knocked two spectators out of his way.

Hemorrhoid almost followed, but people turned their attention from the runway to watch him. At last aware he'd made an unpleasant scene in the midst of a spectacle, he sank back into his chair, pulled out his handkerchief and used it to dab his upper lip.

I pulled free of Richard's grasp and struggled to climb over people. I stepped on someone's foot and nearly fell into the lap of another fashion fan, but I finally made my way to the exit. I pushed past a knot of security guards.

Outside, Orlando was fistfighting his way out of Keith Rudnick's headlock. "Let me go! Let me go!"

"Orlando!"

The boy bit Keith's hand. Keith yelped and released him. Then Orlando rushed out of the warehouse. On the sidewalk, he ran slap into the arms of a small man who'd been waiting at the curb. The man was dressed in a traditional chauffeur's uniform. He held his cap in one hand, but he managed to hug the boy against his gray wool overcoat.

The chauffeur was an older gentleman, with the wizened face and twinkling blue eyes of a leprechaun. "Hey, there, lad," he said. "What's all this?"

Overcome with fury and distress, Orlando could only cling to him.

The chauffeur looked familiar. I approached the two and said, "Gallagher? Is that you?"

He squinted at me, then broke out a grin. "Miss Nora? Why, haven't you grown up pretty!"

I shook his hand with pleasure. "How nice to see you. I'm amazed you're still working for Oriana's family."

Charles Gallagher smiled as he continued to hug Orlando around the boy's pudgy shoulders. "I should have retired years ago, but I'm no quitter."

I smiled. "You used to deliver Oriana and me back to college after holidays. You made us listen to bagpipe tunes in the car."

"I did?" He looked delighted at my memory.

"We pretended to hate it, but now I actually enjoy bagpipes. Does he make you listen to awful music, Orlando?"

The boy's face squinched. "Yeah, sometimes."

"You two seem to be special friends."

"He keeps me busy." Genuinely affectionate, Gallagher tousled Orlando's spiky hairdo, then pulled his hand away and looked at it with surprise. "What's this?" he asked the boy. "Who's put this grease in your hair, son? And how did you tear your shirt?"

"Uncle Hem." Orlando twisted around to look up at Gallagher's face. "He wants me to buy a bunch of gross girl underwear, too."

Gallagher laughed and attempted to smooth over the incident for my benefit. "I bet you misunderstood him. Nobody's going to make you do anything like that."

"Uncle Hem said so. He wants—"

"You hush now," Gallagher soothed. "Don't worry."

I said, "Perhaps this event isn't appropriate for someone Orlando's age. I think he wants to go home."

"Then that's where we'll go." Gallagher gave the boy's shoulders another rough hug. "Ready, son? You can sit up front and read that confounded Global Position computer whatever. Where's your coat?"

"Uncle Hem took it. He said it makes me look fat."

"Let's get you into the car then, before you freeze."

The chauffeur's presence had obviously eased Orlando's spirits, but I followed them a few steps into the cold night anyway. They climbed into a long black Jaguar together. Gallagher waved goodbye from behind the wheel, and I watched as the car pulled into the street and disappeared.

Slowly I went back inside, glad Orlando had escaped, but wondering if things were worse for the boy at home.

I couldn't fight back into my seat, so I stood in the doorway of the show. Nearby, a handful of very young magazine assistants squealed as the fashion parade continued, reminding me it was time to get to work. I took out my notepad and eased along the edge of the crowd. I asked opinions, and people were happy to gush between rapturous glances at the stage.

I soon bumped into exactly the person I needed to balance my story.

"Lexie!"

Lexie Paine, my best friend since day school and my heartless financial adviser since the death of my husband, looked stunning in a black Fendi suit that was both prim and sharp enough to subdue the bulls and bears who dared charge the bronze doors of her brokerage house. Around her neck, she wore three strands of Bulgari fabulousness—pastel diamonds on a delicate platinum chain, the latest thing. As always, her black hair was swept back into a sleek ponytail, refining her slender face and emphasizing the intelligence of her gaze and the wry set to her mouth.

She hugged me with enthusiasm. "Here to buy some undies, sweetie?"

I hugged her back and we moved away from the doorway so we could hear each other over the screech of Led Zeppelin. "I should have known you'd be here. Are you in charge?"

"Lord, no. At the last minute someone asked me to help with the fund-raising, that's all, which meant having my assistant phone the usual suspects. Nora, is this event too tacky for words?"

"Only if it fails to raise a truckload of money for a good cause."

She sighed. "In that case, we're safe. The local blue bloods have come to see and be seen, everybody with checkbooks open, and there's the full-court fashion press, too. But all this sexist flash for brassieres? While we're trying to cure a terrible disease? I worry it's in bad taste."

"The money is green, Lex, and researchers will make good use of it."

"I hope you're right." With a grin, Lexie said, "I saw Libby earlier. She outwrestled Mimi Tarbockle for some gift bags—no easy feat, considering Mimi spends twelve-hour days with her personal trainer."

"Whatever you do, don't ask Libby about her new line of work. You'll end up buying something you can't show your mother."

"Yikes. Is Emma here, too?"

I sighed. "My little sister is back in rehab. We're hoping she stays this time."

Lexie's expression softened. "Oh, sweetie, I know you must be worried sick. Fingers crossed."

"Thanks."

Since my husband had been shot by his cocaine dealer, all my friends felt obliged to tread lightly every time the subject of addiction came up. Coping with Todd's drug problem and death had been a very public ordeal. Friends like Lexie saw me through.

She squeezed my arm. "Tell me what you're wearing, sweetie. Looks like a pink mink!"

"Chinchilla. Don't turn me in to PETA, please. This is the only thing I could grab and know it would keep me decent." I unbuttoned and flashed Lexie a peek of my nightgown under the coat. "No time to be politically correct."

Lexie let out a roar of laughter. "Button up, darling, before the fashionistas mob you. That's a killer nightie. For all his faults, Todd had great taste in lingerie. And the fur? What are we supposed to do with an old one?"

"I was in a terrible hurry. Kitty called at the last minute—hoping I'd miss the assignment, I suppose. I can't lose this job, so here I am despite the snowstorm."

"And not even a minute to grab some earrings? Never mind,

the stars in your eyes are better than diamonds. Can I assume your new beau has spent the holidays lavishing or ravishing you?"

"A bit of both," I said with a smile. "And thank you for the case of wine, by the way. Michael tells me it's worth a fortune."

"I hope it's delicious with hot lovin', sweetie," she said with another laugh. "Thanks for the return invitation to your New Year's Eve bash, by the way. I'm so glad you've decided to revive that tradition. Your soiree was always so glamorous."

"Actually, I thought an intimate dinner might be better this year."

My friend understood instantly. "So Michael can meet your friends in small doses?"

"If he shows up at all."

Lexie's elegant brows rose in delight. "The Mafia Prince is leery of social butterflies?"

"He's more worried he'll sully my reputation."

"We could all use such sullying."

My unlikely liaison with Michael Abruzzo had caused an earthquake in my social circle. His family—that is, the Abruzzo crime family of New Jersey—had made a name for itself in racketeering, illegal gambling and other nefarious deeds that I needed a law degree to understand. Michael had no business with his father and various half brothers—the ones who weren't currently serving sentences, that is. At least, I was almost sure he had no dealings with them anymore. He had served time years ago for juvenile offenses and seemed determined to avoid doing so again. Still, I had not yet worked up the courage to ask for details about his various current activities, and so far he wasn't offering any information either.

My friends knew I had suffered through one apocalyptic relationship, and despite her cheery banter I could see Lexie feared I was facing another catastrophe in my life.

Meanwhile, Michael was reluctant to go on display.

Thing is, I loved to entertain. I liked lavishing my old friends and nurturing new acquaintances. That ever-widening pool of friendship had always been my touchstone. It was time Michael understood. I wanted him to like my friends. And I hoped they would see beyond the crime-lord persona the newspapers tagged him with to the real man beneath.

Lexie correctly read my thoughts and said, "You know what I like best? You look happy. So damn what anybody else thinks. Let me bring my cousins. They'll be in town that night and I simply assumed—"

Against my better judgment, I said, "By all means, bring them."

"Good. They'll adore seeing you again. And meeting your beau has them in a tizzy of excitement. Now, who were you chasing out of here a minute ago? The chubby kid?"

"You didn't recognize him? It was Orlando Lamb."

Lexie stared after him. "That was Orlando? Poor thing! He's like a character in a Dickens novel now, isn't he? First orphaned, and now chained to Hemorrhoid. Does Hem still color code his medicine chest?"

"And use Lysol by the gallon? I suppose so. Hem just told me he's changing his own name to Lamb."

"I can imagine what the Lamb family might have said about that."

"Aren't they all dead? I think Orlando is the heir to the whole empire now. With two dozen guardians, or something?"

Lexie nodded. "He won't see a penny for years. A huge board of directors protects the assets, but they're all in New Zealand. Hem was given a seat on the board when he became Orlando's loco parentis. Now he thinks he's a mogul. I suppose he dreams of Orlando expiring so he gets the whole enchilada himself."

"That's awful. He's Orlando's only living relative, isn't he?"

"Yep."

I noticed her expression. "You have your Wall Street face on, Lex."

She continued to frown as if contemplating a Vatican political plot. "Do I? A rumor just started to make sense."

"Anything I can know about? Or is client privilege at stake?"

"Not at all. I heard Lamb Limited is looking to expand. I wonder if they're thinking of buying the Brinker Bra?"

"Is it for sale?"

Kindly, my friend said, "Everything's for sale, Nora."

I never pretended to understand how large fortunes were made. Personally, I only knew the other end of the tale—how families lost great sums of money. But with Lexie supervising my financial learning curve, I was holding the tax man at bay—at least until my next installment was due. I hated the monthly panic of raising more cash, though.

"Trouble is," Lexie continued, "making a deal like this requires a lot of financial expertise—or else a very solid friendship at the core. Brinker and Hemorrhoid weren't exactly best buddies as kids, remember?"

"Believe me, I remember."

Lexie popped her eyes wide. "Of course! I'd forgotten! My God, Nora."

"Don't worry. I plan to leave as soon as the show is over."

"I've been watching his videos." Lexie indicated the rushing deluge of film that continued to spin over everything around us. "His obsessions haven't changed, have they?"

Brinker's stand-up comedy always felt like one angry man lashing out at people to prove himself smarter or more able to talk women into doing things they wouldn't admit later to their friends. His rage at his parents boiled over. At first large audiences howled at Brinker's routines—crude remarks made while a video of candid bumbling played behind him. Only when his images turned even more misogynistic did people begin to object to him. Finally a woman sued, and his rising star began to fizzle.

Then his comedy club conveniently went up in smoke, and the insurance money made him rich.

Lexie and I heard the music change, an indication that the fashion show was coming to a climactic end. I said, "Before the grand finale, how about giving me a quote for the paper? Something noble, please, to dispel the tacky factor?"

"Okay, I'm delighted to have any ally help us fight breast cancer. I hope Brinker's combination of creative thought and good luck inspires scientists to seek innovative treatments."

"Perfect." I jotted down her remark. "And who's the biggest donor? I'll put their picture in the paper."

"It's me," she said. "But why not ask Sue Mandell?"

"She's here all the way from Maine?" I'd met Sue in college when I dated a naval officer who'd been one of her patients. Long after I parted ways with the young lieutenant, Sue and I remained friends, bonding over Brazilian music and Thai food. Now she was a respected oncologist, the ideal person to picture in the newspaper.

"She's in town to see a patient, I hear. She and Steve are running up to see a show in New York later this week."

"She's the perfect choice. I'll be sure we get her photograph."

"Here comes the big finish," Lexie said as we drifted back to the warehouse doorway. "Hey, see those twins? The models?"

I watched the two young women flaunt themselves for the crowd. "Yes. Are you wondering if their hair is real?"

"Not just their hair. But . . . I think I know them from somewhere."

"The floor of the stock exchange?"

Lexie laughed.

We didn't have long to wait for the big finish. The twin models disappeared behind the curtain at the back of the runway, and the lights brightened. The crowd held its collective breath.

Suddenly the futuristic theme exploded. No more hard rock or outer-space girls. Even the videos changed. The images became deep forests and tumbling waterfalls.

The curtain parted, and the lights struck the gleaming black coat of a magnificent stallion—a gigantic live animal snorting and tossing its thick ringlets as his rider spun him on his haunches and sent him strutting onto the runway. On his back was no astronaut girl in plastic harness but a modern Lady Godiva, clad in little more than a long red wig and artfully cast seaweed and, of course, a Brinker Bra that drew the eye to her beautifully displayed breasts.

Behind her strode Brinker Holt himself.

Brinker—tall and rangy in blue jeans and a T-shirt that clung to his gym-rat physique—accepted his applause with unsmiling aplomb. Then he lifted his camera and began to film the crowd. We could suddenly see ourselves projected live against the walls, then spinning across the floor and climbing to the ceiling. Brinker filmed his applauding audience—an auteur recording his own adulation. An ego trip magnified.

But I wasn't looking at Brinker.

I only saw the model on horseback. And recognized her instantly.

"Emma," I said aloud. "What the hell are you doing out of rehab?"

She had a whip in her hand—a long one. With a strong snap of her wrist, she cracked it over the heads of the audience, then down beneath her horse's feet. The animal danced, causing shrieks in the crowd. But Emma was in total control. She rode the enormous horse straight off the end of the runway and directly toward me. As the crowd behind her jumped to a standing ovation and the music crashed to a climactic conclusion, my sister effortlessly guided the stallion through the crowd and out of the warehouse.

Going past, she leaned down to me with a grin. "Hey, Sis. Happy New Year!"

Chapter Three

*E*mma disappeared, of course. Like a naughty genie evaporating back into her bottle.

Libby and I scoured the warehouse and the parking lot long after everyone else departed, but no luck. Emma was gone, and her horse with her.

"It's not easy to hide a horse," I said.

"Trust Emma to know how." Libby shivered outside her minivan. "Why did she leave rehab?"

"She probably went over the wall in the dark of night like some kind of prisoner of war."

"I thought Emma was getting her problem under control."

"Me, too." I should have known it wasn't going to be as easy as dropping her off at one of Mama's spas. But nothing about Emma was ever easy.

"She looked good, though, didn't she?" Libby unlocked the minivan and got in. As we fastened our seat belts, she said, "I don't suppose she'd like any Potions and Passions gadgets. Emma probably has scads already."

As Libby drove me home to Blackbird Farm, we both thought privately about Emma, whose life was more of a bonfire of insanities than our own. Our little sister had a tendency to self-combust when things went bad, and I always felt the need to step in. But as the headlights swept the bleakly leaning fence posts and finally flashed squarely on the bright blue tarp that flapped on one corner of the roof where a major leak had burst through, I realized my own home sweet home looked more like a derelict ruin every day. And in just a few more weeks I owed another installment on my tax repayment plan. Unless the Publishers Clearing House crew showed up soon, I had more problems than Emma on the loose.

"We'll talk tomorrow," I said to Libby.

"I know you want to kidnap her," Libby said. "You're thinking we shall capture her and take her back to rehab. Well, I have handcuffs now. They're fur-lined, very comfy."

"Do you think that's what we should do, Lib?"

"No," she said. "Emma's an adult."

"But she needs help."

"Nora, I may not be the world's best mom, but I know when my kids need to figure things out for themselves."

"Tomorrow," I said. "We'll be able to think more clearly then."

"The lights are on in your kitchen," she said, suddenly observant.

Hastily, I got out of the minivan. "I hate coming home to a dark house."

"Is somebody inside?"

"Good night!"

I dug my house key out and waved to her. Hugging myself against the biting air, I hurried up the slate sidewalk. The porch was still Christmas-swagged with hemlock boughs trimmed from the trees out near the old canal.

On the porch steps I found a neatly wrapped package tied with a holiday bow. Another fruitcake from one of the neighbors, I assumed. I picked it up and carried it inside.

I didn't need to unlock the door.

But I stepped into the kitchen and yelped.

"Sorry," growled the thug in front of the open refrigerator.

"Who are you?"

"Me? We met once before." He took a beer from the top shelf. "I'm the evil minion. At least, that's what the boss calls me. I'm Danny."

He wore a snug leather jacket over a hooded sweatshirt and jeans. A stringy ponytail straggled out from underneath a navy ski cap with a Nautica logo, a touch of class for the aspiring Mafia wiseguy.

I closed the door, but kept my distance. "What are you doing here? There's no car parked outside."

He opened the beer with a twist. "Boss told me to leave it next door."

"Next door" was now a used-car lot. Michael and I first became acquainted when he purchased five acres of Blackbird Farm, a transaction that had helped me stabilize my tax situation, but ruined the riverfront view as Michael erected Mick's Muscle Cars on the spot. Complete with plastic flags and Muzak, the sales lot despoiled two hundred years of Blackbird family history and also provided a steady parade of Michael's merry band of employees. They usually didn't venture into my house, though.

This one took a slug of beer and looked me up and down. "That's some getup you're wearing."

Involuntarily, I checked to be sure the coat was fully buttoned. "I see you've made yourself at home."

He grinned and lifted the beer to indicate the hospitality of the house. "Thanks."

The kitchen at Blackbird Farm was built under the impression that George Washington and his troops might drop by for breakfast before crossing the Delaware. Large enough for a skirmish to break out, it was decorated by a long-dead Blackbird with a love for baronial melodrama. The high ceilings were perfect for hanging game birds or sharp weaponry. The ancient stove, as big as an iron forge, was capable of baking pies, simmering cauldrons of stew, warming stacks of dinner plates and keeping baby chicks alive all at the same time.

"Where, exactly, is your boss?" I asked.

The man in question made his entrance at that moment, simultaneously shrugging into his coat and terminating a cell phone call. He moved with quick purpose—a man with a mission. Nonetheless, I felt the seismic event that shook me to my molten core every time I saw him.

Tall and looming, Michael said, "Rough night?"

"An interesting one," I replied.

In the light of the kitchen, I was reminded that Michael was not a handsome man. In fact, his looks—brutal and blunt, with a nose broken numerous times and jaw that looked almost cruel—often frightened strangers. He was also very tall, with threatening shoulders and a certain manner that bespoke years of hanging around career criminals. But he could melt me into a puddle of hot hormones with the tip of his tongue, and his body had enough strong planes and curves to keep a woman interested for hours.

I had a bad history with men, of course. All the Blackbird women did. We were blind to their faults or drawn to their dark sides or maybe just plain foolhardy. I'm not sure which, but I knew I was attracted to Michael, and he wasn't Prince Charming.

But he was very sharp. He pocketed his cell phone. "Let me guess. One of your sisters has committed a crime. Or both of them this time?"

"If they had, they'd be safely in jail." I dropped the neighborly gift on the kitchen counter. "No, it's nothing that easy. I thought you went out earlier."

"I got held up. I'm going now. Anyway, somebody had to babysit your dog while you were out."

"Where is Spike?"

"In the basement, digging his way to China. While he's busy, I'll make my escape."

I knew he was joking. Michael liked my new puppy, and Spike adored Michael in return. They were two of a kind. Scoundrels at heart.

Part of me really wanted to know where Michael was going in the middle of the night. His evil minion looked as if he'd lost one fistfight and didn't need another. He had a scratch across his cheek and he held the cold beer bottle against his face as if it hurt.

Michael smiled into my eyes while I considered what they could be up to.

"Want to come along?" he asked.

"Would you let me?"

He laughed like an adventuring buccaneer. But he didn't answer my question.

Instead, he tilted his head at his companion. "You remember my cousin? Danny Pescara."

"Another of your cousins?"

"Well, sort of. Say hello, Danny."

"Hey, baby." Danny sipped more beer, absorbing the vibe, then made a decision. He swaggered for the door. "I'll wait outside."

"Nice to see you again," I said, unable to sound convincing.

When the door was closed behind him, Michael said, "Danny's in a jam tonight. Needs my guidance."

"Does he call you Obi-Wan?" I asked.

He came over and pulled me close, smiling. "You like me a little dangerous."

Michael didn't have a lot of free time between secret forays, but when he did have a few hours to spare these days he seemed to spend them at Blackbird Farm, sometimes cooking astonishing meals, sometimes babysitting my obnoxious dog, sometimes causing a commotion in my bed.

I let him kiss me and felt the now familiar heat of his body against mine. I kissed him back until my brain softened and my toes curled.

Dangerous? Probably. Had he put his life of crime behind him? I fervently hoped so. But my big fear was that for Michael, bending the law was what drug addiction had been for my husband, Todd. It was a natural urge he could not fight for long.

"Stick around," I whispered, holding his shoulders.

"I'll be back before you're out of the bathtub."

"The tub is big enough for two."

"Yeah, but that bubble stuff smells better on you." He smoothed the fingers of one hand into my hair and looked deeply into my eyes. "Tell me what's wrong."

Ruefully, I sighed. "It's ridiculous. My sisters are adults, and I should stop taking responsibility for them."

He nodded. The discussion wasn't new. "But?"

"But Emma went AWOL from rehab. Not only that, she appeared half-naked on horseback in front of several hundred people at a fashion show tonight. And there was a whip involved."

Michael smiled. "That's Emma."

"If I'm any judge of showstopping finales, she's going to New York tomorrow for a repeat performance. God knows what she'll get into there."

"Some guy's pants, no doubt," he said. Then, "Sorry. Was she drinking?"

"I couldn't get close enough to find out." I slid out of his arms.

"You were doing so well with the Emma's-the-master-of-her-fate stuff. You decided you're not her keeper, right?"

"Right."

To busy my hands, I opened the gift left on my porch steps. I unwrapped the paper and found a squished ham inside. With a note. I read the scrawled signature and said, "It's from your father."

"What?" Startled, Michael looked into the package. "Oh."

"What is it?"

"Prosciutto. He makes it."

I studied the food prepared by the hand of Big Frankie Abruzzo, godfather of certain regions of New Jersey where even grandmothers carried concealed weapons. "How do you make prosciutto?"

"You cure it, smoke it, age it. Or you go to Parma and buy it. But it's his hobby. He learned it from Nonna. It's a big family deal."

"Well," I said. "How thoughtful. This is . . . a very sweet gesture. I'm touched."

"Yeah," Michael said. "That's how it starts."

I let him rewrap the ham and went looking for an open bottle of wine in the refrigerator, wondering what had just happened.

"So?" he asked, obviously not yet prepared to discuss his father's acknowledgment of our relationship. "What else? You've got something besides Emma on your mind."

I sipped the cold wine and I tried to organize the confusion of emotion and events of the night. "I saw a little boy tonight—the son of an old friend of mine. She's dead now, and he's . . . well, he's just ten years old and in the custody of a nutty excuse for a human being. And they had a public argument."

Michael leaned against the opposite kitchen counter, his hands in the pockets of his jacket, one ankle languidly crossed over the other. "What happened?"

"Orlando ran away. I followed, but—"

"The first problem the kid has is his name."

I noted Michael's amused expression. "Orlando comes from two distinguished families, and he's going to inherit a huge corporation someday. At the moment, though, he's the saddest-looking rich kid I've ever seen. And I've seen my share."

"Like the granddaughter of that Greek tycoon. The teenage girl who inherited all the dough, only she's living in the Alps or some-thing."

"Well, it's a similar situation, I suppose." I swirled the wine in my glass. "Except Orlando is stuck with someone who doesn't love him—his mother's brother, who probably washes his hands fifty times a day and could teach the Pentagon a few things about regimentation. He refuses to wear socks more than once and replaces shoe laces every week. The company, Lamb Limited, is a huge international textile manufacturer and exporter."

"That's what the kid inherits? Lamb? I hope he watches his step."

"No, no, it's nothing like that. He's just a child who's miserable. I knew his uncle when we were younger. He has lots of . . . issues."

Michael shrugged. "Kids have a way of overcoming issues."

The lousy childhood was territory Michael knew better than anyone.

"I don't know," I murmured doubtfully.

"Does the uncle bat left-handed?"

I cast Michael a wry glance. "Is that a quaint New Jersey way of asking if he's gay? No, he isn't. Just odd."

"Odd isn't life-threatening. So he likes new socks." Michael shrugged. "What doesn't kill the kid will only make him tougher."

"He isn't tough. Not at all."

"He'll develop," Michael promised, reaching for his keys.

"Michael . . ."

Already at the door, he turned.

Uncertainly I said, "Do you think I should do something?"

"For the kid?"

"For his mother. She was my friend, after all."

He studied me with a tender sort of doubt. "What would you do?"

"I . . . I don't know."

"He's got a lot of people in his life already, doesn't he?"

"Yes, but nobody is his friend."

"What makes you think he'd trust you?"

"I wouldn't take advantage like everyone else around him."

Michael strolled back to me. "And how would he know that?"

I sighed. "I can't help wanting to take care of him."

He took my glass and set it on the table. "Nora, I love you. I love this part of you—the woman who wants to save the world. But this boy's life can't be fixed with cotton candy and a trip to the zoo."

"I want to try."

His smile flickered again, and he slid one arm around me. "Don't you have your hands full already? Saving your sisters? Not to mention me?"

I let him fit my body to his larger, warmer frame. "Is that what you think I'm doing?"

"I could keep you busy for a long time, you know," he said. "If you'd marry me."

I laughed unsteadily. "You ask me every day."

"And every day you change the subject."

"Stay here tonight," I said. "We'll talk about it."

He hesitated.

I unbuttoned my coat all the way. And let it drop slowly to the floor.

"See what I mean?" he asked, touching my bare shoulders, then tracing his fingertips down my arms. "You always change the subject."

It was wrong of me, I know. But I let him gather the hem of my nightgown in his hands and draw it upward until all I was wearing were my Chanel boots. I kissed his temples and watched his eyes and let the syrupy wave of warmth grow inside. He touched me and told me what we'd do later.

"Now," I said, catching my breath.

"Later," he promised. "We'll make a baby."

I couldn't keep him. Not when he was hearing the call of something even more seductive. Michael wrapped me up in the coat and went outside into the darkness. When he whistled for his sidekick, he sounded exhilarated.

I had never been able to stop Todd either. Even now—nearly two years after his death—I was trying to convince myself that no one person had the power to prevent anyone else from plunging down the path of his own destruction, no matter how much love was tangled up in the whole mess.

The sound of Michael's whistle conjured my dog. From the depths of the basement, Spike appeared at my feet and barked.

"No," I said, understanding his demand. "You may not eat my coat."

Spike was a remarkably disgusting excuse for a house pet. Part very ugly Jack Russell terrier and part mongoose, Spike was a gift I couldn't refuse and now I was stuck. He'd made me love him. He'd been run over by a car early in December, and his hindquarters were supported by a contraption the vet had invented to outsmart Spike's determined teeth. At least he no longer had to drag his rear end around in the little cart we'd suffered through for three long weeks. He sometimes wore a plastic cone-shaped collar, too, an item of doggy apparel that gave him the look of a cockeyed Elizabethan serial killer.

No medical apparatus could slow Spike down. Only lethal injection could do that, and even then I had my doubts. He had the spirit of a tiger in the body of a circus dog.

I picked him up and carried him along with my glass of wine to the dining room, where my laptop computer was plugged into the wall. I sat down with Spike in my lap and gave him a blank page of my notebook to shred. While he destroyed it, I proceeded to write my piece about the Brinker Bra show.

When I was finished, I e-mailed the short article directly to the features editor, Stan Rosenstatz. If I was lucky, Stan would okay my piece before Kitty got a chance to order a few dozen rewrites.

"Do it again, Sweet Knees," Kitty often screamed across the crowded newsroom. "Cut the polite shit and entertain me!"

I checked my e-mail and discovered two notes from friends who had heard about my New Year's Eve party. Both asked if they could "stop by."

Reluctantly, I wrote back and invited them for the evening. As long as Lexie was bringing her cousins, a couple more guests wouldn't matter. But I noted that the guest list for my intimate New Year's Eve dinner was now up to eighteen.

To Spike, I said, "I don't think Michael will be pleased."

Spike growled in agreement.

After the e-mails, I found myself Googling Lamb Limited. I read about Orlando's board of guardians and how they took care of his business affairs while he grew up.

But who, I wondered, was looking after the boy, not the future owner of the corporation? It certainly wasn't going to be Hemorrhoid.

When I closed my eyes I could clearly remember the summer Oriana and I hung out at the outdoor pool. We had slurped mango Popsicles and leafed through magazines under the shade trees, trying not to be obvious about watching the older boys.

But Hemorrhoid, Oriana's squirrelly kid brother, made a constant pest of himself. He kept obsessive track of how many acorns he could toss down our bathing suits and counted how many paces it took to get to the locker room toilet from various locations around the club. He kept his towel immaculately clean and hated to venture off the concrete on days when the lawn was mowed because he didn't like getting clippings on his feet. Soon he was drawn to the older boys, who had no patience for his behavior and quickly dubbed him with his nickname. He accepted the name joyously, taking it as a sign he'd been made a part of the brotherhood. He tagged after them, imitating their dives, learning their curse words, begging to be a part of the group.

Of course, the older boys began to pick on him.

Their leader was Brinker Holt, a cocky prep school lacrosse player and champion bra snapper. Brinker stole the key to his father's liquor cabinet and supplied his friends with expensive brandy, which they mixed with cola drinks every afternoon. The booze whipped them into high spirits and, eventually, ever-increasing acts of cruelty. At first they stole Hemorrhoid's sneakers. A few days later they stripped him naked and left him cowering and crying behind some azalea bushes until his sister ran to the rescue with a towel.

But Hemorrhoid went back for more every time, and soon the hazing escalated. The bigger boys used pocketknives to hack his hair off. By the end of June they regularly stuck his head in a locker room toilet and flushed. Hemorrhoid sometimes wept, but— bizarrely—returned to his tormentors every day for an entire summer.

His sister and I watched, frightened and intimidated by the intensifying violence. To intervene meant punishment for us, too, of course. And all along Hemorrhoid seemed to want the attention he received from the older boys. We were too young to understand the psychology at work and too scared to stop it.

Then one August evening, we came upon the boys in the parking lot. Holding Hemorrhoid down in the backseat of someone's car, they were burning his back with cigarettes, clamping his mouth shut to muffle his screams. When we ran to get help, Hemorrhoid tore loose and shouted through his tears.

"Leave us alone," he had shrieked.

Oriana took her brother home and finally reported everything. Their mother forbade Hemorrhoid to return to the pool and sent him off to a camp to learn to play bridge, a different kind of torture for some people, but probably a relief to Hemorrhoid, who loved numbers. He came back more obsessive about nose hair and drink coasters, but very good at card games. I'd heard he collected playing cards picturing royalty in erotic poses and figured that was almost healthy, for him.

To Spike, I said, "It was very weird. Hemorrhoid wanted to be hurt so they'd be his friends."

Spike cocked his ear, puzzled.

I rubbed his head and thought about Orlando. What was it like for him, trapped with Hemorrhoid now that his parents were dead?

I said, "He's just a kid."

With a low snarl, Spike asked if he was edible.

"No," I said.

Trying to put it all out of my mind, I took a bath with a novel—my nightly ritual. Around midnight I slipped between the cool sheets of my bed. I lay awake, trying not to worry. Spike twitched in his sleep, and I rubbed his tummy.

Eventually, Michael slid into the bed. I hadn't heard him come in, nor had I been aware of him putting Spike out in the hall, but suddenly he was there, all warm muscle and slow attention.

"Did you have a good night?" I murmured, barely awake.

"It's getting better," he said against my mouth.

I did love him. Despite months of my holding back and pushing him away, he hadn't given up on me. He wanted me with such intensity that I sometimes felt swept into a stormy place that both frightened and excited me. I had delayed living my life almost too long. I wanted a family of my own and had recklessly, perhaps, thrown myself on the winds of chance with Michael. For better or worse, we had come together to create something that I hoped was lasting.

In the morning, Michael woke first and made love to me again while I was still deliciously half dreaming. He headed for the shower a few minutes later, and after listening to him croon some Elvis I wobbled out of bed and into my bathrobe. Outside the bedroom door Spike looked up indignantly from his basket.

"Forgive me," I said to the puppy. "I can only cope with one bad boy at a time."

He accepted my apology and permitted me to carry him downstairs. In the kitchen, I scooped him some Puppy Chow and began making coffee in the new contraption Michael had brought over when he decided my once-very-expensive pot made sludge.

The phone rang, and I picked up, knowing exactly who was calling.

"Good morning, Libby." Her kids were still sleeping off their Christmas excesses, and she was no doubt feeding the baby while waiting for *LIVE with Regis and Kelly* to come on.

"You didn't give me a straight answer yesterday," she said over the wails of her baby. "When can I schedule a Potions and Passions party at your house?"

"This isn't a good time, Lib."

The baby stopped crying as if he'd just latched onto her breast. "Oh, Lord," she said, "you mean That Man is there?"

"I hear you're calling him the Incredible Hulk now."

"How do you know that? Did Rawlins tell you?"

I decided not to reveal that her sixteen-year-old son was still hanging around one of Michael's garages after school.

"Nora," she said, "I don't understand. You could have any number of suitors from our social circle. That nice Jamie Scaithe would love to sweep you off your feet, and you treat him like—"

"Like the cocaine dealer he is."

"Okay, bad example. But why not a nice lawyer with a trust fund? The Incredible—I mean, That Man has a certain sex appeal, I agree, but he's just not your type, Nora. I think it all comes back to you being unable to understand your own needs." She paused long enough to draw a deep breath. "Which makes you the perfect Potions and Passions customer. As your Potions and Passions representative, I can teach you to discern and quantify your innermost desires and effectively communicate your—"

"Let's communicate about your sex life for a change," I suggested.

"Oh, all right," she said happily. "Yesterday you said you didn't want to hear another word, but if you really—"

"I'm joking, Lib."

She sighed. "You're no fun." Then, "Is he really there?"

I went looking for the oatmeal and decided to be brave and damn the consequences. "Yes, he's here."

"Oh, my God! He spent the whole night?"

"Yes. In fact, he's been staying here for a few weeks."

Suddenly understanding in a way only sisters can comprehend, she said, "You're trying to have a baby, aren't you? With *him!* Are you *crazy?*"

"No. Just afraid to wait any longer."

"Oh my God, does he know?"

"Of course he knows. He wants children, too. We both want a life, Lib. Like you."

I knew she was smiling. Libby liked nothing more than being reminded of the joys of family and motherhood. "I'm going to be an aunt? Will you have a girl? I like to spoil little girls. Lucy has discovered baseball, and I'm so disappointed she hates ballet— Oh, heavens, this means I'll be related to That Man, doesn't it?"

"Not if I don't marry him."

"You can't, of course," she agreed. "If you do, he'll die, you know. It's the Blackbird widow curse."

"I know. But I'm afraid to wait much longer. My ovaries aren't getting any younger."

"Blackbirds always have big families. It's in your genes." Libby considered the situation, then said, "Well, if he was with you last night, I suppose that's better than his alternative."

"What alternative?" I carried the oatmeal to the stove.

"Getting arrested," she said. "There was a big bust. A car theft ring. It's in today's paper."

My whole circulatory system turned cold. "What happened?"

"The police chased a bunch of crooks and caught most of them red-handed. In stolen cars—luxury cars they've been chopping up and sending overseas. A police officer was shot."

"Oh, God!"

"He's wounded, not dead yet. The good news is that if That Man was at home stimulating your womb, at least he isn't mixed up in a ring of car thieves. That's a blessing."

"Yes," I said faintly. "It is."

"So, the sex," she said. "Is he all Conan the Barbarian? Or is he aware of your need for satisfaction?"

"Lib—"

"Women have been known to fake orgasm, but men fake fore-play. Remember that singer from Dublin I dated once? He told me Irish foreplay means 'Brace yourself, Bridget,' and he lived up to that, let me tell you!"

"I am not going to discuss foreplay with you, Libby."

"Why not? Maybe it's easier to talk with pictures. The two of you should look at one of my catalogs. I know you're shy, and he's probably completely inarticulate when it comes to the erotic arts. I'm thinking Italian men might be my target customer, in fact."

Spike finished his breakfast and dashed over to scratch at the back door. In my ear, Libby kept talking, but I stopped listening. All I could think about was Michael disappearing with Danny last night. I went to the door to let the puppy outside.

"Lib, what time was the shooting?"

"What?"

"The car thieves. When was the police officer shot?"

"I don't know exactly. Let me look in the paper. It was early, I think— No, let's see. Ten fifteen."

Not long after I had walked into the kitchen. So Michael couldn't have been on the scene when it happened. Could he?

"I hear you're having your New Year's party again this year," my sister said bluntly. "Am I invited?"

"Lib—"

"Lexie says she's invited. And she's bringing people. It's a good opportunity for me to meet potential customers. I'll even bring my spinach dip."

While I struggled with the dead bolt, Spike suddenly stopped capering and glared out through the glass. He barked.

"Bring anything you want. Bring Masters and Johnson for all I care, except—"

"I think they're dead."

"I just don't want you to turn my dinner party into a taste test of edible underwear."

"But I can come?"

"Yes, all right, you can come."

"Oh, you won't regret it! I have my first shipment of products coming tomorrow."

"No products! Don't bring anything!"

She continued to babble, but I couldn't hear her.

At last I got the door open. Spike dashed outside and attacked the heap on the porch. Not another neighborly gift this time.

It was a coat, I realized. Spike seized a mouthful and began to worry it, snarling and clawing.

The coat was tied up with some kind of twine.

And inside was a person.

A dead person.

She had blond hair with white roots and too much makeup for a woman of her years. She was barefoot and bare-legged, having lost her shoes somewhere. A ratty feather boa ruffled in the breeze. She had dried blood in her hair, smeared on her face.

I felt the earth tilt. The morning sunlight darkened. Spike's bark began to echo in my head, and everything began to blur. My heart slammed in my chest as I stared at the dead woman on my porch.

In my ear and a thousand miles away, Libby said, "Nora? Did you hear me? Are you there? Nora? What's wrong?"

"It's Kitty," I gasped. "Kitty Keough. She's dead."

A soundless snowstorm whirled up around me, and I fainted.

Chapter Four

I woke up with an ice pack on my face and Michael roughly wrapping me in blankets. His expression frightened me. In the distance, I could hear Spike barking, barking, barking.

I tried to move, but my hands were tightly captured inside the blanket. "W-what happened?"

He put me back down on the sofa, more gently than before. But his face remained taut. "It's okay. The police are here. So's your sister."

"Michael—"

Libby arrived and shouldered him aside. She had a cup of something steamy in her hands. "Let me handle this. It happens all the time. She really ought to see a doctor."

"I have seen doctors," I said, sounding infuriatingly feeble even to myself.

"A psychologist, then. Someone who can help you deal with emergencies more appropriately."

"Michael," I said again.

He said, "She's got a point. Let her take care of you while I talk to the cops."

He went away, and Libby scrunched onto the sofa beside me. Her hair was wet and hastily shoved into a clip, but she'd managed to dress in a provocative red sweater.

"My goodness, his language goes to Hades when he's angry.

F-bombs all over the place!" She noted where I was looking. "I'm wearing the Brinker Bra. Doesn't it do wonders? Very Jennifer Lopez."

More Anna Nicole Smith, actually. I wrestled one hand out of the blanket and felt my cheek under the ice pack. It throbbed. I was going to have a headache soon, too. "What happened?"

"You fell and hit your face on the porch railing. It's just a bump."

I squinted at her. "How long did it take you to get here?"

"Seven minutes from the time you dropped the phone. I left the baby with Rawlins. He'll babysit his brother if I pay him."

"How many of those seven minutes were spent putting on the bra?"

"None. I slept in it last night." She sat up straighter to show off her décolletage. "It's really amazing, Nora. What support! There's only a teensy problem."

"Just one?"

"I can't seem to get it off," she said. "Here. Drink some tea."

The smell wafting from the cup made me feel weak all over again. "What is this stuff?"

"A special tea blended by Potions and Passions. It's supposed to have reviving properties. Go ahead. Drink."

My mind finally cleared enough to suspect the worst. "It's some kind of aphrodisiac, isn't it?"

"It improves blood flow, that's all. It will help reduce the bruise you're going to have on your face. Here's a tissue. Let's wipe your eyes."

I put the stinking cup on the coffee table and sat back against the pillows. "Libby?"

"Yes?"

"It's Kitty Keough, isn't it?"

"Yes," my sister answered, dabbing a tissue to my face. "She's dead."

Once again I felt my head spin and darken. I could not convince myself it had been a sick nightmare. Kitty Keough's dead body was lying on my porch. The woman we'd jokingly wished might choke on her own poisonous venom was gone.

"How?" I asked. "Did she have a heart attack?"

Libby looked at me pityingly. She reapplied the ice to my cheek with a gentle hand. "Honey, with all that blood, I don't think it was a heart attack. And she was tied up, too. Trussed like a Christmas goose with her own panty hose."

"She was . . . ?"

"Murdered," Libby said. "That's what the police think. And Mr. Abruzzo says it didn't happen here. Somebody shot her two times in the back of the head and dumped the body on your porch. That's execution style, isn't it? Twice in the back of the head?"

"Why was she left on my porch?"

Libby frowned. "I'm sure we'll find out soon enough."

Two state troopers waited until I could put a coherent sentence together before they asked to talk with me in the dining room. The younger of the two had dimples, and the older one seemed to think direct eye contact could keep me from rambling off into hysterics. Michael sat next to me at the dining room table, looking capable of fending off an invading army of Mongol warriors if I said the word. I answered basic questions about what I had seen and heard over the last twelve hours.

"And what's your relationship with the deceased?"

I clamped my hands between my knees to keep the trembling to a minimum. "She's my boss. She works with me at the *Intelligencer*. We're in the Features department. I spoke with her last night. She called around six to ask if I'd cover an event for her—"

"Nora," Michael warned.

"It's the truth. Kitty writes the social column, and I'm her— I *was* her assistant. She said she had somewhere else to go, and I was to cover a fashion show for her."

"Nora," Michael said again.

"Sir," said Dimples, who had not removed his hat, "will you step into the other room, please, while Miss Blackbird answers a few questions?"

"Do I need a lawyer?" I asked.

"Why would you need a lawyer?" The older trooper sat across the table, still peering intently into my eyes.

"I'd like to call a lawyer," I said.

"Have you done anything that requires a lawyer?" the trooper asked. "How did you get that bruise, Miss Blackbird?"

"I told you, I fainted when I found the body. I must have hit my face on the porch. You can't be insinuating that Kitty might have hit me. She was already dead when I found her."

"That's not what they're insinuating," Michael said.

Still, the beady stare from the older cop. "We want to be sure you're safe in this house, Miss Blackbird."

"Of course I'm safe. Until a dead body showed up on my porch and I keeled over, I was perfectly— Oh, for heaven's sake! You think . . . ? That's utterly ridiculous." The complexity of my situation suddenly made me angry. "Look, I want to call my lawyer."

"You're sure? I mean, we want you to be comfortable, but as soon as lawyers get involved, things slow down. The first few hours of any investigation are critical, so if we could just get a little more information, we'd be grateful."

Since I had watched as much television as the next person, I took the phone into the living room and telephoned my friend Tom Nelson, an attorney in the city. The state troopers hovered in the hallway and talked in low voices with Michael.

Tom had been my dancing partner when we learned the cha-cha

from the formidable Miss Markham when we were kids. While determined to avoid learning anything about ballroom dancing, he thoroughly enjoyed scuffing my shoes and telling moronic knock-knock jokes. Now we got along fine. Although his law firm was one of the busiest in the city, he took my call within a few minutes.

"Am I invited to your New Year's Eve party?" he asked when I blurted out my predicament. "Because we'd love to come."

"Tom—"

"Okay, okay. Don't talk to the police. If they want to schedule an interview, I'll set up something tomorrow when you're feeling well enough to talk. Meanwhile, don't say anything else, all right? I mean it."

"Thanks," I said, relieved. "Come about eight o'clock."

"Great! Can I bring my brother and his wife? They want to thank you for writing the letter that got their daughter into Barnard."

I withheld a sigh. "Bring them."

When I hung up and leaned back shakily into the sofa, Michael came over and sat on the coffee table. He handed me the ice pack.

I touched it to my cheek and met his gaze. "The police think you slugged me."

"I know." He said, "It's going to get worse."

"How's that?"

"Chances are," he said calmly, "the cops are going to take me in."

"For hitting me?" I dropped the ice.

"No."

"Not for Kitty's death!"

He picked up the ice pack again and held it gently to my face. "When somebody steals a candy bar, the cops assume it's me. It's not an arrest, just questions. There's nothing to worry about. I've already called Cannoli and Sons."

His lawyers, whom he frequently took on his famous fishing trips and paid enormous sums of money, were known lovers of pastry from a bakery in Newark, and Michael had fondly bestowed them with a nickname.

He said, "There's this other thing."

I didn't like the sound of that. "Oh?"

"The way she was tied up."

"With her panty hose. Libby told me."

"A few years back, there was another killing," Michael said slowly. "A baseball fan owed some significant play-off money. He didn't pay and got himself whacked for it. His body floated up in a toxic retaining pond in Jersey."

Trying to keep my courage up, I asked, "Is there any other kind of retaining pond in Jersey?"

"He'd been tied with panty hose."

I started to sense that huge tidal wave of disaster building over my head. "What does this have to do with Kitty?"

"The killer turned out to be a relative of mine."

I looked into his face and tried to find some emotion. "How can you be so calm about this?"

"It's the usual drill." He shrugged. "I'll go with them and let my lawyers answer their questions."

"You have no reason to murder Kitty."

"These particular officers don't seem to care about that. I'll be back in time for dinner, I promise. I'll take you out, someplace nice."

"No, Michael—"

"Okay, we'll stay in and cook." He smiled, but it didn't last. He kissed the top of my head. "This is what it's like, being with me."

The police asked us a lot more questions, but they could not look beyond the man in my house. Motive and opportunity didn't matter. Michael's connection to organized crime always set off more alarms than a gun-wielding maniac in a convenience store.

An hour later, as the police folded him into the back of a cruiser, Libby said, "Even I can see how unfair this is."

On the back porch, the worker bees of the crime scene team were busy with cameras and little plastic bags and lots of Styrofoam cups of coffee from Wawa. They still hadn't covered Kitty up. Her hair shivered in the winter wind. I could see she needed a pedicure, too. I turned away from the window.

Libby helped herself to a bagel and slathered it with cream cheese. "But the Incredible Hulk didn't seem too upset about it. His arrest, I mean."

"It's not an arrest. And he's not a hulk."

"Well, for all his shady dealings, I can't really see him bumping off Kitty. And leaving her body practically on his own doorstep wasn't exactly the move of a master criminal. I talked to that handsome guy outside, the one with the blue jacket?"

I glanced out the window. They were all wearing blue jackets. "Are you trying to get a date with a crime scene investigator?"

My sister's Cheshire-cat smile appeared. "He might be interested in the Potions and Passions catalog. Maybe law enforcement people should be my target customer. Carrying guns is surely a sign of inadequacy elsewhere, right?"

"I've always thought so."

"Anyway, he told me that Kitty probably died between seven and nine last night, depending on how long she was out in the cold."

"She died during the fashion show," I said.

With a mouthful of bagel, Libby nodded. "That's useful information, right?"

"It only means whoever killed her didn't attend the show."

The phone rang again, and Libby went to answer it.

I took Michael's oatmeal back to the pantry, unopened. The thought that he hadn't had any breakfast suddenly brought a stupid lump to my throat. The police had no evidence against him except that he'd been conveniently on the premises when they arrived and a silly coincidence with panty hose. And now, while they wasted precious hours interrogating him, the real killer could be off enjoying brunch at a picturesque country inn while Michael went hungry. I blinked back tears.

Libby hung up and appeared at the pantry door. "The newspapers have heard about Kitty's death. I guess it's true reporters listen to police scanners."

I leaned against the cupboard. "I can't stand it, Libby. It's happening again."

Libby came over and put her arm around me. Between the two of us, we had coped with a lot of death and loss over the past few years, and we didn't need words to communicate how we felt anymore. But she said, "Let's go to my place, Nora. Tons of people will be tracking you down for quotes and interviews."

"Any reporter worth his salt will find me at your house. Besides, I don't want to hide."

Her face clouded. "Nora, honey—"

The phone rang again. Libby winced.

"Go ahead and answer," I said. "I'll be okay."

She went out and picked up the telephone while I tried to steel myself for what was surely to come. A moment later Libby returned, clutching the receiver to her bosom. "It's your editor. Stan Rosenstatz."

I took the phone. "Stan?"

My editor at the *Intelligencer* managed the ragtag misfits of the Features department—me among them—with the air of a man who calculated his pension twice a day and hoped none of us would screw it up for him. But once in a while, like an old hunting dog seeing the shotguns come out, he woke up eager for the chase.

"Nora, we just heard the news about Kitty. We're all in shock."

"So am I, Stan."

"Was she . . . Do you think she suffered?"

"No, I don't." I spent a quick moment pondering my predicament. Stan definitely was an old bird dog of a newspaperman who knew how to follow the scent of a story. "Listen, I'm not ready to talk to the press yet, okay? I . . . It's too soon, and the police are still here."

"I understand." He hesitated between human kindness and his journalist's instincts. "But our crime desk guys are hoping to get the first break on this story. I'm sorry to do this to you, Nora. Can you just confirm if the Abruzzo guy was arrested?"

I caught my breath. Already the story was breaking. And the news desk was using Stan to get to me.

I said, "I can't talk right now, Stan."

"Okay, okay, I get it. But you'll be available later, right? For one thing, I could use your advice about covering Kitty's stories. Can you take over?"

"You mean, take her job?"

"No, sorry, it's too soon to talk about replacing Kitty."

And they'd probably prefer to hire someone with experience or a degree in journalism or at the very least someone who knew how to run spell check.

"But," Stan continued, "she's got events on her calendar that need to be covered. We've got a photographer scheduled to follow her around today, in fact. Some fashion thing is happening at the train station, and we've saved a lot of inches for it."

"At the train station?"

"It's a traveling fashion show, I guess. Some guy taking a bunch of people to New York. Kitty thought it was a big deal."

Brinker Holt, I thought at once. He was going to New York with the Brinker Bra.

"What time has Kitty noted for today?"

"Two o'clock."

To take pictures of Brinker waving farewell from the station was another brilliant idea of Kitty's—the local boy setting off for fame and fortune in the big city. No doubt he'd have half-naked girls in bras ready to pose for pictures. I had to give her credit: Kitty knew what readers would want to see in the paper.

But another thought occurred to me. "Stan, what appointments had Kitty marked down for yesterday?"

A short silence while Stan checked. "Just one name," he said a moment later. "Brinker Lamb."

"That's two names."

"It is?"

Was something going on between Brinker Holt and Lamb Limited as Lexie had guessed? Kitty must have picked up on that possibility. Immediately, I wondered what in the world her business had been with Brinker.

"Stan," I said, galvanized by the information, "I'll go to the train station for Kitty."

"That's great. You'll e-mail me later?"

The world was going to think the worst of Michael, but I didn't have to contribute to his looking guilty. If I went out in public as if nothing were wrong, surely it would help his cause. And I had a feeling I could learn more about Kitty's death by following her footsteps.

"You're sure I look all right?" Libby asked half an hour later. "I'm hardly dressed for another fashion show."

"It's not a show. It's a bon-voyage party."

We'd managed to get Libby's hair blown out and we applied makeup from my vanity drawers, but it wouldn't matter. Nobody was going to look higher than the jiggle in her red sweater.

"You look fabulous," I said. "Wearing that bra, you're going to blind anyone who looks at you."

Libby gave herself a bodily shake and unlocked the minivan

door. "It's getting a little snug. I wish I knew how to get it off."

"There must be a trick to it."

The crime scene guys turned to admire her as she got into the driver's seat. Libby gave them all a beguiling smile and fingertip wave. At least two of them waved back.

As she drove out my driveway, we saw that more state troopers had blocked the entrance to Mick's Muscle Cars with their cruisers. The cops were methodically searching the automobiles on display, working to build a case against Michael.

Spike crouched on my lap as we drove to Philadelphia. Periodically he hurled himself at the window to threaten all the buses and trucks that passed us. He seemed to have a particular grudge against white Escalades.

Libby careened into town and crossed over the Market Street Bridge and Schuylkill River to the Amtrak station. She parked, and I put Spike into the oversize Balenciaga handbag I used to carry him around. Settling into the soft leather, he seemed content to sleep off his busy morning.

In a freezing wind, we dashed into the palatial 30th Street Station, made familiar to the average American in the movie *Witness*. When years of grime were washed away to reveal its gilt ceilings and magnificent sculptures, the beautiful neoclassical design surprised us all. It was a beautiful place and a photogenic backdrop for a fashion event.

Music for the farewell party drew Libby and me across the cavernous grand concourse toward a milling crowd. People bounced to the beat and waved signs. It looked like a political campaign rally, only with fewer clothes.

On the outskirts of the party loitered a woman dressed head to toe in a silk sari and holding a clipboard.

Libby recognized her first. "That's Sabria Chatterjee," she said to me. "What in the world is she doing here? Sabria!"

Sabria spotted us and immediately looked as if she wished she could teleport herself to the Khyber Pass.

"Sabria," I said, putting out my hand to her. "How nice to see you."

"Hello, Nora. Hi, Libby." She shook my hand with the firm grip of a woman who felt she had a lot to prove.

When I had last seen Sabria, she was an ambitious executive who wore stark business suits and pinned her hair back in a bun to avoid looking anything but seriously career-minded. Now it appeared she had gone to another extreme by embracing her heritage. Her soft figure was swathed in a shimmery silk sari the color of hot curry. Rings glittered on her fingers, and bracelets jangled on her wrists. Even her toes winked with tiny jewels. Put her on an elephant, and she could make a passage to India.

I remembered Sabria as one of Emma's Bryn Mawr friends. The daughter of immigrants, she had resisted the culture of her parents. Now she seemed to have immersed herself in it. Her lustrous hair gleamed, and she had applied a thick ring of kohl around her velvety dark eyes that still flashed with determination to break through the glass ceiling. She had a death grip on her clipboard, and with her other hand she repeatedly clicked a ballpoint pen.

Libby said, "You look lovely!"

"Thank you," Sabria said briskly. "We're currently enjoying an uptick in Indian cultural awareness. It's not often the general demographic shows an interest, so I figured I'd ride the wave. It worked. Clientec Advertising hired me for their New York office. Look, I even pierced my nose."

Sure enough, a tasteful diamond winked alongside her left nostril.

"That's great," said Libby. "How is your sex life?"

Sabria blinked, unable to translate Libby's question into corporate-speak, so I said quickly, "I've heard of Clientec. Congratulations.

Didn't you do the Super Bowl ads for a soft drink last year? The one with that teenage singer?"

"Our clients included a soft drink–based conglomerate last year, yes."

"Looks as if you're on the job right now," I observed, glancing at her clipboard.

"I'm seeking ideas," Sabria said, all business. "Creative input from popular culture, you know." She used her pen to make a quick sketch in the margin of the paper. I noticed it was the only drawing on the page.

"The Brinker Bra is certainly the most creative thing I've seen in a long time," I said. "Is Clientec doing the ad campaign?"

"No, no." Sabria whipped her clipboard behind her back as if we might forget about it. "Not yet anyway. We hope Brinker will bring us on board, but nothing's been inked yet. I'm just looking around. Absorbing. Brinker is a very creative person who provides results for the consumer."

"I'll say!" Libby pointed at her own breasts. "I haven't looked this good since I stopped using the Bust Booster!"

Again, Sabria looked at a loss for a response.

"I don't mean to brag," Libby went on, "but I fill out a bra better than most women. Trouble is, this one doesn't want to let go. Do you know if there's some special technique for releasing it?"

"Uh, no, I don't. I have nothing to do with the Brinker Bra. Nothing at all."

While the two of them struggled to communicate like aliens from different planets, I glanced around to see who else had come to send Brinker off to New York and stardom in the fashion world. No doubt Kitty would have noted all the movers and shakers to list in her column. I looked for someone Kitty would have found worthy of mention.

But the first people I spotted were the twin models from the fashion show. Today they were dressed in pink jeans that laced up the sides, sandals better suited for a Miami disco than a Philadelphia winter, and Brinker Bras embedded with sequins. Their too-shiny hair extensions caressed their tanned, naked shoulders and bare backs. It was hard to ignore their breasts, though. The twins looked as pleased with themselves as if they were the inventors of mammary glands.

They must have been on the lookout for Sabria, because they scampered over as soon as they recognized her.

"Sabria! We've been looking all over for you!"

Sabria's face slackened as the twins approached. "Hi," she said weakly. "Uh, Libby, Nora, these are the Finehart twins, Fawn and Fontayne."

"We're models?" said Fawn, ending her sentence with a question mark.

"We're hoping to become the spokesgirls for the Brinker Bra," Fontayne added cheerfully, flipping her perfect plastic hair over her shoulder to better display her bra. "Get it? Twins for your twins."

"We thought that up ourselves? How's it coming, Sabria? Do you think we have a chance?"

"I have nothing to do with that," Sabria said quickly. "It would be totally the decision of the advertising firm Brinker hires. Which he hasn't done yet, of course, since it would be ethically wrong to choose one advertising firm before the others had a chance to submit their bids."

"Brinker seems to be avoiding us."

"We thought you could help?"

"I— Excuse me," Sabria said suddenly. "But I have to . . . I must make a phone call."

Sabria departed so abruptly that Libby and I were left staring at the twins, who looked disappointed by Sabria's swift exit. They actually pouted. But their breasts remained perky.

Fontayne rallied first with a smile that had more white teeth than should fit into the mouth of a normal human being. "So," she asked brightly, "are you friends of Brinker?"

Sensing a request for career help, I said, "Not exactly, no."

"We're here for the newspaper," Libby volunteered. "You know, the *Philadelphia Intelligencer.*"

"Would you like to take our pictures? We're here to facilitate the media's understanding of the Brinker Bra." Fontayne flipped her hair extensions again, but managed to catch her bracelet in the flaxen strands. She yanked, but the hair only wrapped tighter. She tried using her other hand to disengage the tangle, but more hair got snagged in her rings. In seconds, Fontayne was wrapped up in her own hair and panicking.

Her sister helped untangle Fontayne's hair. "Maybe if we get our pictures in enough newspapers, Brinker will forget about that other girl?"

"What other girl?" Libby asked.

Fawn rolled her eyes. "The one everybody's talking about? I mean, she's gorgeous and all, but come on? She's not really trained? She can't walk? Which is why they put her on the horse?"

"A horse," I said.

Fontayne sighed heavily. "We thought we had this gig sewn up. We're perfect for the Brinker Bra ad campaign, don't you think?"

"No, we really want to become Brinker's muse? Like Kelly was for Calvin?"

"But this horse girl rode in off the street, and suddenly she's the superstar."

"Yeah, Brinker loves her?"

"You can totally see why," said Fontayne.

"But she's got this boyfriend?" said Fawn, rolling her eyes. "What a loser?"

"I think the newspaper will definitely need your picture," I said. "But I must find our photographer. You girls should mingle. Stir up some publicity for yourselves."

"Yeah," said Libby. "We'll find you when the photographer gets here."

"Okay, if you say so. C'mon, Fawnie."

"Okay, Fonnie?"

They skittered away on their high heels, leaving Libby and me to stare at each other.

Libby said, "What has Emma gotten into this time?"

"Think she's here?"

"We'd better find out."

The flash of camera lights led us directly to our little sister.

Fully dressed this time, Emma wore leather pants, spike-heeled boots and a body-skimming turtleneck sweater that framed her fine-boned face. I doubted it was only a Brinker Bra that made her look so sensational. With her long legs and supple body, Emma could pass for a headliner from a Vegas chorus line. Today her hair was short and devilishly spiked, and she carried her whip over her shoulder like a runaway's pack.

"Hey, sis!" she bellowed when she saw me among the jostling photographers. "It's about time my keeper showed up! And Libby, too. What is this? Another intervention?"

Chapter Five

$\mathcal{V}$ery funny," I said as the guys with the cameras reluctantly dispersed.

"A girl's gotta keep her sense of humor."

"Em," said Libby, "you look fabulous."

Of the three of us, Emma was the one who had turned the Blackbird creamy skin and auburn hair into something downright sexy. Libby tended to look like a ravished concubine from another century, and I . . . well, I hoped I managed to appear to be the dignified one. But Michael had laughed when I said that.

The youngest sister, Emma, had come of age during the great Blackbird depression—the time when Mother and Daddy first ran low on money and started their plunge into the morass of massive debt. Emma had a tantalizing taste of the good life, but it was yanked from under her nose when she was a teenager. Unlike Libby and me, she knew how to "make do." Unfortunately, she required increasingly large quantities of vodka to do so.

Emma grabbed Libby's wrist and burst out laughing at her so-called bracelet. "What the hell are you wearing this for?"

"It's my new company bracelet. I'm a Potions and Passions consultant now."

"Do you even know what it is?"

"I like it! It's pretty in a masculine sort of way, and I believe in embracing both your yin and your yang."

"Well, you've certainly got the yang all choked up." Emma hooted.

"It's good to see you, Em," I said. "Your entrance last night was quite a surprise."

Her grin widened. "Yeah, that was a hell of a production, wasn't it? How did you like Stoli? The horse, I mean."

For a while, Emma had parlayed her riding expertise and reckless disregard for her own safety into a decent career on the Grand Prix show jumping circuit. But a few broken bones put a speed bump in her career path. Today she was using the horse as a diversionary tactic, I knew.

I played along. "You were both great. You stole the show."

"Did you see the Vacuous Vixens, too? Those blond twins? Man, are they nuts."

Libby said, "I thought they were cute."

"They follow me around all the time. Give me the creeps." Suddenly Emma narrowed her eyes at me. "What's with you? Something wrong with your face?"

"You won't believe it," Libby jumped in before I could address the subject more decorously. "Kitty Keough's been murdered. And guess where the killer dumped her body? Right on Nora's back porch. Nora found her this morning and fainted on the spot."

"Whoa." Emma reached for my arm. "Are you going to faint again?"

"I'm fine."

"Yeah, you look fine. Let's sit down."

She helped me to a bench, and I sat, trying to force the image of Kitty's dead body out of my mind's eye again. Spike woke up and poked his head out of my bag. He barked joyously at Emma. She pulled him out and gave the puppy a roughing-up. Libby, meanwhile, told Emma the whole story.

When she was finished, Emma cursed. "And Mick's in jail? No wonder you look ready to keel over."

"He's not in jail. He's being questioned. His lawyers are with him."

Emma nodded, stroking Spike into submission. Like most male animals in Emma's thrall, he rolled his eyes and sighed. "Nobody has lawyers like Mick. But hell, what happened to Kitty? Who killed the old bat?"

"I can't imagine."

"Leaving her on your porch was a hell of a calling card. It had to be somebody who knows you."

"That had occurred to me."

Emma frowned. "And while the police grill Mick, the real killer's getting away."

"Yes." I took a deep breath and spilled my guts. "Kitty asked me to cover the fashion show for her last night, and when I got there I was told she had been barred by Brinker himself. But she had his name written in her appointment book for yesterday. Which makes me wonder if they had some kind of argument."

"Did Brinker and Kitty even know each other?"

"I assume so. And there was another name in her book—Lamb. Did you know Hemorrhoid Pierce has changed his name to Lamb?"

She nodded and hefted Spike under her arm. "Yeah. And he's been hanging around Brinker all week."

That news surprised me. "As friends?"

She shrugged. "They weren't throwing punches in public, if that's what you mean."

"What's going on between them?"

"I dunno. You think one of them killed Kitty?"

I rubbed my forehead, feeling my headache coming back. "I feel they're involved somehow. I need to figure out why she wanted to meet with them."

"Who do you plan on asking first?"

"Brinker's not exactly my favorite person."

"Or mine," Emma said.

I shot a glance up at her. "How did you manage to get hired by him?"

"I don't know if Brinker even knew who was hired. One of his assistants called me."

I bet Brinker knew exactly who he had put on his payroll. But I didn't say so to Emma. Had she blocked from her mind what had happened many years ago?

"Right now," I said, "I need to find the *Intelligencer* photographer to take some photos, and then need to get some quotes. With Kitty gone, they need me to get her column written this week."

"Has the poisoned pen passed into your hands?" Emma asked, one brow arched.

"Not yet. Maybe never."

"We could use some help," Libby said to Emma. "And you need to keep your mind off the booze, right? Want to give us a hand? We could be like Charlie's Angels."

"Lib," I said, "take it easy."

"Is that why you're here?" Emma asked me, her voice suddenly cold. "To make sure I'm clean and sober?"

"No, Em," I said. "We only—"

She shoved Spike back into my arms. "I can take care of myself, you know. I don't need to be locked up in a cage."

"If you start thinking of it as a prison, you can't—"

"Just shut up," Emma snapped. "Did you come to get a urine sample from me, too?"

"We love you, Em."

"As long as I'm convenient," she said. "As long as I don't make trouble. Well, I'll never be a good girl like you, Nora, so get used to it."

Libby looked distressed. "Did I start an argument? I only meant— Hey, did you meet any nice men in rehab?"

Emma grinned nastily. "Of course I did. A real find. We tunneled out together a couple of nights ago. You might have heard of him; he's famous. Well, infamous, really. Want to meet him?"

"Emma—"

"Oh, yes, please, Em!" Libby said.

"You're gonna love this one," said our sister. "Right this way."

I stuffed Spike back into my bag and followed.

Emma chose her men on the basis of their shock factor. It started with Jake, her husband, a professional football player who once posed in the buff for a women's magazine. After he was killed, she took up with a defrocked evangelical minister who scouted parishioners for his new congregation in an adult bookstore. After that, she found a skinny kid who went around competing in all-you-can-eat chicken wing contests. And then there was the taxidermist. Don't ask.

So I wasn't exactly surprised when Monte Bogatz walked out of the train station men's room, looking like Buffalo Bill had wandered away from the Wild West. He wore a squashed cowboy hat and lots of fringed leather and a belt buckle shaped like a bucking bull. He hastily tucked a silver flask into his hip pocket.

"Why, howdy, little ladies!" He tipped his Stetson when he laid eyes on Libby and me. "I bet you're Emmy's sisters."

"Emmy's just finished telling us about you," I said. "But, of course, we know you by reputation."

Monte's gap-toothed grin made him famous at the age of six, when he stepped on the stage of the Grand Ole Opry and yodeled his first hit song, "Roller Skates and Heartache." He enjoyed a short career as an aw-shucks country kid with a golden voice until booze got the best of him and better-looking rockabilly stars took over the country music scene. His last hit, "I'm Saving Myself for

Marriage While Mama's Saving Her Pennies for Beer," fell off the charts at least a decade ago.

Looking at him now, I figured Monte was on the fast track to nowhere. His child-star cuteness had given way to a squinty stare and a loose, boozy smile. Thirty years old, but looking forty-five, he had the bowlegged walk of an arthritic cowpoke heading for the bunkhouse. Not long ago, however, I'd seen him on television advertising western-style baby clothes for a huge discount chain, so maybe he wasn't washed up yet.

Spike poked his head out of my handbag and gave a surly snarl.

"Well, hello, little feller. What kind of varmint are you?"

Spike informed his admirer that he was a vicious beast capable of ripping a man's arm off.

Monte Bogatz yanked his hand back in the nick of time. If he was drinking this early in the day, at least it didn't affect his reflexes. I shoved Spike back down into my bag.

Libby, who hadn't spotted the flask, was starstruck. "Oh, Mr. Bogatz, could I have your autograph?"

"Why not?" he said, looking down her cleavage with the air of a connoisseur. "We're practically family. But call me Monte, sugar. Everybody does."

"Hold off on the autograph," Emma said. "Let's get out of here, cowboy. We've got a train to catch."

"Whatever you say, little lady." He snaked his arm around her waist. "You're gonna show this country boy the bright lights of Broadway, right?"

"Right. Let's go take a bite out of the Big Apple."

"Emma, wait," I said.

"Forget it," she said. "If I've got problems, I'm gonna enjoy them."

I couldn't stop her, I told myself sternly. I couldn't change her. I could only stand by and be supportive while she made her own choices. I wanted to repeat my new mantra aloud. I could not make my sister's choices.

But as Emma stalked away with her new boyfriend, I could hardly prevent myself from chasing them. Maybe everyone was right. Maybe I'd been protecting Emma too long. Maybe I should have let her fight her own battles from the beginning.

"What should we do?" Libby asked, distressed as we watched Emma head down the road to ruin with Monte Bogatz. "I don't have my handcuffs with me."

"Let her go."

"Are you sure?"

"No, but that's what she wants."

I sent Libby to scope out the train station in search of Brinker or Hemorrhoid. Meanwhile, I went looking for the newspaper photographer who'd been assigned to today's event. I found Lee Song already snapping pictures of Fawn and Fontayne. He crouched on one knee, shooting upward to emphasize their long, bare legs.

"Enjoying your work?" I asked him.

Lee smiled at me and stood up. "Some days, I'd do it for free. Hi, Nora. You okay? You look—"

"I'm fine."

"I heard Kitty kicked the bucket. Sorry, Nora. You look upset."

"Stan said he was saving space for this story. I hope you can fill up the page with pictures."

"Yeah, but you'll need a quote from Brinker, if you can get close enough."

I never wanted to get close to Brinker, and my expression must have given away that involuntary thought.

"I don't blame you." Lee pointed. "He's over there. Last I saw, he was pouring champagne over some girl's breasts. She was crying."

"He hasn't changed, then."

Chivalrously, Lee tagged along as I headed into the throng that was gathered beneath a cloud of shiny pink helium balloons all grouped in breastlike pairs and each bearing the Brinker Bra logo. Several dozen absurdly dressed people mingled around a makeshift bar while models in Brinker Bras circulated the perimeter.

Steeling myself, I plunged in.

I found Brinker talking with the fashion columnist from the other city newspaper, Dillard Farquar, a refined gentleman who'd been around since Diana Vreeland's heyday.

In his middle years, Dilly had grown bored with his life of inherited wealth and decided to make a career out of what he loved most—clothing. Within a few years, he became the city's patrician arbiter of style, not to mention an instantly recognizable celebrity.

Still the picture of polished elegance at seventy-odd years—the years he admitted to—Dilly wore a natty blue blazer with his own family monogram on the pocket, plus a crisp shirt, flannel trousers and ascot. Like an architect, he kept a pair of round black eyeglasses perched on his aristocratic nose. His primary fashion statement, of course, was the Farquar fortune—a reported $90 million made in cutlery. His great-grandfather descended from a long line of French fencing masters and invented steak knives.

In addition to his long career interpreting fashion trends for Philadelphia, Dilly was best known for an often-repeated story. Minutes before a face-lift procedure, he had supposedly grabbed the hand of his Main Line plastic surgeon and told her, "If I die on the operating table, dear heart, please don't stop. I must look good in my casket."

He caught sight of me waiting for Brinker's attention.

"Nora!" He broke off scribbling with his trademark Montblanc pen. "Don't you look lovely today. My God, is that a Dior coat?"

I had put away the pink chinchilla and found a coat more politically correct this afternoon. "It is. One of Grandmama's favorites. Hello, Dilly."

He kissed both my cheeks. "It's stunning. I've always loved that reversible design, so clever of Dior. Brinker, do you know Nora Blackbird? You should. If anyone in this town innately understands fashion, it's Nora."

Brinker looked as if he'd like to burn my Dior coat with me in it.

It all came back to me in a rush, and I could see he remembered every nanosecond of our fateful summer, too.

A few days after Oriana and I found him branding Hemorrhoid with a cigarette, he'd sought me out and cornered me in the deep end of the pool. He untied my bikini top and threw it over the diving board like a captured flag. I kicked him in his Speedo, which should have been the end of it.

But it hadn't been.

Now in his mid-thirties, Brinker looked like a TV version of a Special Forces agent—head shaved smooth as a bullet, muscles bulging beneath a plain olive T-shirt. He had cold black eyes—surely contact lenses—a hawk nose, and a macho tilt to his chin. My first thought was overcompensation. In one hand, he gripped the neck of a champagne bottle—an empty one, I noted. With his other hand, he pointed his video camera.

As Dilly introduced me, Brinker's camera zoomed in on my face. "Hello," he said from behind the lens.

"Would you mind putting down the camera?" I asked.

The videotaping was his way of forcing people to participate in their own humiliation, and I was surprised when he honored my request. But Brinker also had a mean habit of studying a person before lowering himself to speak. I recognized it now as a comedian's trick of putting his audience in their place before starting on his material. He defied heckling by displaying his own superiority.

I endured his scrutiny for a long moment, waiting for the put-down.

Then he said, "I remember your face, but not your name."

I managed to smile despite his inability to remember Dilly's introduction. "I'm Nora Blackbird."

"Oh, yes. You're thinner now. It suits you."

During his short time in the fashion business, he'd learned the advantage of remarking on everyone's weight. I said, "Congratulations on your success."

He smiled, too, suddenly turning on the force of a powerful personality like a sunlamp. "Have you tried it yet? The Brinker Bra?" He let his gaze slip down to my breasts and linger there.

"Not yet. Do you expect every woman in America to buy one?" I had my notepad in hand, pen poised.

"She's going to buy several," he said. "In various colors, all the styles. The Brinker Bra will become an indispensable part of every woman's wardrobe."

Dilly Farquar glanced wryly at me as if to say Brinker had already given him the same canned baloney.

"What was your inspiration?" I asked.

"It came to me in a dream. What man's dreams aren't full of women's breasts?"

Except he didn't use the word *breasts*. Once again, a comedian's trick—using a crude word to score a crude laugh.

When the laugh didn't come, he asked me, "And how do you rate being a fashion expert in this town?"

"I'm not. I simply wear old clothes because I can't afford anything new."

"But she always manages to look stunning," Dilly interjected.

I decided to take the bull by the horns. "I'm working for the *Intelligencer*. In Kitty Keough's place. I understand you requested she not come to your show last night."

He looked startled. "I did?"

"Or someone in your organization did."

"Well, that old bat deserves a slap in the face now and then."

Kitty had once called him "Baldy Brinker" in her column, when Brinker's receding hairline started to become obvious. Now he shaved his head but I imagined her remark still stung.

"Nobody likes Kitty much," Dilly agreed, "but that doesn't mean—"

"Let her find somebody new to kick around. Besides, even the Brinker Bra can't help those sagging udders of hers." Brinker gave me a sneery, triumphant smile.

"It doesn't really matter," I said, "since Kitty passed away last night. In fact, she was murdered."

Dilly's jaw dropped. "Good Lord!"

Brinker looked as if he'd swallowed a hand grenade.

I said, "She was barred from your show earlier in the evening."

"We had to limit the guest list." As if seizing on a good idea, Brinker said quickly, "Fire regulations. You expect us to invite the entire city to these events? We had to cut somebody."

"I see. But she had your name written in her appointment book for yesterday."

"So?" Brinker began to look belligerent. "That doesn't mean anything. I didn't know the bitch."

"That's odd," Dilly said. "I thought your family knew her quite well. In fact, I clearly remember your father throwing a drink in her face once. Because of something she wrote about your grandmother?"

If possible, Brinker turned pale. "One old broad writing about another? Who cares?"

"Care to comment on Kitty's death?" I asked.

"No," he said shortly. "No comment at all."

"Are you sure?"

"I know who you are." He suddenly pretended to recognize me. "I've got your little sister working for me, did you know that?"

Brinker lifted the camera to his eye and turned on his heel. He walked away, already filming other people.

"Hard to believe a young man can be so pompous," Dilly said.

"He's not my favorite person either. What do you know about his grandmother?"

"Old Biddy Holt? You never met her? Now there was a barracuda! She was very strict. Used to lock the family butler in his room when he slipped up. She thought she was punishing him, but he read the whole Zane Grey oeuvre several times."

"Brinker gets his cheery personality from his grandma?"

"Very likely. She and Kitty had a feud for years as a matter of fact. Something about an umbrella at a garden party. Biddy claimed Kitty stole hers or visa versa. There was hair pulling and retaliation involving dog shit in somebody's limousine, as I recall. You must have been away in college at the time. Otherwise you'd remember the sordid details. It was a pitched battle."

"Sounds awful."

"It was actually quite entertaining. Don't let Brinker spoil your day, dear heart. He's beneath you. Now spill the beans." Dilly pulled me by the elbow until we stood apart from the crowd. "Ding-dong, the witch is dead? And murdered, no less? What does Brinker have to do with it?"

"Maybe nothing," I said, relieved that he was gone. I smiled at my old friend. "What do you know about Brinker's arrival on the fashion scene, Dilly?"

"It was incredibly sudden," Dilly observed. "One minute he's telling jokes in a dive, and now he's heralding himself as the next Marc Jacobs? You and I both know it doesn't happen this way. He should have spent years working his way up, designing for some Italian divas or in a Hong Kong sweatshop. It's very suspicious."

"Have you heard anything?"

"The truth is bound to come out. But," said Dilly, "if Brinker Holt designed that bra, I'm going to take up brain surgery."

I gave his arm a grateful pat. "Don't buy your scalpel yet, Dilly."

"Are you going to assume Kitty's column, Nora?"

"They haven't offered me the job."

"Yet," Dilly predicted. He reached into the pocket of his blazer and came up with a silver case. From it, he delicately removed a business card. "Why don't you call me sometime? We'll have lunch. You need a friend in the biz, someone to talk through professional matters with—from the point of view of someone who shares your background."

"Thanks, Dilly. I can use all the good advice I can get."

He presented his card to me. It was vellum with embossed letters, not a quick card from Kinko's. "You'll do fine on your own, Nora. Just don't let the corporate bastards get you down."

I gave him a heartfelt kiss. "I'll keep in touch."

We parted ways, and a minute later I literally bumped into Richard D'eath.

Richard's cane clattered to the floor, and I hid my surprise at seeing him there by bending to pick it up. Tartly, I said, "You career journalists sure know a hot story when you see one."

"Actually," he said, accepting the cane without thanks, "I was looking for you. Can we talk?"

I couldn't have been more surprised if he suggested we run off to Disney World. "Talk about what?"

"Kitty Keough's death."

I should have known he was on the job. And he wanted information from me.

His gaze narrowed. "Is there something wrong with your face?"

Without thinking, I touched my cheek. "No, nothing."

He shrugged. "You disappeared last night. You have some time now?"

"Not really, no. You see—"

"It will only take a few minutes."

"I'm—"

"Got something to hide?"

"I have a lot on my mind today."

"Like Kitty Keough's death? Or your boyfriend's arrest?"

He watched my expression as an icy chill washed over me. I should have known Richard was way ahead of me.

"Don't try to kid a kidder, Miss Blackbird. We both know you're not chasing front-page news. I heard your boyfriend got himself arrested this morning."

"How do you know who my boyfriend is?"

"There are some people who make news when they sneeze. Mick Abruzzo is one of those people."

"He wasn't arrested. Michael is being asked some questions. When bad things happen, the police automatically assume he has information."

"Especially when the bad things concern you?"

"Kitty's death has nothing to do with me."

"If the dead body turned up on your doorstep, the murder very much has something to do with you. And, by extension, the man you're involved with. I hear he's not exactly the tea-and-crumpets type."

"Let me guess," I said, adding up all the clues. "Your story is organized crime."

"Not yet, it isn't. Talk to me. Maybe there's an angle I'm missing."

The last person I wanted to talk to today was Richard D'eath, especially if he had decided to write about Michael. I felt certain he could twist my words into an unflattering story, and I didn't have the strength to outwit him today. But ditching him obviously wasn't going to be graceful.

"All right," I said, "but I have to speak with my photographer first. Even the society column has a deadline."

"Sure," he said, suspiciously good-humored. "Do what you have to do. I'll wait. It'll be interesting to watch you work."

"You might notice other things that are more interesting here."

"You mean all these women in Brinker Bras?"

"They're hard to ignore, aren't they? Even for a seasoned reporter like yourself."

He remained unflustered. "I like women with a little mystery. I'll wait for you right here." Richard leaned against the marble wall by the exit I'd have to use to make my clean getaway.

I looked for Libby, but didn't see her in the crowd. So I found Lee Song again.

"Lee, can I ask you a favor?"

He still had a grin on his usually impassive face. "If it involves hanging around with these models for a few more hours, I'm your man."

"Sorry to disappoint." I smiled. "Will you find my sister and give her a message for me?"

"Happy to."

Lee listened carefully and agreed to help.

I glanced over my shoulder and saw that Richard had been approached by Fawn and Fontayne Finehart, who could surely distract even him with their attributes. I had a minute, at least.

I found a ticket counter blessedly open, and I bought my ticket quickly. In another moment I was headed for the trains. A fully dressed woman hardly rated a glance from the transit cop. But once out of Richard's sight, I whipped off my Dior coat and turned it inside out to show the other side—small checks instead of big attention-getting blocks of primary colors. Then I plunged downstairs toward the trains.

As I boarded, Spike poked his head out of my bag and demanded to know where we were going.

"We're making our escape," I told him, sliding into the ladies' room and closing the door behind me. Safely inside, I used the time to gather my wits and powder my nose.

At last, the train gave a lurch and began to move. Spike dashed around my feet, panting with excitement. He loved moving vehicles.

As the train cleared the station, I felt safe enough to let myself out of the loo. With Spike once again stowed in my bag, I found plenty of open seats. I slipped into one in a middle row. As Spike struggled to look out the window, I whispered, "Don't draw any attention, please. Behave yourself."

"Who, me?" asked Richard, taking the adjacent seat.

Chapter Six

I blushed like a teenager caught shimmying down a drain spout.

"Can we have a conversation now?" he asked.

Spike told Richard to get the hell off the train.

"Take it easy, pooch," Richard said. "I'm already a wounded man." He looked closer at Spike with his plaster cast. "And what the hell happened to him?"

"It was an accident a few weeks ago," I said, trying to stuff Spike back into my handbag.

"How does the other guy look?" Richard relaxed into his seat with a short, pained explosion of breath, then glanced at me. "Do you always dress like you're in an Audrey Hepburn movie?"

"Would I look more professional in a safari jacket?"

"I think you'd look great in just about anything."

Before I could completely absorb what he'd said, he added, "From the way you just tried to disappear down a rabbit hole, I figure Audrey has something to hide."

I decided to come clean and apologize. "I'm sorry. I shouldn't have run away."

"I understand. You're trying to protect somebody."

"He doesn't need my protection. He's innocent. You'll have to find yourself another story."

Spike chose that moment to chomp his jaws around Richard's cane and growl.

Richard wisely allowed Spike to take possession. "I don't know what my story is yet. That's what I'm trying to find out. But if the clues point to organized crime, that's where I'm going."

"Why were you at the fashion show last night? To watch the launch of the Brinker Bra? Or to watch me?"

He met my gaze, and I was surprised to realize he had one blue eye and one hazel. The discovery shook me. I had hoped to keep Richard out of my head completely, and here he was insinuating his way into my conscious mind.

"Why don't we make a pact," he said, noticing the moment that stretched between us, too. "I'll tell you something useful if you tell me something useful."

I hesitated.

"I'll go first. Brinker Holt is involved with something besides women's underwear."

Still gripping Richard's cane in his teeth, Spike cautiously settled down on my lap, keeping one eye cocked on Richard to make sure there were no false moves.

"Brinker is your story?"

"If the Brinker Bra catches on like everybody's saying, Brinker stands to make hundreds of millions of dollars."

"As far as I know, that's not illegal."

Richard shrugged. "Where that much money is involved, there's usually something else going on. Especially when the guy has a track record."

"As in his comedy club burning down."

"Conveniently," Richard said. "From the insurance money, Brinker had enough cash to get his fashion venture off the ground. My question is, did he light a match to his own club? Or have some help from a pro who knew how to torch the place without getting caught?"

"What are you suggesting?"

He risked bodily harm by reaching out to scratch Spike behind his ears. "I'm not suggesting anything. I'm just asking questions."

"You think Michael is an arsonist now?"

"Abruzzo has a lot of talents," Richard observed. "One of them is his skill at avoiding convictions."

I decided to dislike Richard on a permanent basis. "So you *are* investigating organized crime. Okay, smart guy, what does the comedy club fire have to do with Kitty Keough's death?"

"I don't know yet. Do you?"

"They're totally unrelated events."

"You sure?"

No, I wasn't. What had Michael said long ago? Something about two crimes happening at the same time tended to be connected.

Under Richard's fingertip massage, Spike gave up growling. Traitor that he was, my dog let out a contented gurgle and began to suck on the handle of Richard's cane.

"All I know is that Michael has been detained for Kitty's murder because he happened to be in my house when I discovered her body. He'll be out of police custody very soon, and then the real investigation can begin."

"Why do you think her body ended up at your house?"

"I don't know," I said at once, automatically defensive. But when Richard didn't react, I said more slowly, "Somebody's trying to throw blame."

"Or send a message?"

"To me?"

"Maybe," Richard said. "Or to Abruzzo."

"What if somebody is trying to frame Michael?"

"Why would anybody do that?"

I looked out the window. The train had gathered momentum and left the city limits behind. I couldn't begin to guess how many enemies Michael had. I knew scant few of his friends, and most of those made Tony Soprano's crew look like a Little League team.

"Look," Richard said, "I don't know what your relationship is with the Abruzzo guy. I've heard a few things around the news desk, that's all. I find it hard to believe a woman like you could be seriously mixed up with a character like him, but—"

"You don't know anything about him."

"Only what's in the papers," he agreed. "Money laundering, illegal gambling, maybe the biggest car theft ring in the nation. It's not inconceivable that he could be an arsonist, too."

"The Abruzzo family might be mixed up in that kind of crime, but not Michael."

"Does he know Brinker?"

"Of course not!"

I could feel Richard looking at me. Softer, he said, "So you're really seeing him?"

"I'm not explaining myself to you."

"Okay, let me try explaining to myself. Tell me if I'm right. Mick Abruzzo is a lying sociopath who says whatever it takes to get a woman into his bed. And right now that woman is you."

"He doesn't lie!"

"No? What does he do? What happened to your face, Nora?"

I fought down the urge to kick Richard right in his lame leg.

Michael told me the truth; that I was sure about. He might occasionally leave out information he knew I didn't want to hear. There was a small difference between that and lying, perhaps, but I could live with it.

"We might look like opposites," I said slowly, "but we're alike. I know it doesn't make sense to you, but we've both been places we don't want to go back to."

"Meaning jail for him."

"Yes. His jail wasn't much different than where I was."

"You're a rich girl with fancy clothes and powerful friends. How is that life remotely like a prison cell?"

"My clothes have nothing to do with who I am inside. Michael sees that. We've both made some foolish choices in the past, and we paid a price. Now we both need— Oh, never mind." Suddenly I found I couldn't swallow and my words dried up. I took a steadying breath. "If you're on a crusade to put Michael back in jail, you're asking for help from the wrong person."

Richard shrugged. "A smart, beautiful woman like you doesn't need my advice when it comes to your love life. But I've seen some heartbreak in my day. People have been known to turn to the wrong kind of person to help them through tough times."

"Is this the part where you warn me not to get hurt? That's very sweet, Richard, but it's transparent. Don't try to befriend me—or my dog—so you can get information."

"No need for coddling," he said, removing his hand from Spike's ears. "Okay, I like that. Tell me what you know. Last night you were all over that kid. The one with the Game Boy. Who was he?"

"Are you always this insulting? You already know who he is."

He nodded. "Orlando Lamb. Who—speaking of hundreds of millions of dollars—is the nephew of Hemmings, who's been sniffing around the Brinker Bra for weeks. What's going on?"

"I have no idea."

He sent me a disbelieving smirk. "You were pretty quick to chase after the kid last night."

"I wanted to make sure he was okay. He was running away from his uncle, and I— Come to think of it, you held me back!"

"A reporter's job," he said, "is not to interfere with the news. We're supposed to observe, not go sticking pretty noses in places—"

"Let's not talk about my nose, shall we?"

Richard's gaze slid to the bruise on my face again. But he said,

"The kid said something about not wanting to buy women's underwear."

"I've only heard rumors."

"Maybe I've heard the same ones."

"All right, one theory is that Hemmings wants the Brinker Bra to become a subsidiary of Lamb Limited. It will be a very profitable investment and have the added advantage of establishing him as a real asset to the Lamb company. Right now, he's only Orlando's babysitter."

"You know Hemmings Lamb pretty well, right?"

"A little."

"He's a nut."

"He's complicated," I said. "And his relationship with Brinker is . . ."

"Is what?"

"Even more complicated."

"Are they friends? Enemies? Lovers?"

"Maybe all three, in a way."

Richard raised his brows thoughtfully.

I said, "If they are forging a business relationship now, I'm sure it's volatile. Years ago, Brinker— Well, it doesn't matter. It's Hemmings who has the power now. He's got the Lamb fortune behind him, and that has certainly turned the tables. I can't begin to guess how the two of them could function as a team. Some very screwy dynamics are at work."

Even as I spoke, my thoughts played hopscotch.

I knew Brinker and Hemorrhoid had found perfect partners in each other before. The sadist inside Brinker had been drawn to the masochist in Hemorrhoid, and the two of them were like tinder and flame. Had their relationship escalated even beyond what I had witnessed in their teenage years? Had one of them turned violent enough to kill?

And why had Kitty Keough wanted to meet with Hemorrhoid and Brinker on the day of her death? What had she known about them that I wasn't seeing?

My brain made another leap. I remembered what I had found when I went home after the fashion show.

I walked in to find Michael's new evil minion, Danny Pescara, in the kitchen looking as if he'd gone three rounds with Mike Tyson.

And Michael had gone off into the night to help him fix something.

Richard said, "What are you thinking?"

Nothing I wanted to share with a reporter bent on investigating organized crime. I needed to see Michael.

Chapter Seven

Both Richard and I got off the train at the first stop. He went looking to buy a ticket back to the city while I went outside. Libby was waiting for me in the parking lot, thanks to the message Lee Song had communicated for me.

"I made my first sale!" she cried as soon as I climbed into the welcome warmth of her minivan. "That nice photographer bought the bracelet right off my wrist!" Her eyes gleamed with the fanaticism of the newly converted. "He said it was— Well, do you think it's true that Asians are the least endowed men in the human race?"

"Libby, could we please agree that my coworkers are off-limits to Potions and Passions? How am I supposed to look at Lee with a straight face now?"

"I'm doing a public service! Maybe I should make Asians my target customer." Libby adjusted the switches on the dashboard so that the heater began blasting my frozen toes. "By the way, Emma didn't get on the train with Brinker's entourage."

"Where is she?"

"I don't know. I guess she and Monte had bigger fish to fry."

"Were they planning to marinate the fish in vodka first?"

"Judging by the way his hands were all over her, something else was on their minds. How does Emma do it? Put her in the middle of the scorching desert, and she'd come home with somebody yummy."

"If you think Monte is yummy, you need your head examined."

Libby helped me pat Spike dry with a handful of aloe-scented tissues. "Okay, so this one may be a new low for her. You'd tell me if I was such a twit, wouldn't you?"

"I'm your sister, Libby. You can always count on me to call you a twit. But Emma can take care of herself." I hoped I might believe my own words if I said them often enough.

Libby stuffed the wet tissues into a small trash bag and began wiggling as if she'd dropped a jelly bean down her sweater.

"What's the matter? What are you doing?"

She lifted up her sweater and tried to wedge her fingers under her Brinker Bra, without success. She blew a sigh. "It's still really stuck."

"Are you serious?"

"I can't get this thing to budge. Can you help?"

I reached over tentatively and gave her Brinker Bra a tug. She was right. It didn't budge. I tried a more vigorous yank. No luck.

"I think it's starting to constrict my blood flow," Libby said. "What if my breasts start to atrophy?"

Wouldn't hurt. But I said, "I don't think you need to worry."

"Try again. Maybe you can loosen it."

Spike popped his head up to watch us.

With a deep breath, I tried to get a double-handed grip on the Brinker Bra. I braced my feet against the floorboard and give it a long, steady pull.

"Ow!"

"Boy, that's stuck like concrete."

"Try one more time."

"Lib—"

"Just once more."

Spike climbed into Libby's lap and sniffed the bra. Then he propped his front paws on her collarbones and began to give her chin a commiserating licking.

I got a firm grip on the Brinker Bra while Libby put her hands on my shoulders. "Ready?"

Just then a passerby with a briefcase stopped in front of the van and gave us a curious stare through the windshield.

Libby rolled down her window. "Take a picture; it lasts longer!"

He scurried off.

"Pervert." Libby sighed and looked down at herself. "I have to say, at least it still looks great, right?"

"If there was something seriously wrong with all the Brinker Bras, we'd have heard by now. There would be publicity."

"So I got a defective one?"

"Well . . . why don't you try soaking it off in the bathtub when you get home?"

"Good idea." Libby pulled down her sweater. "Where is the handsome reporter? I saw him go after you. Did he get on the train? Or did you manage to ditch him?"

"He found me. Lib, I need to go home."

She spun the van around in the parking lot. "Are you going to tell me what happened?"

"I'm not sure what happened."

Libby heard my tone and sent me a speculative glance. "Oh, yeah? Did he try something? I hear there are men who like to have sex in moving vehicles. On the train, did he—"

"He didn't try anything! I need to talk to Michael."

She dropped me at Blackbird Farm and roared off, her mind already working on a new Potions and Passions sales plan.

The bright yellow crime scene tape wrapped around my back porch was the only sign of the earlier catastrophe. Kitty's body was long gone. The forensics team had cleaned up everything but a lone paper coffee cup sitting on the porch railing. I picked it up and went inside. The house was empty. I put Spike on the floor, and he scrambled off to find something to destroy.

I threw the coffee cup in the kitchen trash and called Michael's cell phone. No answer.

Starving, I made myself two slices of toast with crunchy peanut butter and ate them while listening to the phone messages on my answering machine. Three people had called to ask if I'd accidentally forgotten to phone them with invitations for my New Year's Eve party. After those came the voice of Tom Nelson, my lawyer.

"Nora, it's Tom. The police have scheduled your interview for tomorrow, nine in the morning. The fact that they're not anxious to talk to you right away makes me a little uncomfortable. It means they think you might hurt a case they're building against somebody else, and I have a suspicion you know who that is. Call me anytime, here or at home."

Calling Tom wasn't going to change anything, so I sat down and wrote up a short article for the *Intelligencer* about Brinker's send-off party. It wasn't exactly sparkling prose, but it got the job done. But I read it again and heard Kitty's voice bawling me out for doing a half-assed job, so I rewrote the paragraphs, adding some sparkle, and felt much better about myself.

"One for you, Kitty," I said to the air.

I e-mailed my piece to Stan, then dashed to the phone when it rang. I was almost disappointed to hear the voice of Jill Mascione, an old friend and the part owner of her family's catering business.

"I wanted to thank you," Jill said after we exchanged pleasantries, "for sending me the hospital auxiliary job, Nora. We're going to get a lot of business from them—at least a dozen events plus their outdoor festival in July. We're even thinking of expanding the kitchen this year, no small thanks to you."

"It's your service that attracts customers, Jill, not me. I'm glad I could help a little."

"Hey, I'm free on New Year's Eve. Want to go out on the town?"

I had to admit to her that I planned to entertain at home that night and cordially invited her to come.

"Great!" she said. "Usually I have to work. It'll be wonderful to be a guest for a change."

So I couldn't suggest she bring along some food and drink, could I? Jill worked so hard, she deserved a night off to relax with friends.

She asked, "How's your job going?"

"It's going," I said. "But I'm living paycheck to paycheck."

"Don't worry. I see a great future for you, Nora."

I wondered if Jill had a clue what kind of salaries newspapers paid these days, but decided not to bring up the subject. We chatted for a few more minutes, then said good-bye. While the phone was still in my hand, I tried Michael's cell phone again. He didn't answer.

I ran a load of laundry and cleaned up the stack of magazines Spike had massacred in the living room.

There had been a time when I didn't think I could start my life over. After Todd died, I couldn't face trying. But Michael and I made each other laugh, and pretty soon we were talking about things I'd never say to my own sisters, and all of a sudden it had seemed like a great idea to have a baby—a life together.

Now I wondered how I had ever gotten along without him.

And why was I starting to feel as if I might be forced to?

Feeling disloyal, I wiped down the kitchen, sorted my mail and wrote a check for my electric bill with some of the precious few dollars left in my checking account. I looked at the balance and knew I didn't have nearly enough money to cover the next install-ment on my tax bill. But I wasn't going to give up the home that had been in my family for two hundred years, dammit. So I went into the library.

I looked through my favorite books in the collection of first editions. The first one I pulled out was a copy of *Walden,* and I found myself thinking Michael ought to read it. The bits about living a deliberate life would appeal to him. I withdrew a few more books and tried to decide which ones I could bear to part with. A dealer had once offered a princely sum for the whole kit and caboodle. I wondered if I still had his phone number. But was selling the book collection as bad as selling the house?

I put my laundry into the dryer and eventually gave up waiting for Michael. I went upstairs to take a bath. Later, with Spike curled up in bed next to me, I tried to sleep, but the swirl of people and their convoluted lives kept me awake for a long time. I must have fallen into an uneasy doze at last, because when I woke in the morning, my head was fuzzy.

No Michael.

Tom phoned at seven thirty.

"Sorry for the early call, Nora, but the police have postponed your interview."

"Why?" I blurted out. "Tom, did they tell you anything?"

"No, they didn't, sweetheart, I'm sorry. They're holding Abruzzo a little longer, but after twenty-four hours, they have to arrest him or release him."

When Tom hung up, I got dressed. Since Libby hadn't solved her problem with the Brinker Bra, I decided to forgo wearing my freebie and instead slipped into a camisole with matching panties before taking a tour of my closet.

If you don't know where you'll end up at the end of the day, always choose Armani. I put on a black suit with a thin fuchsia thread. I had fuchsia leather gloves to match.

Then I telephoned for my car service to pick me up.

Due to my annoying tendency to faint at emotional moments, I did not possess a driver's license. That hadn't been a problem when I lived in the city and could use public transportation and cabs to get around, but now that I was camping out in the wilderness of Bucks County, I needed more flexibility. Fortunately, my employer—and my grandfather's former tennis partner—had rolled the services of a car and driver into my *Intelligencer* employment contract, which had seemed like a perfectly civilized part of any employment package at the time. It was a perk I now sheepishly recognized not every reporter enjoyed.

My driver was Reed Shakespeare, a part-time college student who earned a few extra dollars by driving a town car for one of Michael's many business ventures—a limousine service. Although I'd been riding with Reed for several months, we still hadn't developed a comfortable driver-passenger dynamic. Reed took himself and his identity as a young, urban African-American male so seriously that driving a Miss Daisy around town was more embarrassing to him than if I'd asked him to sit with me naked on a park bench. But he accepted the job because his mother insisted, which I found rather endearing, although I wouldn't dream of telling him so.

Michael tried to make Reed feel more like a member of his posse than a chauffeur, and I let him be the boss when we were together. Still, Reed resisted getting chummy.

"Does that animal have to come with us?" Reed demanded when Spike ran out of the house and began to joyously jump up on Reed's leg. "Shouldn't he be recovering at home?"

"He chews his cast when he's alone," I said. "The vet says he's better off with me. Us, I mean. He still thinks you're his family, Reed."

Spike had come to me as a gift from Reed's mother, who owned a terrifying terrier that had tangled with a stray.

Spike lovingly peed on Reed's shoe.

"Did you get a chance to pick up any newspapers, Reed?" I asked, climbing quickly into the backseat.

"No," he said. "No time this morning."

"Usually you make time," I observed. "Is there something you don't want me to read today?"

He shoved Spike onto the seat beside me and closed the car door without answering. We drove into the city with Spike panting at the window.

After reluctantly agreeing to keep Spike in the car, Reed dropped me at the Pendergast Building, home to offices of the *Intelligencer*.

Instead of taking the elevator to the ninth floor, I went to the security desk and used the house phone to call Stan Rosenstatz, my editor. The company's automated telephone system routed me through three different menus before I was finally encouraged to press 5 for a real person, who picked up and immediately connected me to Stan.

Ten minutes later he came down to meet me, a lanky drink of water tying a worn, hand-knitted scarf around his neck. "What's wrong with your cheek?" he asked.

"I fell."

His own face—usually careworn and pale from a lifetime spent molelike in the newsroom—was unusually animated this morning.

"Let's go up the street to talk," he said. "I know a place."

We walked a couple of blocks to the Turf Club, a wood-paneled betting parlor just a short walk from City Hall. A welcome blast of heat hit us as we stepped inside, along with the noise of televised horse racing.

In the middle of the morning, the place wasn't crowded, but a gang of regulars hung around the televisions, mostly men and mostly smoking like dragons. With stubby pencils and well-thumbed copies of the Daily Racing Form in their hands, they were intent on the races televised from tracks in Europe. I could see a rainy gray racetrack on all the screens, with graceful horses flickering like lightning.

Stan took me upstairs to the Clubhouse, where each booth boasted its own television set. As the horses rounded the turn and headed for home, a handful of racing enthusiasts intently watched the screens.

No shouts rose as the horses flashed across the finish line. In silence, tickets were torn, and the only noise became a few groans and mutters.

"Back here," Stan said. "Nobody will bother us."

He found us a table in a quiet corner and shut off the television there. The bartender brought Stan a cup of coffee before we had time to sit down. Stan asked for a Reuben sandwich, and I said I'd have a BLT. I peeled off my gloves and asked for a tomato juice, no vodka. The bartender nodded without a word and went away.

Stan hung up my coat, then sat on the opposite side of the table and pushed a stack of photocopies across to me. "It's Kitty's schedule. We made a copy before the cops came yesterday. They took the original book for their investigation, and she may have kept a pocket version with her. If so, the cops have that. This one is all we have to go on. Trouble is, it's in some kind of code."

I flipped open the pages and clumsily found my way to December. Not only would the book provide us with a way of piecing together Kitty's coming plans, we could also check where she'd been recently.

I glanced down at a few of the entries and nodded. "I can read this, Stan. The organizations are in initials, and the locations of the events are here, too. I can decipher her coming schedule. Fortunately, this week isn't very busy. It's the social season's post-Christmas lull."

I ran my finger down Kitty's notations. The Brinker Bra launch had a line drawn through it, and my initials were printed in the margin. Below, alongside the hyphenated names Brinker Lamb, she had written the number seven with the word *Oaks*.

"We checked," Stan said, "but there's no Number Seven Oak Street in the city or any of the suburbs. I thought you might recognize it."

I shook my head. "I'm sorry."

He took a small sip of his coffee, like a man who knew how to nurse a drink in a betting parlor. I knew Stan ducked out every afternoon for his AA meeting and suddenly wanted to ask him how he worked to overcome his problem. Did he have siblings who pestered him to stay sober?

He said, "There's another thing."

"Yes?"

"When we went through Kitty's desk, there was a letter. It outlined what she wanted after her death."

I looked up from the photocopied pages. "You mean a will?"

"There was a will, but another document, too. It's newer. The company lawyers are reading it now. It specifies about her funeral. For people with no family, I guess it's common to find such letters in desks at work."

"What's it to be? A pyre in Rittenhouse Square?"

"Actually, that's up to you."

I laughed shortly. "To me?"

Stan didn't blink. "That's right. Kitty wanted you to take charge of her funeral. Or memorial service—whatever. She said to leave the details up to you."

"Why me?" Flummoxed, I asked, "Doesn't she have *any* family?"

"Apparently not. She may not have acted like it, Nora, but Kitty respected you. She knew you'd do the right thing."

I muttered a word that seldom crossed my lips.

Stan let me think about things for a minute while he sipped another quarter teaspoon of his coffee. Then he said, "We're running her obit today. But the space for her column on Sunday should probably include some kind of tribute to her. I was hoping you'd write it."

Still stunned, I said, "What would I write?"

"You'll come up with something appropriate. You're a good

writer, and you have good instincts. Consider it an audition piece." He set his coffee cup in the saucer. "I wish I could offer you Kitty's job right now, Nora. I can make a recommendation about Kitty's replacement, but nobody's going to take me seriously if I suggest you right away. Especially after somebody delivered her body to your house."

"I know it looks bad."

He nodded. "The guys at the news desk have heard that your sister was making public remarks about Kitty—how you'd be better off if she weren't around anymore."

I groaned as I remembered Libby's stupid exclamation. "My sister is no diplomat. She wasn't serious, Stan."

"I assumed so." He leaned forward on his elbows to tell me more. "The police didn't just go through Kitty's desk, Nora. They wanted to search yours, too. The company lawyers stopped them, but . . . Look, I've spent a lot of time around cops, and I can guess what they're thinking. They want to believe somebody might have killed Kitty as a favor to you."

"A favor?"

"So you'd get her job."

"That's ridiculous."

"Yeah, they haven't taken a good look at our working conditions yet." He allowed a grim smile. "Nora, I'd love to interview you for the *Intelligencer* and get the whole story—everything about your boyfriend, the whole nine yards. But that's not my job anymore. My job is to edit a Features section that will sell papers. I believe you can help me do that. Fact is, I want you to have Kitty's column. But until your connection to her death is cleared, my hands are tied."

Out of nowhere, I heard myself say, "I can't believe Kitty's gone."

I hadn't liked Kitty. She had certainly made a public display of hating me. But her death unnerved me just the same.

"Me neither," said Stan. "I hated her tantrums and bullying and all the diva stuff. But she was the most reader-savvy writer in my department, and the paper is going to take a hit now that she's gone. You can write, and you know the people who count. Her beat is really your turf. But can you take your assets to the next level?"

"What do you mean?"

"Kitty had ideas. She had opinions. She made people mad, but her work always got attention. In the newspaper business, that means something."

"I can't write like Kitty. I can't smear people. She ruined lives, Stan."

"Bull. People ruin their own lives. She might have made their falls more public, but she didn't stick out her foot and trip anybody up."

"Then what . . . ?"

"She had a vision. And she used her skills to back it up. You need to figure out a way to use your own talents to support a viewpoint that's distinctly yours. I don't want another Kitty. I want somebody new and fresh."

The bartender brought our sandwiches and my juice, then warmed up Stan's coffee. Stan picked up half his Reuben.

I sat staring at my BLT, wondering why I'd ordered it. "I'm not a journalist, Stan. I never claimed to be."

"Do you want to sit at Kitty's desk?"

I didn't need to look farther than my bank account to know that I needed a better job than the one I had at the moment. But as Stan waited for me to respond, I suddenly had a new answer. I hadn't enjoyed being Kitty's handmaiden. She had made me feel devalued and foolish even while I contributed to her column. But I knew her world better than she had, and I was sure I could do her work better, too.

"Yes," I said before I could stop myself. "I really do."

"So make it happen. Quit worrying about being so damn polite. Come up with your own concept of the social column."

"What if my concept isn't what the newspaper wants?"

"Convince us," Stan said, around a mouthful of sandwich. "What have you got to lose?"

Stan was right. I didn't have much to lose anymore. And I had a lot to gain. It was about time I had more going for myself than a broken-down farm and a lover who spent a lot of time in and out of police custody, not to mention two sisters who weren't exactly Mary-Kate and Ashley.

"Thanks, Stan," I said. "It's nice to know I have a mentor."

He snorted. "A mentor? I just want the least likely pain in my ass to get Kitty's job. That means you."

"You're a dear." I picked up my sandwich and forced myself to eat a few bites.

He drank more coffee and studied the tabletop for a moment. "Funny thing. I have a hunch Kitty was on the trail of a story when she died."

"A news story?"

"Something beyond her usual beat. I don't know what it was."

"Maybe it got her killed."

Stan smiled wryly. "That only happens in the movies."

I had a brainstorm. Suddenly I knew exactly what Number Seven Oaks meant.

Across the table, Stan blinked at me. "You okay?"

"Yes," I said.

I ate quickly and thanked Stan for meeting me away from the office and the news reporters. Then I telephoned Reed from the public phone. Twenty minutes later, he pulled up to the curb in the black town car. I slipped into the backseat, and Spike leaped at me in a frenzy of joyous puppy kisses.

"Reed, I need to get to Bryn Mawr."

The tony suburb of Philadelphia included a few well-manicured colleges, dozens of estates that could pass for Hollywood sets, and a patchwork of upscale shops, restaurants and luxury car dealerships. Litter didn't linger in the streets for long, and a corner patisserie did a brisk afternoon business in low-fat lemon tea cookies. Some of my dearest friends entertained each other at Chez Nous, just around the corner from a pricey day spa.

"This some kind of park?" Reed asked when he drove the car through a towering gate and into a beautifully designed landscape of graceful hillocks and mammoth trees.

"No, it's a private home," I replied.

Cast in the bronze gate was the name of the estate. Tall Trees. Those of us who grew up visiting the house and grounds knew the place by its original name, Seven Oaks. During a storm fifteen years ago, half the trees had been knocked down, so the new name made sense. Unless you'd been invited to parties on the old estate, you'd not know its former name.

Reed glanced over the trimmed bushes to the Henry Moore statue that sat stolidly in the east lawn. "Scarlett O'Hara live here?"

"No, just an old family."

Reed mumbled something under his breath. I directed him to drive me around the back of the gracious brick home.

When we arrived at the back door I checked my face in my compact and touched a little powder to my cheek before I hopped out. I asked Reed to wait for me.

"What about the dog?" he asked, eyeing Spike as if he'd like to see him roasting over a campfire.

"Maybe he'd like a walk," I suggested. "There's an old croquet lawn beyond the big garage." I pointed.

"That's a garage?"

"It used to be a barn. I bet there is something interesting to keep him busy there."

"That's what scares me." Reed sighed.

A cold wind whipped my coat as I dashed up the stone steps to the servants' entrance. A simple wreath of magnolia leaves with a unfussy tan ribbon decorated the door. I rang the bellpull and waited only ten seconds before a white-clad figure appeared on the other side of the window. She unlocked and opened the door.

"Is Miss O'Toole at home?" I asked. "I'm Nora Blackbird."

The sturdy middle-aged woman invited me inside. She wore an immaculate white apron over a white cotton shirt and—once the door was opened wide—blue jeans and running shoes. She shook my proffered hand. "Nora, I'm Agnes Harley. Forgive my cold hands. I've been cleaning."

"I didn't recognize you at first, Agnes. You've lost weight."

"South Beach diet," she said with a grin. "Eighty-two pounds. Come into the kitchen. I'll call Mary Margaret."

I waited in the large, modern kitchen, where a king's ransom in silver had been laid out on the long center island along with cleaning supplies. Two candelabra, shined to perfection, stood in a splash of sunlight on the round table in a breakfast alcove. The scent of fresh-brewed coffee wafted in the air. I could see my reflection in the gleaming marble countertop. It could have been a kitchen in *Architectural Digest*.

"Nora?"

Mary Margaret O'Toole crossed the kitchen in three athletic strides and hugged me with her long arms. "Isn't it wonderful to see you? I loved your Christmas card this year. You make your sisters sound so funny, don't you? How are you, dear? Aggie, let's have some of your delicious coffee, shall we?"

Irish to the bone, Mary Margaret was fair-skinned, prematurely white-haired, and shaped like one of those warrior-women statutes that stand at park gates with their swords raised and bosoms flaunted.

Except Mary Margaret didn't wear armor. Her no-nonsense blue jeans were better suited to the housework that kept her busy. She managed to stylishly elevate the casual jeans with a faded green cashmere sweater and ballet-slipper flats that showed off her slim ankles. I often thought of her with a feather duster carried aloft like a sword, though. She managed the household with more fervor than a crusader marching into Jerusalem.

"I'm fine, Meg. And you? I should have called ahead, but—"

"Am I ever too busy for a chat with a friend?" She pulled me to the breakfast alcove. "This house isn't going anywhere, is it?"

I had met Mary Margaret when she first came over from County Cork, employed by the family to look after Oriana.

"She's not a governess," Oriana had firmly assured me at the age of ten. "She's my *companion*."

As well as her personal maid, tennis instructor and bodyguard.

All jobs that hadn't used up Mary Margaret's boundless energy. At twenty-nine, she had quickly assumed more important roles around the household by making herself invaluable to the whole family. Within a decade she was running the house with an iron fist—so much so that Oriana's father, industrial titan and a man who had faced down Joe McCarthy, had once asked Mary Margaret's permission to smoke a cigar in his own library.

Now, with the family nearly all gone, she continued to manage the housekeeping at Tall Trees with as much attention to detail as if the place were her own. It *was* her home, of course. I knew she lived in a spacious third-floor apartment that enjoyed the most picturesque views of the estate. She had served me coffee and raspberry scones in her sitting room when I came calling two weeks after Oriana's memorial service.

"What brings you all the way here?" Mary Margaret asked when she'd taken my coat and urged me into a chair at the table. "Come to ask my opinion of your young man, have you?"

"How do you know I have a young man?"

"It's in the papers, isn't it?" Her green eyes sparkled. "They say you're having an affair with a very naughty boyo. What's his name? Is he Irish, then?"

So the morning's newspapers had included Michael's latest brush with the law. No wonder Reed had kept me in the dark.

"He's Michael," I said. "They call him Michael 'the Mick' because he has blue eyes. His mother was Irish."

"Was she, now? And how's he behaving for you, this half-Irish mongrel?"

I couldn't stop my fingertips from touching the bruise on my face, which she'd noted, of course, despite my careful attempt to cover it. "He's a perfect gentleman," I said. "I've never known anyone kinder."

"But?" she prompted, only half believing me.

"He's been known to get into trouble," I acknowledged. "This time it's not his fault."

Mary Margaret ended her false gaiety. "The newspapers say he's the one who killed that awful woman. Kitty Keough was the one who scorned Miss Oriana for marrying so young, wasn't she?"

"Yes. But Michael had nothing to do with her death. I hope you'll trust me when I say he's innocent."

Agnes brought coffee on a tray—three flowered cups with saucers, a silver coffeepot, sugar and cream in matching china and a clutch of demitasse spoons. But after putting the tray on the table, she quietly picked up the third cup and began to carry it out of the room.

"Agnes, please stay," I called after her. "I'm not revealing any secrets you can't hear."

Mary Margaret smiled and companionably patted the chair next to hers. "You'll have a sit-down, won't you, Aggie? I think Nora's come to pick our brains."

I accepted the cup of coffee she soothingly passed to me. "I need to know whether Kitty Keough was here night before last."

"Here?" Mary Margaret and Agnes exchanged startled glances.

"She was supposed to attend an event in the city, but canceled at the last minute. And her date book indicated she might have had an appointment here. At least that's what I'm guessing."

"She wasn't in the house," Mary Margaret said. "I'd have known that, wouldn't I? We keep the place locked up tight. And when was the last time a soul came calling here?"

"The week before Christmas," Agnes volunteered. Her flat American accent contrasted with Meg's Irish lilt. "Mr. Hemmings had a party for some friends. He entertained in the old gardener's house. A dozen people came. At least, I prepared food for twelve and delivered it at four. Mr. Hemmings insists on punctuality. Cocktails at five, just like his mum. No green olives, only black. Always pour the glasses exactly seven-eighths full. No getting back into the gardener's house until eight the next morning."

So Hemorrhoid was still bizarrely rigid, even at home. "He doesn't live in this house?"

"He does. But he doesn't entertain here. He prefers the privacy of the gardener's house. We don't speculate about what goes on there. It's none of our business, really."

Mary Margaret had pursed her lips and kept silent during Agnes's explanation of the living arrangements.

"Have you met any of Hem's guests in the past?"

"A few. I don't remember Miss Keough being here, though. Hemmings tends to have younger people to his evening parties."

I took a chance. "What about Brinker Holt?"

Mary Margaret frowned. "That name's familiar, isn't it? Is he an unpleasant fellow with a shaved head? Carrying a video camera, perhaps?"

"That would be him."

"He was walking all over the place, filming one evening. I suggested he get himself back to the cottage before the guard dogs found him." Mary Margaret smiled. "Of course, we haven't had guard dogs in years."

I said, "Could Kitty have gone to the gardener's house night before last to meet Hem without your knowing?"

"That's not his schedule. He only entertains in the gardener's house on specific nights, and that wasn't one of them."

"Could she have gotten onto the grounds without your knowing?"

"Normally, we hear cars that arrive by the driveway. I didn't hear anyone arrive, but I suppose someone could have slipped through. The security system runs the perimeter of the grounds," Mary Margaret explained to me. "There used to be an alarm on the gate that beeped when somebody drove through, but that was shut off since Mr. Hemmings requested it about a year ago. The beep annoyed him."

I could see the strain in Mary Margaret's face and knew she had been engaged in a battle of wills with Hemorrhoid. I said, "It must be hard living with a young man like Hemmings."

"It's good to have challenges," Mary Margaret said with diplomacy.

"And we wouldn't dream of leaving," Agnes added staunchly. "Not while Mr. Orlando is still here."

"I don't want anything to happen to Oriana's child." Mary Margaret's eyes misted briefly, but she controlled herself.

I touched her hand. "I'm glad you're looking after him. I saw him night before last, and he seemed . . . well, I know he's had a hard couple of years."

"He's at school most of the time," Mary Margaret said. "We only have him on holidays now. And then Mr. Hemmings wants to be in charge. Has the boy on a strict schedule and an even more strict diet, but we do our best to spoil him a wee bit when he's here."

"Just a bit," Aggie agreed.

"There's a firm schedule when Orlando is here. Breakfast at eight, then a brisk walk, a visit from his tutor, a reading hour—"

"Sounds as if Hem is as regimented with Orlando as he is with himself."

"Oh, yes," Agnes said. "Mr. Hemmings likes things just so. If we deviate from his usual schedule, we'd better have a good excuse. I forgot to deliver Orlando's nine-thirty hot cocoa once, and Mr. Hemmings was so upset I almost called nine-one-one."

"It was worse the night I tried to iron an old copy of *TV Guide* instead of putting a fresh one by his bed," Mary Margaret said.

"Oh, goodness, yes. What a tantrum!"

"How does Orlando handle the rigidity?"

"He does his best to be good. And we try to ease things a bit."

"So the other night," I said, getting back on track, "you didn't see Kitty?"

"Aggie and I were here in the kitchen until half past eleven, having a glass while we watched that Naked Chef fellow poaching a salmon." She sighed into her coffee cup. "I still love a Guinness."

Agnes admiringly wagged her head. "The Naked Chef surely knows how to make a simple fish into something glorious."

"Mr. Hemmings was out, of course," Mary Margaret added. "He drove Orlando to a fashion show."

"But I saw Gallagher at the fashion show. He picked up Orlando."

"Gallagher went later, to bring the child home so Hemmings could spend the evening with friends. That's his Tuesday schedule."

"Sending Orlando's nanny off," Mary Margaret snapped, rapping her cup into its saucer. "Was that the wisest decision anyone ever made? The boy needs an ally. A young person to be his friend."

"Wasn't Minky his nanny?" I asked. "When we talked last summer, she was still looking after him."

At the mention of Mary Margaret's daughter, the two women exchanged a fond glance.

"Minky would still be working here if Hemmings hadn't enrolled Orlando in that ghastly school. At his age and what with just losing his mum and dad, I ask you, was that the right choice?"

Agnes shook her head. "Minky was wonderful with him, too."

Mary Margaret smiled. "Isn't she the best thing I ever did?"

Agnes slid her hand across the table to join Mary Margaret's, and the two of them looked very proud.

The whole reason Mary Margaret went into service at all had been the birth of her out-of-wedlock child, Melissa. In the years she first worked for Oriana's family, Mary Margaret's baby had been like a doll for us to play with—a perfect little child with a sweet temperament. In later years, we'd spoiled Melissa with candy, taught her to French-braid hair and throw water balloons off the conservatory roof onto guests who lounged around the pool. After Oriana and I went off to college together, Agnes had come along and helped Mary Margaret raise Minky into an intelligent, gracious and empathic young woman. When Orlando was born, his mother had known exactly what nanny could best look after him.

"No child should grow up the way Orlando is," Agnes said. "Mr. Hemmings is so fussy about his clothes and his manners. And don't get me started on the toothbrush ritual! Plus he's isolating the boy from everyone who loves him."

"Giving Orlando only one person to turn to, see?" Mary Margaret said. "And that person is Hemmings, isn't it?"

"Well," said Agnes, shooting a furtive look at Mary Margaret.

The two blushed.

"What's going on?" I asked.

"It's harmless," Agnes assured me.

"And isn't Gallagher an old softie?" Mary Margaret said. "Not a bad influence on a boy, is he? He may not be the perfect companion for Orlando, but he's the best we've got."

"We let Orlando hang around Gallagher in the garage. Keeps the boy active. Takes his mind off his troubles."

"And if Hemorrhoid doesn't know, who's going to tell him?" asked Mary Margaret.

Watching the two women smile, I put a few facts together and made a decision.

"Maybe I'd better go talk to Gallagher."

They put on their parkas and Wellies to accompany me outside, claiming they both needed a breath of fresh air, but I knew they had seen Reed from the alcove window and they wanted to meet him.

I led the way myself, knowing the path to the garage after years of playing on the grounds of the estate with my friend. Even covered with snow, the dips and curves that skirted sweeping beds planted with perennial flowers and ornamental bushes were familiar. We chatted about the small changes that had been made, and Mary Margaret pointed out the new orchard of spindly young fruit trees. Peach preserves had been Oriana's favorite.

At the croquet lawn, we came across Reed standing on the walk. A few yards away, Spike barked and ran circles around Orlando, who stood stiffly, ankle deep in snow and wearing an immaculate parka over a shirt and tie. I couldn't believe my eyes. His uncle made him wear a tie?

As we approached, the boy bent down cautiously to pet Spike. Seizing the opportunity, Spike snatched Orlando's knit cap from his head and took off galumphing as best he could with his plastered hind legs.

"Hey!" Orlando called.

"What kind of animal is that?" Mary Margaret demanded.

"He's a dog, believe it or not," I said. "But I think his species would prefer not to claim him."

"Orlando seems to like him," Agnes observed as the boy plunged after Spike through the snow. The two of them were clumsy and yet bursting with energy.

"And who's this?" Mary Margaret asked as we approached Reed.

I made the introductions, and Reed tried hard not to look appalled at finding himself introduced to people who actually lived in such splendor.

"Have you gotten your shoes wet?" Mary Margaret asked him. "Do you want to come inside and dry off?"

"No," said Reed.

"You're more than welcome," Agnes added. "And there's coffee."

"I have to watch the dog," he said.

Mary Margaret's brows rose at Reed's devotion to duty, but she said nothing.

Orlando arrived then, panting and pink-faced from exertion. His tie was askew and his clean parka already showed filthy paw prints. To me, he said, "What's the dog's name?"

"Spike. Uh, be careful, Orlando. He's been known to bite."

"He won't bite me."

Spike ran up to Orlando and jumped against his knee, flourishing the cap. Orlando hesitated for an instant, then grabbed it and they played tug-of-war, Spike growling ferociously.

Reed and I exchanged a nervous glance.

Spike won the fight and dashed off with the cap. Orlando looked up at Reed. "Do you know Shaquille O'Neal?"

"Orlando," Mary Margaret said sternly. "Get your hat before the dog chews it up."

He knew better than to disobey her, so he romped off in pursuit of Spike.

"Sorry," Mary Margaret said to Reed. To me, she said, "Gallagher's in the workshop." She pointed. "That side door. Half-hidden by the bushes, see?"

"I'll find you after I've talked with him."

Mary Margaret headed back to the house with Agnes right behind.

Reed had both hands thrust into the pockets of his coat. "Those women. Do they own this place?"

"Agnes and Mary Margaret? No, they run the household."

Reed frowned. "Run it?"

"Mary Margaret is the housekeeper. Agnes is the cook and the . . . well, just about everything else. They're a team."

"They're servants," Reed said.

"Employees."

He nodded, still frowning in the direction of Spike.

"What are you thinking, Reed?"

"The way you talked to them," he said finally. "I don't know."

"They're my friends."

Which wasn't quite true. My grandmother had called it "maintaining the wall." She could sit in the kitchen and drink coffee with her housekeeper, and I was allowed to visit the housekeeper's room and watch her television or play Go Fish with her. But I could not ask to borrow money—even a quarter for the bubblegum machine. I was forbidden to yell for her from another room, sulk in her presence or make demands upon her time beyond certain limits that we all, instinctively perhaps, understood. I could treat her as a friend, and yet I was not permitted to make the assumptions one friend might make of another.

Reed scowled as he tried to decide if there was social injustice at work at Tall Trees.

"I'll be in the garage," I said, pretty sure I wasn't going to change his mind about anything very soon. "You should wait inside if you get cold. They won't bite you."

He shrugged, watching Orlando wrestle with Spike. "I'm okay here."

I picked my way across the mud-spattered sidewalk to the door of the garage. Here it became apparent that Mary Margaret's obsessively neat housekeeping gave way to the habits of someone less fastidious. No magnolia wreath hung on the door, but a wild tangle of shrubbery grew haphazardly close to the unpolished knocker. Hunks of rotting leaves and torn-up grass blew against the stones.

Stepping gingerly over the mess, I knocked, then went inside.

Chapter Eight

The first thing that hit me was the music. Screaming bagpipes, turned up loud enough to be heard over a North Sea gale.

Next I was assaulted by the sight of junk heaped and hanging everywhere. The jumbled mess made Santa's workshop look like a Zen temple.

The workshop was an airy space originally intended to be a stable for horses, later converted to a garage. Sunlight streamed through the tall windows. From the roof beams hung a bizarre mobile of crooked wheels, swinging gears, bicycle tires and assorted wreckage that must have been looted from a toymaker's trash can.

"Mr. Gallagher?" I called over the wail of recorded bagpipe music. An Irish rebel tune, no doubt, glorifying some gallant lad's sacrifice of love for country.

I edged my way around a pile of empty plastic jugs with their handles lashed together. My boot struck an anvil on the floor. I ducked under a unicycle hanging from a wire and decorated with lampshades.

"Mr. Gallagher?"

When I straightened up, I faced an enormous model train layout. Spread before me on a series of waist-high tables was a miniature landscape with rolling mountains, tiny forests and little Victorian towns complete with houses, street lamps and human figures.

Throughout the picturesque landscape wound train tracks—even disappearing through a mountain tunnel at one end of the huge table. As I watched, a model train suddenly burst out of the tunnel and charged down the tracks in my direction.

The train flashed past me. A whistle tooted, making me jump.

And I heard a human cackle.

Gallagher, wearing an engineer's cap on his head and a red bandanna around his neck, was perched on a stool in front of a lighted console, looking like a demented elf as he controlled the train's progress.

I waved. He saluted me by raising his cap.

I climbed over several coils of Christmas lights and a stack of wooden reindeer, cautiously dipped my head to avoid whacking it on some low-hanging electric fans and finally managed to slide into the tiny empty space beside Gallagher at the console.

"Pardon me, boy," I bellowed over the thunder of bagpipes. "Is this the Chattanooga Choo Choo?"

He laughed, eyes alight. "Hey, there, Miss Nora! How do you like my train set?"

"It's fabulous," I shouted. "Can we turn down the music?"

He reached over and flipped a switch with one finger. Instantly the dramatic skirling crescendo subsided into a tinny whine.

"I had no idea you loved trains," I said. "This is magnificent!"

"It's for the boy." He settled his cap back on his head. "Orlando. We've been working on it for a couple of years. Since his mama and papa died, you know."

"He must love it."

"We both like tinkering. Here. See this corner of the table? We're building a circus. He finished painting the animals just yesterday. He's not a bad artist, is he?"

"It's lovely. There's a lot of detail here." I admired the platoon of miniature animals that stood ready to be inserted into the tiny model menagerie. I could see the individual stripes on the zebra, and the spots on the giraffe had been painted by a very careful hand.

After studying the train layout, I let my gaze roam over the weird mishmash of things collected around us. "You're quite the inventor, Gallagher. I'd forgotten that."

"Oh, it's gotten out of hand these last few years," he admitted. "I don't drive much. Mostly I stay here and make things. Why, I invented a gizmo to clean out the house gutters; did Miss O'Toole tell you?"

"She didn't have time to mention it."

"And a slick way of taking marks off the linoleum in the garage, too. It's a chemical compound I mixed up."

"So you're a chemist, too?"

"Well, I like to keep my hand in," he said modestly, then waved at the junk overhead. "See all these inventions? I haven't even tried to patent half of them yet. It's the paperwork I don't like."

"Maybe Orlando could help."

"Oh, he's still a boy. He ought to be playing."

I wondered fleetingly if Spike had managed to bite him yet and decided I'd better speed things up.

"Gallagher, I'm wondering if you had a visitor here night before last."

"Visitor? I don't— Oh, we were out, remember? At that warehouse fashion thing. You were there."

"I know, but before that? I understand Hemmings drove Orlando to the fashion show, and you picked him up later. What time did you leave from here?"

He scratched his ear. "I don't quite recall."

"Did anyone come to visit before you left?"

He grinned. "Who did you have in mind? Some lovely lass, maybe? No, I'm past those days."

I smiled, too. "You didn't see Kitty Keough, perhaps?"

Gallagher's brow twitched. "Keough? The one who died? I remembered her before I saw her picture in today's paper. Years ago I did a piece of moonlighting, and she hired me to drive her around. She was a handful—very rude. But she didn't deserve to die so young."

I nodded. "She died shortly after the fashion show. It's important that I find out where she was that night. I believe she had an appointment here."

"Here?"

"At this estate, yes."

"I didn't see her," he said. "I worked on the trains a little, because the boy had his heart set on playing that night. I promised if he'd behave for his uncle, we'd have a midnight session."

"And did you?"

"Yes. Earlier, while he was with Mr. Hemmings, I got things ready here. I made our popcorn, but don't go telling on me. The boy needs a treat once in a while. He can't always be on a diet. I made a special heater to pop the corn. Would you like to see it?"

"No," I said, smiling. "Thanks."

"I thought it was broken. I heard popping and thought for sure it had blown a breaker. But the noise I heard must have been outside, not here."

"Noise?" I asked.

"Two big popping noises. I blow breakers all the time, but the lights didn't go out. No, it was outside."

"Big popping noises," I repeated.

"Almost like gunshots."

I don't remember how I got outside. I left Gallagher with his train and hurried away. Standing in the doorway to the garage, I looked at the mess on the sidewalk again. Leaves, dirt, twigs, bits of grass. Why was there grass, I wondered? In the dead of winter?

It shouldn't have been on the sidewalk.

I walked around the overgrown bushes that ran along the garage and looked at the snow. A gate stood half-open behind the bushes, allowing access to the area behind the gardener's shed and the alley used by landscaping trucks that came when the trimming was done. A path ran from the gate down to the shed.

I could see that the snow had been disturbed by someone walking there recently.

And something else showed in the snow.

A shoe. A medium-heeled, outdated silver pump with an orthodic device inside. Kitty Keough's evening shoe.

I leaned against the gate, staring at the shoe and suddenly starved for oxygen.

Behind me, Reed said my name.

"Call the police," I said.

"What?"

"I think this is a murder scene."

Reed appeared beside me. "No way."

"Way," I said.

The police came. While Agnes had a weeping meltdown, Mary Margaret took charge of the police as if they were dragoons in need of a commanding officer. Under her tight-lipped observation, they gave me a thorough cross-examination about who I knew and what footwear they favored. Then the officers wanted to talk in detail to the people who lived at Tall Trees. A sniffling Aggie made me comfortable with coffee in the kitchen while they spoke with Mary Margaret first, then Gallagher. Reed waited with me, looking nervous that he'd tracked snow onto the floor.

"I think I should take you home," he said over and over.

"Not until we find out what happened."

But at last I felt I couldn't subject Reed to the torture any longer. We went outside to leave. By that time, police vehicles and a crowd of people swarmed the estate. I could see someone unwinding a reel of the familiar yellow crime scene tape, and I blanched. Some people surround themselves with chintz. For me, it was police tape.

"Wait here," Reed said. "I'll go get the car."

I stood obediently on the sidewalk and looked at the scene. A crowd of people had gathered already. Two television trucks idled in the driveway. A cameraman was checking his batteries by the holly hedge. Some reporters were rapidly scrawling in their notebooks. The first person I recognized was Richard D'eath.

He came over, moving with surprising speed despite his cane. He wore a worn raincoat with a faded Burberry lining. "I heard you were here."

When my heart lifted, I realized it was a relief to see him, and for a stupid second I wanted him to hug me. But I said, "Tell me what the police are saying."

"There's blood in the snow over by the garage." He turned and pointed his cane. "The cops think it's Kitty Keough's. I hear you suggested it might have been her. Something about a shoe?"

"Have they found anything else?"

"No murder weapon." Richard took another look at me. "How'd you know to come here?"

"I read something in her schedule book. It was an old nickname for this place."

"What was she doing here?"

I hadn't figured that out yet for certain, and I didn't want to theorize in front of Richard. Too much was at stake.

He put his hand gently under my arm. "You look like you're going to keel over. Let's go sit in my car."

"I never liked Kitty," I said without thinking, resisting his pull. "I know she's dead, and that's bad enough. But the idea that somebody actually killed her . . . makes me feel . . ."

His hand tightened to support me. I was absurdly glad to feel a human touch at that moment.

Which was when Michael walked around the corner of the house, looking dangerous but out of jail. Richard released my arm instantly, as if we'd been teenagers necking on a front porch when a light came on.

Michael said to me, "If you're here, it must be a crime scene."

I wanted to fling myself into his arms and bawl with relief. But I didn't. "Reed called you? He probably thinks you'll fire him if I break a nail."

"He'd be right."

"Hello," said Richard, clearing his throat. "You must be Mick Abruzzo. I'm Richard D'eath, a friend of Nora's."

A friend? Since when?

I occasionally forgot what impact Michael had on mere mortals. Not only did his body seem to heat the air around him, but he had a face people associated with brutal murders committed in abandoned factories. Even grown men gave Michael plenty of space.

But Richard looked intrigued, and I gave him credit for not being frightened.

Michael shook his hand and gave the standard male New Jersey greeting, the phrase "How are you doing?" only shortened to a three-syllable mutter.

Richard responded with the same greeting, only the slightly more civilized four-syllable version. Then he said, "The cops think Kitty Keough was murdered here last night."

Michael cast a glance around, taking in the cops, the trees and the snow-covered flower beds with the casual but practiced eye of an expert. "Not a bad place for a shooting. Lots of cover. Stupid to do it here with all this snow, though."

Richard nodded. "Yeah, no way to cover your tracks."

"Cops know where the shooter waited?"

Richard shook his head. "What do you think?"

Michael turned around and visually measured the distance between the street and the garage. Then he observed a few more details that probably didn't include an appreciation for fine landscape design or meticulous garden maintenance. "Not a bad security system," he said at last. "A little outdated, maybe, for this neck of the woods."

The town car glided up to us just then, and Reed rolled down his window. Michael strolled over and leaned one elbow on the side of the car for a private conversation.

I harpooned Richard with a glare. "Don't do this, please."

"Do what?"

"He's not going to give you a quote for the paper."

"Are you his babysitter?"

"He's smarter than you think, Richard."

"I think he's plenty smart. Doesn't exactly look like a choirboy, though, does he? And it takes balls to stroll in here like this. The cops have spotted him already. See?"

Two police officers standing under the oak trees were sending furtive glances in Michael's direction, as if working out a plan to capture a loose tiger.

Reed drove off, and Michael sauntered back to me. "I'll take you home."

"I'm ready now."

"What about the shooter?" Richard asked. "Think he hung around long waiting for Kitty? Should we go look for cigarette butts or something?"

I thought Michael was going to ignore the question. He looked distracted and—I finally saw it—a little angry. But he lingered. He inclined his head past the croquet lawn. "I think he probably parked a few blocks away and climbed through those bushes that overgrow the fence over there. We had a breeze last night, and the moving branches probably confused the security sensors. If he had a lookout, that's where to put him, but a partner would have been a complication."

"Uh-huh."

"See the tracks he made as he hiked across the yard? Then he waited under those trees." With a jut of his chin, Michael indicated a clump of rhododendron that so far the police had taken no notice of. "He had to hang there until he got a clear shot at his target coming up to the garage door. Except if the spotlights work the way I think they do, he had a glare in his eyes."

"Which means?"

Michael shrugged. "Half a chance he shot the wrong person."

I opened my mouth but couldn't make words come out.

Even Richard couldn't hide his surprise. "The wrong . . . ?"

"An easy mistake," Michael said. "He was probably cold, his feet were wet, he picked a bad spot, wanted to get out of here. Amateur night, but there you go. Homicide cops will figure it out when they get here."

"Then who was supposed to be killed?" I asked.

Michael smiled at me. "That's your department, isn't it?"

We were interrupted again when a police officer gave a yelp.

Spike had bolted out of a snowbank, ears flat, teeth flashing. Like a stealth fighter, he had made a beeline for his target and attacked. He had seized the trouser leg of one of the loitering cops, who leaped into the air with more strangled cries. The cop landed on one foot and danced frantically on tippy-toe, trying to dislodge Spike by kicking, his shouts hoarse and his arms pinwheeling. Spike hung on, snarling ferociously. Another cop pulled his gun.

"No! Wait!"

I moved to head off Spike's attack, but the puppy caught sight of Michael and happily surrendered his prey. He broke loose, dashed over and leaped at Michael, who scooped him up and effortlessly subdued my dog by tucking him into the crook of his elbow—all with a mildly amused expression that conveyed the idea that Spike had only been teasing. Spike similarly endeavored to look angelic. But some kind of debris clung to his teeth as he panted smilingly.

The cops glowered at us.

"Let's go now," I said, "before Animal Control shows up."

For a moment, Richard looked as if he wanted to tag along. But when I set off to follow Michael, Richard merely waved. "See you around."

As Michael and I walked up the sidewalk with Spike, Orlando appeared out from between two police cruisers. The boy was nearly unrecognizable—dirty and sopping wet from playing in the snow. His hair dripped and his tie was in shreds—exactly matching the fabric in Spike's teeth—but Orlando's cheeks glowed pink.

Orlando eyed Michael. "Is that your puppy?"

"Hers."

"Oh."

"You can visit him anytime, Orlando," I said.

His face was very tight, and he tried to smooth the wrinkles from his wet parka. "I don't need to. He's just a dog."

"He doesn't make friends easily, though," I said. "I'm amazed by how much he likes you."

Orlando shrugged and turned away. "Dogs are stupid. I'd rather have a caiman. They eat live rabbits."

I wanted to run after Orlando and give him a hug, but the hunch of his shoulders told me it would not have been welcomed.

"Some kind of alligator," Michael said. "Now there's a nice cuddly pet for the kid who has everything."

"He didn't mean it."

Michael had driven one of his favorite vehicles, a sea-foam-green muscle car with a ridiculously long hood and the rear wheels jacked up as if ready to run moonshine across some county lines. He tucked me into the soft upholstery of the front seat before wrapping a filthy Spike into a towel he produced from the trunk. When Spike was clean and safely nestled on my lap, Michael slid behind the wheel and closed the door. He didn't start the car.

Something in his manner prevented me from sliding across the seat and wrapping my arms around his neck. He ran one hand down his face.

Calmly, I said, "Have you been absolved by the state police?"

His smile was weary at the edges. "For the moment."

"They kept you a long time."

"I'm out now."

He had changed his clothes since yesterday, which probably meant he went home for a shower as soon as the cops let him go. The clothes were things he hadn't kept at Blackbird Farm, so he'd gone to his own place. He had wanted to rid himself of the smell of the state police barracks as quickly as possible, I guessed, and out of my sight. I wondered if they'd put him in a cell.

An easy relationship required two people who had no pasts, I thought in that second. What had happened before we knew each other was starting to jeopardize what we hoped to build together now.

Looking out the windshield, Michael said, "Who's the professor?"

"Richard's a reporter, not a professor. I wish you hadn't spoken to him. Not about the murder."

"How long have you known each other?"

"A couple of months. He's a good journalist." I suddenly wondered if Michael was asking to be reassured.

But he said, "What does he think? About the Keough woman's death?"

"I don't know. At first I thought Richard was working on a story about Brinker Holt and Hemmings Lamb. But now he's after something else."

Michael hadn't been listening. "Nora, a lot has happened."

He didn't look at me, and suddenly I forgot how to breathe.

I said, "Are you out on bail?"

He laughed shortly and put the key into the car's ignition. "No, I'm out free and clear, thanks to Cannoli and Sons."

"What, then?"

"Danny Pescara was arrested a couple of hours ago. He confessed."

"Confessed? To what?"

Michael finally met my eye. "To killing Kitty Keough."

"Your cousin Danny killed Kitty?" My voice cracked. "How? Why?"

"How? By waiting for her here and shooting her. As for why, I have to assume he was hired."

"You mean as a hit man?"

"Yes. The moron stole her credit cards and used one to buy gasoline a day after he killed her. Arresting him was a piece of cake. I think the cops threatened to take away his comic book collection, so he screamed like a girl and gave up."

"Who hired him?"

"He's not talking about that—not yet, anyway—and the police only have a theory."

"Who do they think hired Danny?"

Michael said, "Me."

Chapter Nine

*H*e looked out the windshield at two approaching men, one in a wool topcoat, the other wearing a shapeless orange jacket. They had already made eye contact with Michael through the glass. Michael said, "Here comes Homicide."

His phone chirped, and he pulled it out of his pocket. "Yeah?"

He listened for a moment, then handed the phone to me.

"Hey, sis," called my sister Emma when I said hello. "I figured this was the best way to find you. The Love Machine giving you an extended nooner?"

Michael got out of the car to speak to the police. Spike scrambled across the seat to watch through the window.

"Where are you, Em?"

She gave a yawn. "Climbing out of a very comfy bed, as a matter of fact."

"Emma—"

She cut me off. "I just got a look at the morning papers. Sounds like Mick was in some trouble. But he's out of jail now, I gather? Or are you sitting in the visiting room?"

"He's free," I said. And I told her that Danny Pescara was under arrest for Kitty's murder.

"No shit," she said. "That weasel? The one running the betting racket?"

"How do you know about that?"

"Nora," said my little sister, "sometimes you're so naïve it's like I'm related to Shirley Temple. What's happening now? The cops think Mick hired Danny? Why would he do that?"

"The police are looking for any reason to put Michael in jail. This seems like the easiest way at the moment."

"So," said Emma, "is your stud muffin planning an escape to a southern climate with nice beaches and flexible banking laws?"

That possibility struck me silent.

Instantly contrite, Emma said, "Sorry. Look, I don't see Mick running away from a fight. And I can't picture him turning into a beach bum. I was just kidding. You still there?"

"I'm here."

"So what are you going to do?"

"I don't know." I craned around to look out the window at Michael. He was leaning against the side of the car, and the homicide detectives seemed to be entertained by a story he was telling them. I heard laughter. I said, "I have to find out why Kitty was wandering around Tall Trees when she was killed."

"How are you going to do that?"

"I'll talk to Hemorrhoid. My other option is tracking down Brinker Holt."

"What does Brinker have to do with this?"

I told her about finding Brinker's name in Kitty's appointment book. Then I asked, "Do you know where he is?"

"In New York with the Brinker Bra, I presume. It's all over the news. Even Dan Rather talked about the hype. It's like America has rediscovered boobs."

"How long is Brinker staying in New York?"

"What am I? His social secretary?"

"I'm surprised you associated with him at all," I snapped, irritated by my sister's attitude.

"I can associate with anyone I please. Even a serial creep like Brinker."

"Can you blame me for wondering if you need a keeper?" I asked. "Brinker, Emma! Why are you working for him?"

"It's a free country."

"You know what he's capable of."

"I can handle him. I'm all grown up now."

"And his games have grown up, too. Do you remember what he did, Emma? Or has all the vodka pickled your memory?"

Emma hung up on me.

Rightfully so, I thought grimly. I was trying to run her life again.

Spike climbed into my lap. Michael got back into the car, and I returned his cell phone to him.

He pocketed the phone. "You okay?"

"No."

"What did Emma have to say?"

"She was checking up on you, I believe."

"You look steamed."

"She's an idiot. And I'm supposed to keep my mouth shut while she acts like—"

"—an idiot, I know," Michael said. "Who's the guy this time?"

"Brinker Holt. She's not sleeping with him—that honor is reserved for a rhinestone cowboy with a drinking problem at least as bad as hers. But she's working for Brinker, and that is so colossally stupid that I—"

"Why is it stupid?"

"Because Brinker is a sadistic monster, that's why."

"I thought he was just a lousy comedian."

"The truth?" I was shaking hard and unable to control my voice. "He nearly raped Emma when she was twelve. His pack of animal friends held her down while he— Well, let's just say I happened to arrive just in time, which was what he planned all along. It was me

128

he wanted to punish. It was so horrible to see Emma pinned down like that, and I—"

"Hey." Michael reached for me. "Take it easy. It's over."

"No, it isn't!" I pushed his hand away. "Emma has conveniently forgotten that she was tortured by that horrible kid, who's grown up into an even more horrible man. She is scaring the hell out of me right now. She has no judgment. None of you do."

"Me? How do you figure?"

I faced him. "Michael, tell me the truth." I knew I was getting hysterical but I couldn't stop. "What were you doing with Danny night before last?"

He turned his face away. "You don't need to know."

"Yes, dammit, I do! This time I really want to know what's going on."

"Nora—"

"Just tell me!"

Spike began to bark.

"All right," Michael snapped over Spike's noise. "Danny wanted to get rid of a car. He didn't tell me why, and I didn't ask, understand? I know a guy, so we took the car to his place in Jersey. I didn't look in the car, and I didn't ask any questions. By now it's on its way to Venezuela."

"You saw same people who were involved in the car-theft ring that night?"

"Yes. We went to a different garage, though, and missed the bust."

"Do you know who shot the police officer?"

"That's not— No, not yet. All I did was help Danny make a car disappear."

"How can you do it, Michael?" I burst out. "How can you help a person cover a crime?"

"The crime I assumed he was covering wasn't murder."

"Other crimes are okay? Which ones, exactly?"

"Don't lecture me. Crime is a natural part of the world. Gambling? People like to gamble! My father provides a service even little old ladies want! If he didn't do it, they'd find some other way to throw their money away. And who doesn't want to fix a parking ticket? Break the speed limit? Get a freebie once in a while? It's all illegal! But it's what people want."

Suddenly I was shouting, too. "But Danny killed somebody! And you helped!"

"I didn't help. I had another agenda that night. We set him up, get it? I'd had enough of the shakedown shit he was running while calling himself an Abruzzo. We set him up to get busted. Ditching his car was part of the plan, and you don't need to know the rest. . . . No, you really don't. It went wrong, and part of that's my fault. But what the hell he was doing over here capping some broad when he was supposed to be in south Philly sure as shit beats me."

"So now you're involved in covering up a murder."

"I'm not happy about it."

"Was Kitty in the car while you were with Danny? Or did he put her somewhere and come back later to leave her body on my porch?"

"Damned if I know. Maybe he had some help. He's too much of a mutt to figure out anything more complicated than a parking meter by himself." Michael slammed the steering wheel. "He's a fucking, stupid mutt. Now I've got to fix this mess. But no matter what, goddammit, until I do, you are going to keep your nose out of it!"

With the speed of a striking cobra, Spike lunged from my lap and bit Michael.

He cursed, and I pulled the puppy back, but the damage was done. Michael's hand began to bleed.

In my lap, Spike fell silent and didn't move a muscle.

Michael got a handkerchief out of his pocket and wrapped it around his hand.

In the quiet, I said, "Does your cell phone keep track of incoming calls?"

"Yes."

"I need to know where Emma is staying."

I put Spike on the floor. One-handed, Michael retrieved his cell phone and punched a few buttons. He looked at the tiny screen and passed it to me.

The name of Emma's hotel appeared in little blue letters.

"Is that where you want to go?" Michael asked.

"Yes, please."

"All right, I'll drop you," he said. "I have something else to take care of."

He reached across the seat and caught me gently around my neck. Leaning close to kiss me on the mouth, though, he suddenly stopped himself, and we looked at each other.

"I love you," I said.

"I love you," he said. But it sounded different this time. I could see his mind was already far away.

An hour later, I was downtown and knocking on the door of my sister's room in one of the city's most luxurious hotels. I crossed my fingers that she hadn't trashed it.

She opened the door herself, wearing a hotel bathrobe and carrying a can of Red Bull. Her hair was wet and standing up on her head. Spike yipped with glee and leaped into her arms.

Emma caught him without spilling a drop. "Hey, Sis."

Behind her, doing sit-ups on the floor in his underwear and a Stetson that looked as if a herd of cattle had stampeded across it, was Monte Bogatz. "Hello there, little lady," he yodeled, hands behind his sunburned neck. "Come on in, and welcome to Paradise!"

"Speak for yourself, cowboy," Emma said, closing the door behind me and giving Spike a roughing-up.

Monte got to his feet and held my hand with a smile that

looked overmedicated. "It's a real pleasure to lay eyes on you again," he drawled. "Such a pretty gal as yourself must have more important people to talk to than little old Monte, but I'm sure glad you stopped by."

Emma leaned against the wall by the door and held on to Spike. "Actually, cowboy, we need a little sisterly chat. How about if you go down to the bar and find the jukebox?"

"Oh, sure, I know how you sisters need your chats," he said. "Why, I bet you talk each other's pretty little ears off, don't you?"

Monte picked his jeans up off the floor and went into the bathroom with a cowpoke swagger.

Emma sighed. "He's talkative, but he gets the job done."

Their hotel suite had two rooms plus the bath, and through an archway I could see an unmade bed the size of a tropical island. The living room had a big-screen TV tuned to *Junkyard Wars* with the sound turned off. The minibar door hung open, and various items of clothing had been abandoned on the carpet.

"So it's Sexcapades with a singing cowboy now?"

"Why not?" Emma said, matching my testy tone. "He's got stamina. And plenty of enthusiasm."

I glanced at the television. "I'm sure the postcoital conversation is stimulating, too."

"I'm not with him for the conversation."

I did not ask if she was with him for the vodka he could supply. Instead, I glanced around the lavish suite. "And Monte's paying for all this?"

"Even chocolate-covered strawberries. You want some room service? We're running a tab."

"No, thanks."

"Want to smell my breath?" she asked in a harsher tone.

"No, I don't, Em. Your breath is your business now, I think."

"Always has been," she shot back.

"Look, I can't help it sometimes. I love you and I care about what happens to you. I go too far, maybe."

We heard a flush, and Monte came back into the room, buttoning on a yoked western shirt and looking for his boots. The whole time, he talked. I don't know what about because Emma and I were glaring at each other. Finally Monte found a pair of two-toned rat-stabbers partially hidden under the sofa. He sat on the floor to pull them on.

"Now, are you the sister who has a passel of rugrats?" Monte asked me.

"No, that's the other sister."

Monte continued as if I had not spoken. "I know how hard it can be to keep those little buggers in good-quality play clothes. I am the official spokesperson for Big Box, the people's store, and we carry a fine line of quality duds for the young members of your family." He wedged one foot into the first boot and didn't pause to draw a breath. "We carry overalls and cargo pants and T-shirts and even embroidered jumpers for the little cowgirls, not to mention a complete collection of socks and other unmentionables that will suit your budget."

He reached for the second boot. "You can be sure Big Box makes darn sure their goods are manufactured in safe, well-ventilated factories where the workers are treated just like every member of the Big Box family—with big hearts and big smiles. So you know all the fine products you buy are making the world a better place for all of us."

With one hand, Emma stuck a cigarette in her mouth, picked up a Zippo lighter and snapped it. She inhaled. "Monte takes his shilling very seriously. He already knows his lines for a commercial he's shooting in two weeks."

"Anyhoodle," Monte continued, getting to his feet to admire his boots. "I believe in Big Box. And you can trust Monte Bogatz to steer you into the right store for the right price for the right family."

"Hit the road, cowboy," Emma said.

Monte smiled suddenly, as if stepping out of a trance. "Sure thing, sugar. See you downstairs?"

"I'll catch up with you," she replied, putting the sofa between herself and Monte's farewell kiss.

When he was gone, Emma put Spike down on the floor.

I said, "I'm sorry. I shouldn't judge you. My own life isn't exactly letter-perfect these days."

She stretched out on the sofa and smoked. "I thought yours was going pretty well. The Love Machine moved in with you, right? And he lets you out of bed once in a while?"

"Em—"

"Oh, loosen up. Admit it. The sex is great."

I sat down on the upholstered chair and kicked off my shoes. "Better than great."

She grinned. "I knew it. You pregnant yet?"

"Not yet."

"Not for lack of trying, I'm sure, at least on his part. You surprise me, though. A kid outside the sacred bond of marriage. You're supposed to be the good girl in the family."

"Good girls don't always get what everybody else gets. And none of us can keep a husband alive, so I can't marry him, can I?"

"You suddenly watching the biological clock?"

"And a few other things."

"Well, if you're looking for a lovefest, at least you picked one who doesn't talk your ear off. And I bet he isn't hung like a hamster or doesn't develop carpal tongue syndrome after only two minutes."

"Em—"

"Best of all—he cooks!" She laughed and threw her arms wide. "The perfect man."

"Well," I said.

"Okay, so he may be the next Godfather. Small glitch. What else do you want?"

"Someone I can trust not to drive his life off the edge of a cliff."

"Yes, but think about the exciting ride down."

I laughed, then hiccoughed and realized I was barely holding back tears. The possibility of losing Michael was so real I almost choked on it.

And if all our baby making had been successful, I was in an even bigger mess.

"On top of everything else," I said when I could speak, "half the city has invited themselves to my house for New Year's Eve. And I can't afford to serve pretzels."

"Am I invited?"

"Sure, why not?" I laughed drunkenly. "Just bring chips or something, okay?"

"What, no caviar?"

"Libby might bring some tasty massage lotion."

"Well, then, nobody will starve."

We smiled at each other.

Then Emma said, "I remember, you know. Brinker grabbed me in the swimming pool and took me out behind somebody's cabana." She looked up at the ceiling.

"I should have watched you more carefully."

She shook her head. "I thought they were going to let me be a part of the gang. But they yanked off my bathing suit. Remember that suit? It was blue and white stripes. I loved that one. They tore it, and I froze. All their slippery, wet hands on me." She closed her eyes and smoked. "I'd never been so scared before. Next thing I knew, you were hitting Brinker with something."

"An inflated plastic alligator."

"Right." She laughed shortly.

"Not exactly a weapon of mass destruction."

"They let me go, though. At the time I was mad at you because I didn't have my nice bathing suit anymore." Emma opened her eyes and her gaze steadily met mine through a thread of blue smoke. "But now I know what you did for me, Nora."

"I was afraid of him then, and I'm afraid of him now. He's a sadist. The things he did to Hemmings . . ."

"Hemorrhoid was nuts long before Brinker got hold of him." Emma stubbed out her cigarette. "You said you wanted to talk to Hemorrhoid."

"Yes."

She sat up. "Funny, I think I know where he's going to be tonight."

"Where?"

"Time for a makeover," she declared, getting up and putting her hand down to me. "You can't go to a club dressed like a French housewife. You're classy, Nora, but sometimes you need to show a little leg." She pulled me upright.

Although Emma spent most of her days training horses and rarely wore anything but breeches and boots, she knew more about makeovers than the Fab Five.

"Let's do something with your hair." She dragged me to the bathroom. "And we'll think about the clothes after."

"This is my very own Armani," I protested. "You're not destroying it."

"Well, take off the sweater underneath at least, will you? You look ready for a polar expedition."

"It's winter, Em."

Her hotel bathroom was all marble and brilliantly shined chrome, with gilded mirrors that might have been copied from Buckingham Palace. Emma used her brush on my hair, forcing me to bend at the waist so she could produce enough volume to rival any Hollywood starlet. I let her work, barely looking at my reflection in the mirror as she sprayed hunks of my hair into unnatural positions.

Emma's grin grew as she played. I was so glad to have her on my side that I suddenly remembered climbing a tree at the farm one summer. She was faster than a monkey and clambered up ahead of me in the branches. I slipped and barely caught my sneaker on a foothold, but Emma turned back and put her little hand down to me.

"C'mon," she had said. "I'll help."

After the hair project, she made me strip off my suit and re-dress. No stockings, no sweater, no bra under my jacket. She rolled my skirt at the waist until my knees were naked, then found me a pair of heels from her suitcase.

"You took high-heeled slingbacks to rehab?" I asked, staring at my reflection—suddenly more long-legged and sexier than was possible.

"These are my emergency pair. Red buckles, see?"

I wanted to hug her. And not for the clothes or the new hair-style.

Emma dressed herself in snug jeans that clung like rain on a roof, boots and her Brinker Bra. Over it, she pulled a sweater—backward—and instantly transformed herself into a goddess.

"Can you get that thing off?" I asked.

"The bra? Sure, why?"

"You should give Libby a call."

"What's she done now?"

"It's a long story. What should we do about Spike?"

"Leave him here," Emma said. "Monte will pay for the damages."

We rode down the elevator and walked across the lobby without glancing into the bar. Outside on the sidewalk, a line had already begun to form for the club that was attached to the hotel. Emma strode past the murmuring crowd and went straight to the bouncer, who sat on a stool at the door to prevent suburbanites from storming the gates of urban trendiness.

"Hey," she said to him.

His face came alive as if she'd waved a tube of ammonia under his nose. He reached for the clasp on the velvet rope before he could summon any words. Then they were, "Hey, doll-face. Come in. And who's this hot topic with you?"

"Careful with her, sugarplum." Emma patted his cheek. "She runs with the big dog."

We slipped into the club.

Chapter Ten

The club was called Beddy-Bye, but I didn't understand the name until we stepped inside and confronted an enormous round bed covered with dozens of satin pillows and draped with overlapping curtains as if to make things private for Scheherazade or a pair of honeymooners who missed the bus to the Poconos.

Two giggling young women sprawled on the coverlet, simultaneously trying to sip their umbrella drinks and keep their skirts pulled down on their thighs. A handful of male patrons hung around the bed, holding their beers and working up the courage to join them.

Emma and I skirted the bed and went into the main room of the club. The place was dark and air-conditioned to the temperature of a meat locker. Despite the frigid air, the dress code was nearly naked for the women, whereas most of the men seemed to send the message that they would grab their skateboards any minute to do some rad grinding. Backward baseball caps, low-slung shorts and T-shirts proclaiming various Caribbean islands was the wardrobe of choice.

"It's the dead of winter," I said to Emma as we inched our way through the mob. "Isn't anybody freezing?"

"Okay," said my sister, "so this isn't your usual crowd. Nobody's drinking Cosmopolitans or talking about their ski trips to Jackson

Hole. You want to talk to Hemorrhoid, you gotta get a different mind-set going."

Monstrously loud music from the dance floor made my solar plexus vibrate. It was turntable music—half rap, half static. Neon tubes glowed at floor level, but otherwise the space was dimly lit. I could make out a hundred people or so, all animated, some dancing. Mostly young. All draped around each other as if sex had just been invented.

Emma knew her way around, and in the doorway that separated one demographic from the next, she slid past a nodding doorman and into a new group of patrons. A tight knot of young men in Zegna suits and Hermès ties all slugged shooters and looked shiny-faced. A couple of women were with them, but they hovered on the edge of the group, holding martini glasses and smiling uncertainly.

The second room was clearly VIP territory.

Luxurious beds lined the entire room, each one occupied by a group too large for the space, so people were reclining against each other and swooning to the music—R & B this time. Waiters in black silk shirts swiftly carried trays of glassware as if making offerings to impatient deities.

Emma headed to the bar, which was tended by a busy man with a crew cut who seemed capable of concocting drinks quicker than a juggler.

"Robin," she said.

The bartender stopped pouring and shaking long enough to stretch across the bar to kiss her cheek. He had arms like a heavyweight boxer. "If it isn't the lovely and elusive Emma Blackbird." His accent was distinctly British, and his well-worn MANCHESTER UNITED T-shirt gave him away, too. "Let me guess. You checked yourself out already?"

She laughed. "A caged bird doesn't sing, Rob. You know that. This is my sister, Nora."

Robin reached over the bar to shake my hand. His was wet and slightly sticky. "Sorry, luv," he said, and handed me a wad of napkins.

"We're looking for Hemmings Lamb," Emma said. "Seen him tonight?"

Robin cocked his head. "Not exactly your type, Emma."

"Who is?"

He laughed. "Hemorrhoid just came in a few minutes ago." Robin nodded toward a far corner. "I think he's trying to score some X, but he's such a horse's arse, he'll be lucky if he gets his hands on an aspirin."

"Thanks."

We wound our way through the beds and found ourselves at a large, round bed that was covered with a lush spread and heaps of pillows and surrounded by votive candles. Two champagne coolers stood beside the bed. In the center of the bedclothes, Hemorrhoid lolled, holding court with half a dozen Britney wannabes with bare midriffs and lots of blond hair hanging in their eyes. Most of them were sucking on the fingers of one hand while stiffly holding champagne flutes with the other, all preening. Their attention was riveted on their host as if he were about to award a sash and crown.

"What's this?" Emma asked when we arrived in front of Hemorrhoid. "Cheerleading tryouts?"

Finding himself staring up Emma's towering lean body, Hemorrhoid looked startled. "Hi." Then he saw me and blinked at the transformation Emma had supervised. "Nora, hi."

One of the girls said nastily, "Who are you?"

"Doesn't matter, Miss Tan-orexia. You never heard of skin cancer?" Emma took the teenybopper's golden-brown arm and pulled her from her relaxed pose. "C'mon, kiddies. Let me buy a round of diet Sprite, okay?"

Her air of command successfully got the girls to their feet, and Emma spirited them away like a dyspeptic prom chaperone.

I hesitated, then slid onto a vacated spot on the bed beside Hemorrhoid's, keeping one foot on the floor. I noticed a dish of candy amidst the pillows. Gummi Bears. Someone had organized them by color.

"Let's have a talk, Casanova," I said to Hemorrhoid.

He tried to sit up in the bed, but looked even more uncomfortable. "I was just . . . you know, interviewing potential models for Lamb Limited. There's nothing wrong with that. We're thinking of launching some new products in the States, and—"

I cut across his sniveling. "Have you been in touch with your house in the last few hours?"

"My house?" His stupefied expression morphed into terror an instant later. "You mean . . . ? Oh, God, has something happened to Orlando? Is he all right? Has he been hurt? If something's happened to him, I'll be in—"

I grabbed Hemorrhoid's wrist and pulled him back onto the bed. "Nothing like that. Orlando's fine."

I had his full attention. "What's wrong?"

"The police are at Tall Trees. It seems something happened there during the fashion show."

His voice was barely a squeak. "What?"

"Someone killed Kitty Keough outside your garage."

"Kitty Keough? Why would she . . . Was there an accident?"

"No, she was executed." I decided to channel my sister and turned on the tough act. "Listen, Hemorrhoid, we've got a problem, and you're going to help me solve it or risk some very bad consequences, understand? I want you to shut up with the stupid questions and start answering me, got it?"

He clapped one hand over his mouth to smother his own whimpers. A lifetime of being a victim kicked in, and Hemorrhoid was suddenly, pathetically ready to do anything I wanted. He nodded, subdued, and looked as if he wanted to crawl under the covers and hide.

"Okay." I tried to keep up my charade despite the sick wave that rolled up from inside me. "Good. Now, what business did you have with Kitty?"

He slid his hand off his mouth. "None, I swear. I barely knew the woman."

"She didn't just waltz in off the street for no reason. She had your name and address in her schedule book. She obviously had an appointment at Tall Trees."

He grabbed a Gummi Bear and put it into his mouth. Three more followed rapidly, all red. "The appointment wasn't with me. I've never spoken to her in my life. My father hated her. She wrote terrible things when Oriana married so young."

He reached into his pocket and came up with a foil packet. For a mad moment, I thought it was a condom. But he tore open one corner and unfolded a Handi Wipe. He used it to remove infinitesimal traces of the sticky candy from his fingers.

"Then tell me about your relationship with Brinker Holt."

"Who?"

An almost irresistible urge bubbled up inside me. Looking at Hemorrhoid, I wondered what it was about him that just seemed to be asking for abuse. I could see why people longed to slap him—the combination of mealymouthed whining and the weird perfectionist mannerisms drove normal people crazy. "Hem, you've known Brinker since you were Orlando's age. We all went to the same swim club, remember? The two of you weren't exactly best friends. Yet you went to his fashion show the other night. Why? Just to look at women's underwear?"

"No, of course not. I mean . . . well, yeah! I like women's under-wear as much as the next guy." He ate more candy—popping them into his mouth without regard to color.

"Why did you take Orlando to the show?"

"I was— It's time he had a little polish, that's all. He needs to get out into the world. He's going to control an international con-glomerate someday. Why not give him some sophistication?"

"I overheard your argument with Orlando, Hem. Half a dozen people did. You're thinking of buying the Brinker Bra for Lamb Limited, aren't you?"

"I don't have that kind of power! I'm only one guardian in a committee of—"

"But you have influence. Not to mention ambition, right?"

Hemorrhoid proceeded to devour the whole bowl of candy. "What do you mean? I'm nothing at Lamb Limited."

"Do you like it that way?"

"Of course not. I have a lot to offer."

"So you do have hopes for a career with the corporation? You're trying to buy the Brinker Bra as a professional coup. To in-gratiate yourself with the rest of Orlando's guardians?"

"No, no—"

"Because that sounds like a smart move."

"I . . . I can't say anything. It's confidential. Strictly need-to-know."

"Hem," I said.

Hemorrhoid swallowed with difficulty, and his lower lip began to tremble. "Please," he said.

"Is it a secret?"

"If the deal fell apart before— I just can't tell you."

"Tell me."

"Don't make me say it," he said. "Please."

Sweat began to shine on his face. I knew the only thing that could have prevented him from answering me was fear of something more threatening than I could muster.

"What's the matter? Who are you afraid of? Somebody at Lamb Limited? Or Brinker?"

"I can't talk about it." He dropped the Handi Wipe onto the bedclothes and put one hand to his stomach. "I think I'm going to be sick."

"Calm down. I only—"

"I'm going to be sick."

He crawled off the enormous bed and made a run for the bathroom.

I sat on the bed awhile longer, tugging my skirt down and feeling nauseated myself. Bullying Hemorrhoid had gotten me some answers, but I didn't feel happy about it. Around me, people talked and laughed. The music rose and fell. Life went on, with me wondering what kind of person I had become.

As I waited for him to return, a woman in garish blue pajamas suddenly appeared beside the table.

The pajamas were a sari, I realized. And I noticed assorted bracelets, bangles and rings, too.

"Sabria," I said.

Sabria Chatterjee looked just as startled to find me sitting on Hemorrhoid's bed. Her eyes, rimmed tonight with three carefully blended shades of eye shadow, widened as if I had pulled a dagger. "Nora. What a surprise."

An unpleasant surprise, I could see by the expression on her face.

Uneasily, she glanced around the crowded room. "Have you seen Hemmings?"

"He's indisposed at the moment," I said. "Why don't you wait with me? We can have a chat."

Sabria's expression said she'd rather bathe with live tarantulas than talk to me. She toyed with the bracelets that winked on her wrist. Her sari, a little limp, revealed one bare shoulder. It was hardly the uniform of a woman bent on hacking her own career path through the corporate jungle, but her posture was rigid and ready.

She held up the little brown paper bag for me to see. "He sent me on an errand."

I gave up being polite. "Sit down, Sabria."

She surprised me by sliding onto the bed beside me. She sat alertly on the edge of the mattress, like a dog who'd been promised a treat if he performed well.

"So," I said, "you and Hemmings are . . . what? Seeing each other? Working together?"

"We're acquaintances," she corrected, holding the bag in her lap. "Friends."

"Interesting. How did you meet, exactly?"

"Oh, you know. Around."

Even in the dim light of the club, I could see that she wanted to leave. But my tone of command kept her planted on the bed. "Tell me more about your work at Clientec. It sounds very interesting."

"Really?"

"I'm interested, yes. Advertising is a fascinating peek into the American psyche. Popular culture, appealing to the masses, communicating ideas . . . It's all intriguing. What campaigns have you worked on?"

"We represent many clients."

"Like Lamb Limited?"

"Uh, yes," she said, still careful but obedient. "And others."

"Such as?"

"West Texas Bare Ass Barbecue."

"I bet that advertising campaign is fun."

"It's not much different from our other accounts, like Chantilly

Soap and Big Box," she said soberly. "We give full service to all our clients."

"Big Box," I said. "That's interesting. What does Clientec do for Big Box? Print ads? Television spots?"

"A bit of everything."

Using a pair of sturdy pliers to yank out her teeth would have been easier than dragging information from Sabria. Either she was very discreet with her clients' business or she had things to hide. I tried again. "Do you know Monte Bogatz?"

"Monte . . . ?"

"He's a spokesperson for Big Box. I'm a big fan of Monte's," I said. "I love his singing."

She blinked. "You do?"

"Sure." I thought fleetingly of warbling a line from one of Monte's songs to make my claim authentic, but couldn't remember one. "Do you work closely with him? Maybe you could get his autograph?"

"I could try," she said at last, eyeing me as if I'd be needing a straitjacket soon. "But now I must go. I must find Hemmings."

"He'll be back in a minute."

Sabria fingered the paper bag in her lap. She was torn. She wanted to escape, but she felt responsible, I could see, for delivering the little bag to Hemorrhoid.

I said, "I'm sure he's depending on you."

That got her. She sighed and shifted the bag to her other hand.

Hemorrhoid came out of the bathroom paler than before, and mopping his brow with a handkerchief. I thought he might try to make an escape, but he looked across the room and saw Sabria on the bed. He pulled himself together and came over.

"You have no idea how disgusting the men's room is. There aren't any hand towels! Somebody should call the health department."

Sabria scrambled to her feet at his arrival.

"Hemmings," she said, obsequious and secretarial. "I found the . . . um . . . throat lozenges you wanted."

"Throat lozenges?" As a newbie to the recreational drug scene, Hemorrhoid was slow to catch on.

"With echinacea," she volunteered, suddenly inspired.

Hemorrhoid hastily stowed his handkerchief. "Oh, right. Yes. Thanks. You did well."

Sabria smiled and looked ready to roll over on her back to show her tummy to him.

Hemorrhoid said, "Is it . . . ? Did you get the name brand?"

"Name brand?"

"Yes," he said more harshly. "The specific brand I requested."

Sabria's smile faltered.

"You nitwit," he said. "Can't you do anything right?"

"Hem—"

"It was a simple task, and you blew it!"

Sabria lowered her head.

He grabbed her elbow and yanked, spinning Sabria around in a whirl of blue silk. Still gripping her arm, his nails digging into her flesh, Hemorrhoid propelled her toward the door.

As I stood up to stop them, I caught sight of her expression. Sabria didn't look frightened. It stunned me to see it, but her face looked almost happy.

I'd had way too much weirdness for one night to follow them. I went looking for Emma.

I found her in the bar, teaching the Girl Scouts how to tie cherry stems with their tongues. My sister could do it in fifteen seconds and earned their applause.

She saw me coming and got off her bar stool. "Now what?"

"I'm ready to go," I said. "I'm disgusted with myself. And the human race, come to think of it."

"What happened?"

"People are sick, Em."

"You've just observed that fact?"

"Are those the Finehart twins?" I stared down the bar. "Those models from the fashion show?"

She spun her head around. "They're back from New York already?"

"Must be." I noticed my tough sister actually looked nervous and tried to hold back a grin. "Want to go talk to them?"

"Hell, no!"

"I get the feeling they want you snuggled under their bedsheets watching *Xena, Warrior Princess*."

"Very funny."

Perched at the other end of the bar, Fawn and Fontayne wore their Brinker Bras under sheer blouses for the world to see. Their straight blond hair was unmistakable, and they appeared to be carrying lollypops—red to match their glossy lipstick. Already they were drawing a crowd. Fawn leaned out and waved to Emma.

Em turned pale.

"She likes you," I said.

"They can't possibly be as vacant as they pretend," she said. "Can they?"

"Would they be more appealing to you if they were smarter?"

"No!"

As we watched, Fontayne spilled her drink on the bar. Four men leaped to her assistance.

"They might act stupid," Emma said, "but they know how to get what they want."

"Hussies."

"You can laugh. They seem willing to do a lot to get the Brinker Bra gig." Emma shivered and grabbed my arm. "Let's jet. I don't feel like getting my tonsils tickled by the Doublemint Twins."

We returned to the hotel to get the rest of my clothes. We found Spike sound asleep in the wreckage of what once had been the sofa.

"Wow," said Emma, impressed by the destruction. "How'd he manage to shred all the cushions so fast?"

I tucked his limp, exhausted body into my handbag. He gave me a feeble lick and snuggled down with a sigh of contentment. "At least he didn't chew the wooden legs. I won't have to worry about splinters in his stomach."

"Heaven forbid."

Emma took me home in Monte Bogatz's Hummer, which was like riding in a giant carnival ride. It had desert camouflage upholstery and more interior lights than the cockpit of a jumbo jet. Lesser vehicles dodged out of our way, and Emma left them behind in a wake of slush.

Over the roar of the engine, I asked Em about Sabria Chatterjee.

"I didn't know her very well in college," Emma told me. "She was a good student. Lots of drive. Big ambitions. I got the impression her parents wanted her to be perfect, poor kid. They came around on weekends to check her homework and talk to her professors."

"About what?"

"Giving her extra assignments. They wanted her to be class valedictorian, but they wanted her to get it the hard way."

"Did she make it?"

"I dunno. I didn't hang around to find out."

Of course. Emma hadn't finished college. She dropped out when our parents couldn't afford the tuition, and she never looked back.

I said, "I wonder what kind of personality results from such high expectations."

"Lots of people manage. Sabria seems to be okay. Maybe she's a little wacky about her job. But buying drugs for Hemorrhoid isn't exactly a good career move. Those two are an odd match, aren't they?"

"My impression was more master and slave, actually."

"Sound familiar?"

"You mean Brinker and Hem?" I shook my head. "Hemorrhoid was always the victim then—a masochist who went looking for people to pick on him."

Emma shrugged. "So he's flipping. It's not impossible."

"Has Monte ever mentioned Sabria?"

Emma sent me a puzzled glance. "Sabria? Why should he?"

"Her ad agency probably hired him for Big Box. Now he's hanging around Brinker. It's a suspicious coincidence, that's all."

"I'm not up to speed on the cowboy's career plans."

"Em, about Monte. Is he . . ."

She shrugged. "He's no Rhett Butler. I know that. But he's not bad. He's . . . resilient."

Carefully, I ventured, "Are you taking out some frustration on him?"

She considered my question seriously. "Maybe. It doesn't matter. This is a short-term thing. We both know it. Not like you and the Love Machine."

"Uhum," I said.

"Mick's trying, you know. To clean up his act for you." Keeping her eyes on the road, Emma was able to say things she couldn't say to my face. "It's a whole redemption thing for Mick, Sis. Because you believe in him, he's trying to be good. It's pretty sexy when you think about it. But if you stop believing . . . I don't know what he'll do."

"Are you about to give me some sisterly advice?"

She grinned. "Not me. I'm a Blackbird too, you know. I always pick the wrong men."

Em dropped me off at Blackbird Farm and declined my invitation to spend the night.

"No, thanks. I've got to return the cowboy's toy." She patted the steering wheel of the Hummer.

"Em—"

"Don't worry about me," she said. "You've got a lot of stuff on your mind. I'll call you tomorrow."

Smiling a little, I took Spike inside.

Michael was not in the house.

Nor had he left me a phone message.

My machine, however, was clogged with calls from old friends angling for invitations to my party.

With a groan, I went to bed.

In the morning, I woke up alone except for Spike.

When the phone rang, I grabbed it, hoping to hear Michael's voice. But the call was from another potential New Year's Eve guest, a pal who fortunately volunteered to bring a bottle of wine. I hoped it would be a very big bottle.

When I hung up, I wrote down her name and looked at my guest list. It had gone so far beyond my control that I might as well invite the whole city.

The thought of providing food and drink for such a crowd that size gave me a dizzy spell.

"Maybe I'll make hors d'oeuvres out of you," I said to Spike while cleaning up one of his near-misses by the door.

I went into my closet and decided not to endanger any of Grandmama's clothes for a daytime foray. I put on a classic sweater set with a Zac Posen layered skirt, one of the last things I could afford for myself before my trust fund evaporated. I checked the mirror and decided I didn't look half-bad for a woman whose life was imploding.

Cross Your Heart and Hope to Die

Reed picked me up at ten and delivered me to a Philadelphia department store where a Mensa reject had scheduled a fund-raiser for the literacy foundation during the after-Christmas sale. Kitty had assigned the event to me before her death, presumably so I could be trampled by frenzied shoppers returning unwanted presents.

I rode the escalator behind a woman wearing a Juicy sweat suit and matching lavender flip-flops. The Juicy logo was written across her buttocks. She turned around and I realized she was Gretchen Schwartzenhauser, the air-bag heiress.

"I just came from a pedicure," she said when I remarked upon her footwear. "I leave for Palm Beach in the morning. I can't stand winter, can you?"

I admired her toes, which weren't frostbitten yet. "Are you here for the literacy foundation event?"

"Are you kidding? I'm returning a blouse. When will my stepmother stop getting me things that aren't on my list?" She rolled her eyes. "I mean, Ralph Lauren is so old-school. I wore it once, but I don't think anyone can tell."

Those gifts from the heart sure could spoil a girl's Christmas.

"Say," she said, "you always know cool stuff. Where can I get a Brinker Bra?" She pointed at a huge banner that pictured Brinker's smirking face.

"I don't think they're for sale yet."

"Are you sure?" Gretchen narrowed her eyes. "You're not pretending, are you?"

"I have no idea when they'll be available."

"Hm." She continued to look suspicious. "If you hear anything, let me know, huh? I want to be first in line."

Spike poked his nose out of my bag, and Gretchen recoiled. "Yuck! Is that a pet rat or something?"

Spike's snarl hinted that Gretchen wasn't exactly Miss America either.

"Yes," I said. "Rats are the latest thing in pets."

"Oh, yeah? Where can I get one?"

I escaped before Gretchen could invite herself to my party.

Although the rest of the store was a zoo, the corner where the literacy foundation had set up a table was a sea of tranquility.

English Hubble looked forlorn. "Bad timing," she said after I commiserated about the low turnout. "Live and learn."

I liked English. For generations, her family had owned the city's two most popular tourist restaurants. She aspired to be an actress, but now that she had reached the ripe old age of twenty-eight, she spent a lot of time recording books for the blind.

"Better luck with the next event."

English ventured to scratch Spike's head. "Funny puppy, Nora. But then, you always did get attached to underdogs."

"He's ugly, but he's sweet."

English nodded and sent a sideways glance at me. I knew she noticed my bruise. "Are you okay?" she asked. "I mean, you know I'm happy to do something if you need help."

I put my hand to my face. "This? I fell, that's all."

"You sure? I don't mean to pry, but if you've got relationship problems—"

"I don't. Really, I fell."

"Okay." She accepted that, but followed up one more time, just in case. "How about if we get together for lunch soon?" She grinned. "I love to eat at restaurants my dad doesn't own."

"Sure. That will be nice."

I appreciated English's instinct to help and her willingness to press a friend in need. She was one of the good ones. I asked her if she had plans for New Year's Eve. She happily accepted my invitation.

As I made my way out of the store, I noticed a store crew on ladders hanging another huge banner from the store's marble mezzanine.

BRINKER BRA! COMING SOON!

Already, shoppers were pointing at the banner and buzzing with excitement.

I was supposed to meet my friend Lexie Paine at the Ritz-Carlton's Grill for lunch. I walked up the windy street with Spike. On his new Christmas leash—patent leather, from Libby—Spike checked the sidewalks for terrorist threats and left a few dire warnings along the way.

We found Lexie standing outside between two of the hotel's massive neoclassical columns, speaking rapid-fire Japanese into her cell phone. She looked so beautiful that the hotel's two uniformed doormen were practically throwing themselves at her feet.

Her face lit up with a grin when she saw me. She waved and terminated her call. I put Spike into my bag.

"God," she said as she stowed the phone in her coat pocket. "If the Japanese would spend less time being polite and focus an equal amount of time on the yen, we'd have a stronger world economy. How are you, sweetie? I'm so glad you called." She gave Spike's head a rub and me a heartfelt kiss. "I'm simply— Heavens, what's wrong with your face?"

"I fainted over Kitty's body."

She winced. "What a perfectly ghastly business. Are you all right?"

"Not bad." I told her I had just left the department store. "Half the city is returning their Christmas gifts in there right now."

"And buying more stuff, sweetie, which is very patriotic these days. Must keep the economy marching along. Speaking of which, I have just enough time for lunch and a gossip before rushing back to save a major telecommunications company from going bust. Or we could hike down the street to Bojo's and look at shoes for an hour. What do you think?"

"No contest. Shoes."

To the disappointment of the Ritz-Carlton doormen, we linked arms and my friend whisked me to a secluded storefront, where she rang the bell and showed her face to the security camera to gain entrance. In the inner sanctum, the general public was not invited, but as Lexie stepped inside, the staff abandoned their intense study of fashion magazines and sprang to our service. Lexie waved them off graciously.

"We're just snooping," she announced.

"I keep this place in business," she confided when we were admiring the glass shelves of beautifully displayed footwear, backlit like priceless artifacts in a museum. "I send my assistant over here every week to buy herself a bonus, can you believe it? I hate keeping her late at night, but there's just nothing to be done about that until Alan Greenspan pours oil on the waters, so I must spoil her. What about this kitten heel? Too matronly?"

"It's sensible, yet chic. But the bow is maybe too adorable."

She nodded sagely. "A shoe must reflect current styles, but also one's commitment to career."

Lexie had inherited her father's share of a venerable brokerage house, but the remaining partners soon surrendered and left her entirely in charge of a vast financial empire, which she ruled like a benevolent tyrant.

"I always think of you in killer stilettos," I said.

"Excellent for meetings with misogynistic hedge fund pooh-bahs, but hell on my ankles." Lexie ran her forefinger up the four-inch heel of a Prada pump with a skinny patent-leather ankle strap. "This, however, is definitely a shoe for a woman who wants to be tied up and spanked. Speaking of which, tell me what in the name of all that's holy has gotten into Libby? She left the most bizarre message on my home machine yesterday."

"She's become an Avon lady for X-rated gadgets."

Lexie dropped the shoe. "I thought she wanted me to join some sort of cult! You mean all that talk about personal satisfaction in-volved batteries?"

"And some lotion she's addicted to." I picked up the shoe from the floor.

"She's still trying to convert me." Lexie shook her head. "I swear, she has enough sex drive for half a dozen women, and I could care less. The last man I dated only wanted to take me to the opera, and even that required more estrogen than I was willing to sacrifice."

"My biggest worry is that Libby's going to show up New Year's Eve ready to demonstrate her gadgetry."

Lexie laughed. "How does Michael feel about her new product line?"

The mere mention of his name gave me an odd flutter in my stomach. I turned my face away from Lexie to avoid explaining my feelings.

"He doesn't know," I said, manufacturing a light tone. "We haven't reached the stage of intimacy where we can talk about things electrical. Or our relatives, for that matter."

"A good lifetime policy, if you ask me."

Lexie had met Michael and liked him, I thought. The two of them talked about money. Sometimes I thought Lexie believed he kept his savings under a mattress, and he liked to listen to her rant about chickenhearted investors and their mutual funds. I wasn't ready to confide in her about his latest exploit.

"Now, what about New Year's Eve?" she asked, moving along the display shelves with the concentration of a big-game hunter on the trail of a trophy kill. "I may have mentioned your bash to Posie Beedlewine, and she's dying to come with all her bipolar book club pals." Lexie swept on without noticing my pained gasp. "And Jake Jacobson, the drag queen, is back in town for his little brother's bar mitzvah, so I suggested he stop in. He always brings hijinks to a party, and you'll need somebody to cause harmless mischief to divert attention in case the real thing breaks out."

"Which it undoubtedly will."

"What about Kenny Whatshisname—he's on your list, surely? You'll need somebody to play the piano."

Feebly, I said, "It hasn't been tuned in years."

"Even better. It will be so festive that way."

I decided to throw my cards on the table. "Lex, I can't afford to throw a party of this size. And certainly not now that all hell has broken loose in my life."

"Nonsense, sweetie." She patted my hand. "Hell looks much better through the bottom of a cocktail glass—Emma will be the first to tell you that. And you've heard of stone soup? When everybody brings something to the pot? We'll all contribute, I promise."

"Lexie, people in our crowd send flowers and thank-you notes. That doesn't help. I'm going to have to buy cheap gin and make nothing but martinis so everybody gets headaches and goes home early."

"Brilliant strategy! What about food? In college, weren't you the one who always ordered white pizza from a takeout joint, cut out tiny squares and stuck them with frilly toothpicks? And you always got credit for throwing the most fabulous soirees."

She found a pair of black beaded sandals and eyed them with the serious consideration of a connoisseur while I contemplated my options.

"I'll need some dark chocolate," I muttered at last. "A party needs good chocolate."

"There you go! I knew your party-giving endorphins would kick in. It will take your mind off your troubles. Nora, those shoes are so you. Try them on."

I gazed longingly at the pink suede pump in my hand—delicate heel, pointed toe, snakeskin trim. "It's insane to spend five hundred dollars on something I can't wear in the rain."

"Okay, I'll try them on."

We sat in upholstered chairs while the staff brought us green tea and twelve pairs of shoes, all size seven and a half, which happened to be right for both of us.

When the staff retreated to a discreet distance and Lexie was frowning at the reflection of her feet in the low mirror, she said, "So tell me now about Kitty. Are all the newspaper employees dancing on their desktops? Flinging confetti out the windows?"

"It's a mixed reaction," I said. "She was universally disliked, but Kitty's column was one of the most popular among readers. She's going to be missed."

I told Lexie that Kitty had specified me to plan her funeral.

Lexie stopped looking at her feet and stared at me. "What will you do? Light fireworks? Sacrifice some virgins?"

"I was thinking of a memorial service. Suppose anybody would come?"

"If you promised a celebrity or two, yes."

"I thought of that. But what celebrity can I blackmail into attending a memorial for Kitty?"

"Politicians are easy. They'll go to anything."

"But they're no fun. And a good funeral needs just a sliver of something amusing or it's too awful."

"See? You're the expert on parties, even funerals. No wonder Kitty wanted you to plan her last send-off."

"Hm. I'm thinking of a memorial in three weeks—enough time for the general anger to subside and everyone's sense of humor to be restored. People will start to feel more kindly disposed then. Maybe I can coerce a few speakers from organizations that benefited by Kitty's help with fund-raising. And a bighearted clergyman who's good with a joke—maybe that nice Paul Wilmott from First Espiscopal. I could do it in a hotel ballroom with cocktails and nibblies after. What do you think?"

"That you have the best taste of anyone I know, Nora. I'd like you to plan my funeral, too, please, although not right away." Lexie came back to sit beside me. "I heard the news, sweetie. They say a member of the Abruzzo family shot her."

"Danny Pescara. He's a . . . some kind of cousin of Michael's."

Lexie eyed me. "Okay, it's time to come clean. I can see you're in pain. Are you going to tell me what's going on?"

"Oh, Lex."

She sighed, too. "The police visited me yesterday. They wanted to know if I thought you hankered for Kitty's job badly enough to ask the mob to rub her out. I told them such an idea is utterly ridiculous. Darling, I'm so sorry. What a terrible mess for you."

I rubbed my forehead to keep it from exploding. "I can't throw a party, Lex. It's the wrong time, the wrong everything. What am I thinking?"

Suddenly serious, Lexie said, "Listen to me, Nora. You have two important reasons for throwing this bash. One, it shows the world that you believe in Michael and have the utmost confidence in him."

"And two?"

She sighed and took my hand in hers. "I'm your friend, sweetie. Your very best friend. The second reason is to prove to yourself that he can live in your world."

"I have a bad history with men. I know that. I choose the ones who are trouble."

"You're drawn to people you can help."

"Michael doesn't need my help. Not like Todd."

"I watched you with Todd, sweetie. You fought for your husband long after he disappeared into that sucking swamp of addiction. And he almost dragged you down with him. I watched you fall apart. You were half-dead, Nora."

"No, I wasn't."

"You were dead inside. And now you're fighting for Michael. Is he slipping too? And dragging you down with him? You've started a career, Nora—"

"He's not a criminal, Lexie. I just know it."

"The way you knew Todd could be coaxed away from cocaine?"

Softly, I said, "Don't do this to me, Lex."

She squeezed my hand hard. "I won't make you choose between him and me. I wouldn't dream of it. I know how protective you can get when it comes to the people you love. And you do love him, don't you?"

"Yes."

"But self-preservation needs to figure into your life, too, Nora."

"I can't think my way out of how I feel. It's not an intellectual problem."

"There's a lot of chemistry between you, I know. I may not understand it, but I certainly see it."

"I've never felt this way before. It's more visceral with Michael. More . . . consuming somehow."

"What about Richard D'eath?"

I was surprised. "What about him?"

My friend stuck out her foot to look once more at the shoe on it, but I knew she was trying to decide whether or not to hold back. She shook her head and took it off. "He's an attractive man. And I saw the way he watched you at the fashion show. He's intrigued."

"Richard is looking for news, not women."

"I think you're wrong," Lexie said. "He wouldn't be a bad

person to wake up with in the morning. Newspapers at the break-fast table. Clever conversation over dinner. And I'll bet he's thor-oughly housebroken."

"Meaning I could introduce him to my friends without embar-rassment?"

"That's not what I meant," she said, looking contrite. "Okay, forget I said any of this, sweetie. Just tell me how I can help."

Chapter Eleven

exie's cell phone rang and she apologized before answering it. While she spoke with her assistant, I checked to be sure Spike was still asleep in my bag, then tried on a pair of Manolos that sported a price tag of a mere seven hundred dollars. I thought about what Lexie was trying to tell me.

Within a minute, she snapped her phone shut. "I'm truly sorry about that. The cell phone is my enemy and my best ally."

"You're my best ally, Lex. I know you only want to help me."

"If you want my opinion, you should buy those pink suede shoes. If you want my opinion on your love life, though, I'll keep my lip buttoned from now on."

I smiled a little. "Tell me what you know about Brinker Holt's business."

"I'll do even better. My assistant is sending over somebody right now who can answer your questions better than I can."

"Who?"

She grinned. "An investigator for the SEC. As the governing body of the stock exchange, the Securities and Exchange Commission wants to make sure that if Lamb Limited buys the Brinker Bra, the deal is kosher. They've been asking around my firm all morning."

"What's the upshot?"

"Well, everybody knows the Brinker Bra is going to be huge and make Brinker a millionaire. If he sells it to Lamb Limited, he'll probably become a billionaire. Trouble is, his past is starting to circle back to bite him in the tushie."

"You mean Upchuckles?"

Lexie nodded. "Nobody could prove Brinker torched his comedy club, but the place burned down at a very, very convenient time for him, financially speaking."

"Arson was never proved."

"Not then. But the SEC wants to reopen the case. Despite current publicity to the contrary, the stock exchange takes a dim view of crooks. They also want to know why a murder took place on the grounds of Hemorrhoid's estate at precisely the time a big deal is in the works with Brinker. Kitty's death is suspicious, just like Brinker's fire. I thought you might like to talk to one of the investigators."

Lexie called the clerk over and requested three more pairs of shoes. The second clerk ventured his opinion about the pumps Lexie had already tried on, and they chatted about toe boxes while I sat and thought about Kitty. Why had she gone to Tall Trees that night? Had she been working on a story about the Brinker Bra?

While Lexie tried on more shoes, the chime on the door sounded and the clerk permitted the entry of two more customers. Fawn and Fontayne Finehart teetered into the store on their superhigh heels. Fawn had dressed herself in a fake-fur stole and an acid-washed micromini short enough to freeze her assets. Fontayne looked more sensible in a black wool coat and trousers.

I recognized which twin was Fontayne because she caught her toe on the rug and took a header onto the floor. Her briefcase flew in one direction, her cell phone in another. She let loose a string of curses.

I helped her up and dusted off her knees.

"I swear to God," she snapped, "I'm putting in for a transfer. I can't wear these stupid shoes another day."

Her sister picked up Fontayne's cell phone and handed it over, looking dismayed. "But Fonnie, how can we be the first twin supermodels if you stop wearing shoes? Don't you want to be Brinker's muse? Like Kelly was for Calvin?"

"Fawn, I'm not going to explain it all again. And shut up about Calvin, will you, please? Who needs a muse to sew clothes? He makes sportswear, for crying out loud." She accepted her briefcase from me. "Thanks."

"Fontayne!" Lexie cried from the rear of the boutique. "Tell me what you think of these sandals!"

Fontayne plopped into the nearest chair. "Burn 'em."

"Nora," Lexie said, "this is Fontayne Finehart, the SEC investigator I was telling you about. Remember how I said she looked familiar at the fashion show? Well, I almost didn't recognize her with all that extra hair and gunk on her face, but—"

"Gunk?" Fawn objected. "This is expensive makeup?"

"Fawn," said Fontayne, "go shop for something."

Fawn brightened. "Your treat?"

"Why not." Fontayne took off one stiletto with a groan of relief. "After this, I'm declaring a fashion fatwa. No more high heels."

"Let's hear it for Dr. Scholl's," said Lexie.

Fontayne glanced my way. "Lexie, I'm supposed to be undercover on this case, you know."

"We won't give you away, sweetie, honest. You've met Nora Blackbird, haven't you? I trust Nora with my life."

Rubbing her foot, Fontayne bit back a moan of pain. "Sure. You're Emma Blackbird's sister."

"Yes. And your interest in Emma is . . . ?"

"Purely business," Fontayne said. "I can't speak for my sister, but all I want to know is what Emma is doing with Monte Bogatz."

Emma would be relieved to hear the twins weren't chasing her for romantic reasons. Not both of them, anyway.

"Lexie said you were interested in Brinker Holt."

"Of course. But Emma was our way to Monte. And Monte to Brinker."

"I don't get it. Emma and Monte are friends," I said. "Well, maybe more than that at the moment, but—"

Gently, Lexie said, "Monte is a spokesperson for Big Box stores, Nora, but he was hired through Clientec, the advertising firm. And Clientec's biggest client is . . . well, am I giving too much away, Fontayne?"

Fontayne said, "It's public knowledge that Clientec would be little more than a local ad agency selling spots on cable TV if it weren't for Lamb Limited. They have other clients, of course, but Lamb is their raison d'être."

"You mean," I said slowly, puzzling it out, "Monte Bogatz works for Lamb Limited?"

"It's complicated," Fontayne agreed. "All three companies are in bed together, and we're trying to sort it out. We know the rodeo clown is for sale, and Clientec pays him to do a lot of things besides sell baby clothes."

"What kind of things?"

"Snooping," Lexie guessed. "Better known as industrial espionage."

"Right. We think Lamb had Clientec hire him to spy on Brinker Holt," Fontayne tried to clarify. "We thought your sister might be able to tell us for sure."

"The only thing my sister knows about Monte right now," I said, "is the size of his belt buckle. You're telling me that Emma's acquaintance with Monte is not one of those happy rehab coincidences?"

"Probably not. Somebody set it up."

Lexie asked, "How did you get this assignment, Fontayne? I thought you were strictly in mergers."

Fontayne took off her other shoe and gingerly wiggled all toes to make sure they still functioned. "When the call went out for lingerie models, some asshole at my company water cooler came up with the brilliant idea that my sister and I should audition for Brinker so I could work on the case from the inside. You should have heard the Deep Throat jokes. Fawn does a little modeling back home in Wilkes-Barre, so we gave it a whirl."

Fawn hadn't strayed far and returned to us. "Mostly I do department-store ads and some bridal shows? I look great in Vera Wang? But who doesn't?"

"Fawnie," said her twin, "I think I see a pair of boots over there with your name on them."

"Really?" Fawn scampered off.

"Anyway," Fontayne continued, "once I was on the inside, I heard Brinker wanted a special model so he could end his fashion show with a horse. He immediately hired Emma, which sounded suspicious to me. Why would he pick her without even seeing her? I mean, he had a hundred models to choose from, and surely at least one of them knows how to sit on a pony."

Lexie said, "Emma's reputation with horses is well-known. She trains jumpers for the Olympics and looks like a Playgirl of the Month. She was a logical choice."

"But when she turned up with Monte, we knew something else was going on."

"Is Emma in danger?" I asked.

"From Monte? I doubt he could do anything more damaging than hit her with a handful of beer nuts. But if he's being used for keeping an eye on Brinker for Clientec—"

"For Lamb," said Lexie.

"Right, then something more devious is under way."

My head spun with all the convolutions. "What has your investigation learned so far?"

She told me essentially what Lexie had already outlined—that Hemorrhoid wanted to buy the Brinker Bra for Lamb Limited. But no doubt Brinker was also pulling strings.

"Both parties want to walk away with the biggest piece of the pie. And they're both playing dirty."

I remembered what Dilly had said to me at the train station— that Brinker was an unlikely lingerie designer. Musing aloud, I said, "Do you think the bra is Brinker's to sell in the first place?"

Fontayne looked more sharply at me. "What do you know?"

"Brinker's hardly a design genius."

Lexie said, "Did Hemmings design the bra? He's not exactly the brightest bulb in the chandelier either."

"Whatever business sense he has," Fontayne agreed, "he sucked it out of somebody else's brain."

"Sabria Chatterjee," I guessed.

Fontayne nodded. "She's the Clientec account exec in charge of keeping Lamb Limited happy these days. That means following Hemmings everywhere and wiping his nose, as needed."

"She's in a tough spot," Lexie said.

"Yes, do or die. If she fails to please Hemmings, there's a good chance he'll choose another advertising agency."

"And Clientec will basically go out of business."

"Sabria might as well practice her burger-flipping skills."

"So what the hell is she doing? Playing double agent? Or go-between?"

"Mergers like this one are brokered in weirder ways. Often, it takes a third interested party to negotiate a merger. But something's fishy."

"The SEC takes a dim view of murder?"

Fontayne glanced around the store to make sure her sister hadn't wandered off. "Yes, we think the Keough lady's death is connected to the Brinker–Lamb deal, but we haven't figured out how yet. The police are no help. They think they've got some kind of mob hit on their hands, so they're not listening to us."

Lexie shot me a sympathetic glance. "If somebody comes up with more specific information about Kitty's death, I'm sure the police will start listening."

"Okay," I said, grabbing my bag. "I have an idea who really designed the bra. That information will definitely help. Let me find out for sure and get back to you."

Fontayne forgot about her sore feet and perked up. "Can I come along?"

"Let me find out for sure first. I don't want to drag any innocent bystanders into this mess. I'll contact you as soon as I know more. Lex, can I borrow your cell phone?"

She handed it over without question, then gave me some privacy by engaging the Finehart twins in a footwear discussion.

I checked my watch and knew Reed would be taking his mother and her friends to their weekly bingo game. I couldn't disturb him. I tried Michael's cell phone. No answer. I dialed my own house, then his, but he didn't pick up. I wanted to shriek at him. Where was he?

On impulse, I called information and asked for the number of the most respected newspaper in the city.

A minute later I heard Richard D'eath's voice on the line.

"Hi," I said without preamble. "Do your injuries prevent you from driving a car?"

"What? No. Nora?"

"Yes, it's me. Do you have a car? I need a ride back to the Lamb house in Bryn Mawr."

"You going to tell me what this is about?"

"I thought ace reporters acted on hunches now and then."

"My hunch is you're getting desperate to prove your boyfriend is innocent."

"Can I have a ride or not?"

"What's in it for me?"

"The pleasure of my company isn't enough?"

Long pause during which my joke fell flat.

"Where are you?" he asked once I was fully embarrassed.

I gave him the address.

He said, "Okay," and hung up.

After further consideration, Lexie decided to buy two pairs of shoes for herself. She offered to buy the Manolos for me as a very early birthday gift, but I refused. Although I was sorely tempted.

To keep her sister quiet, Fontayne Finehart bought her a pair of beflowered sandals with ridiculous heels.

"Great?" Fawn cried with unabashed delight. "Nobody's going to make fun of my shoes anymore?"

"Nobody's making fun of your shoes now, Fawn."

"That awful woman from the newspaper did?" Fawn pouted. "I wanted to, like, punch her in the nose?"

"What woman?" we asked in chorus.

Fawn blinked, prettily confused by our interest. "That woman who was killed? She got what's coming to her, y'know? She was totally rude to me?"

"Kitty Keough?" I asked. "When did you see her, Fawn?"

"The day of the fashion show? She went to Brinker's condo? And they had a fight?"

Fontayne said, "You didn't mention this before, Fawn. What were you doing at Brinker's condo?"

Fawn flushed. "Oh . . . I . . . I was visiting Brinker, that's all? To ask if we could be the Brinker Twins?"

"Oh, my God, you didn't sleep with him, did you?"

Fawn got so angry her implants actually began to tremble. "Of course not? What kind of girl do you think I am? I took him some jam, that's all? In a basket?"

"Jam," Fontayne said blankly.

"It's a universal gift? But he was busy fighting with that woman, so I left? But before I got on the elevator, she made fun of my shoes? I thought about killing her myself? I'm glad she's dead?"

"You could have mentioned this earlier, Fawn."

"Like, who cares what I have to say?" Fawn asked.

"Hm," said Fontayne.

"Look," I said. "This only supports my idea. I'll call you as soon as I know more."

As platinum credit cards flashed, I said my good-byes and dashed out to the street.

Richard had pulled up in a nondescript sedan—a newspaper pool car.

"Do I get a hint?" he asked as I climbed into the passenger seat. "Or are you trying to dazzle me with your Lois Lane impression?"

"Take it easy, Superman. I've got an idea, but I need a promise that you won't use the information yet."

He squinted at me. "Do you know anything at all about the profession of journalism?"

"I just need enough time to—"

"I know what you're trying to do," he said, pulling into traffic. "But you're supposed to be a reporter, too. Do you understand what that means?"

"No reporter can write a story that's short on facts. I think I know who really designed the Brinker Bra. And if I'm right, it's why Kitty was killed."

"Brinker didn't design it?"

"Only if the laws of the fashion universe have changed." I put my handbag on the seat between us and checked on Spike. He gave my hand a groggy lick. "I think Brinker stole it. I also think Kitty figured out who really deserves the millions the bra is going to earn."

"And the killer wanted the secret to die with Kitty."

"Why, Richard, you almost sound like a tabloid headline. Did you learn that in journalism school, too?"

He ignored that. "Has it occurred to you that the killer still has the same intent? And you're walking into a trap?"

"A lot of people could be in danger."

"What people?"

I just wanted to see Orlando for myself. With everything happening so close to him, I needed to know he was safe.

We arrived at Tall Trees in the midafternoon, and Meg opened the door to us herself.

"I'm so glad you're here," she said to me, looking strained.

"Meg, this is Richard D'eath, a friend. He's a reporter."

She shook his hand briskly. "Hello. I'm sorry. I'm not myself at the moment."

"Is it Orlando?" I asked.

"He's upset, yes. But it's . . . Mr. Gallagher is gone."

"Gone?" Or dead? I wondered.

I followed Meg into the kitchen, which smelled of fresh baking. A rack of oatmeal cookies cooled on the counter. Spike poked his head out of my handbag to better assess the fragrance.

"Do you know where Gallagher is? Have you spoken with him?"

"Yes, of course. He's gone to Ireland. He called me from one of those expensive telephones on the airplane, didn't he? First class! Now, tell me, who would spend money on a first-class ticket when he's going home to look after his poor mum, who hasn't got two pence to rub together?"

Somebody who really wanted Gallagher out of the country would buy him a first-class ticket, I thought.

But I asked, "Where is Orlando?"

"In his room. Aggie's keeping an eye on him. The lad is so sad! I was just about to take him a snack to cheer him."

"And Hemmings? Is he here?"

Mary Margaret shook her head. "He left for his manicure appointment this morning before we learned Gallagher was gone. He doesn't know yet."

"Meg, I think we need to talk about Orlando's safety."

Mary Margaret was already ahead of me. She said, "After that woman was killed here, I telephoned Orlando's guardians in New Zealand. I give them weekly reports, but this murder! And now Gallagher walks out without a word! You can't tell me all's right with the world when a trusted employee leaves flat after a lifetime of service, so I called them again."

Her cheeks flamed with two pink spots. I patted her hand. "You did the right thing, Meg."

She had to bite her lower lip to keep it from trembling, but she burst out, "That dear boy needs to be protected! The board of guardians is sending someone to take him back early to New Zealand, but it's a bloody long trip, and I don't expect anyone to arrive before tomorrow, maybe even the next day. I don't mind telling you, Nora, I'm worried."

"I'm worried, too."

"I tried to hire a guard, but the security company sent over a boy who's barely older than Orlando himself and carrying a big ugly gun on his hip, too! What do people imagine they carry a gun for except to use it on other people? I just despise a weapon! So I sent him packing."

"But," Richard said reasonably, "how can anyone protect the boy if—"

"I can't abide a handgun," Mary Margaret said smartly. "Now, shooting for sport is another kettle of fish altogether, and I've enjoyed bagging the occasional partridge myself, haven't I? But I simply don't—"

"Meg, how can we help?"

Mary Margaret hugged me impulsively. "Oh, Nora, you're so kind to come. I know you're thinking of Miss Oriana, aren't you?"

No, I was thinking of something Michael had said about Orlando. That the young heir should watch his step. As Orlando's only living relative, Hemorrhoid stood to inherit Lamb Limited. Now, with Gallagher gone, there was one less line of defense between the boy and someone who wanted control of the company badly enough to murder.

"I'm afraid for Orlando," I said. "He could be in danger."

"What can we do? If I ask the police for protection, there's going to be publicity, and that's a sure way to make things worse. What kinds of crazy people might come out of the woodwork as soon as the television trucks show up?" She sat down abruptly at the table, her anger flagging.

I glanced at Richard. "I'm afraid publicity is going to be hard to avoid at this point. We just need to figure out how to protect Orlando until his other guardians get here. Can you phone another security firm?"

"If I trusted them to be sensible, I would, but I don't. They call themselves professionals, but all they do is practice on a gun range and presto, they're protectors! Why, if my own father were here . . . He knew how to take care of a nasty business, if you know what I mean. Give me a strong man with his own way of doing things— that's the ticket."

"Ah," said Richard. He took a cookie from the rack. "I think we might just have the man for the job."

"We do?"

Chapter Twelve

Mary Margaret looked hopefully at Richard. "Somebody who can protect Orlando?"

I said, "Wait a minute."

From inside my handbag, Spike looked at Richard's cookie and moaned a soft request.

Unaware of Spike's attempt at good manners, Richard bit into the cookie and looked at me. "It's only for a day or so. Why not take the kid yourself? You've got the best protection in the country, don't you? Who would dare cross the Abruzzo family?"

"That is—"

Mary Margaret said, "It's not a bad idea, is it?"

Spike growled.

To Richard, I said, "You're just creating a better story for yourself. Vulnerable young heir under the protection of the mob? What a headline."

"Great cookies," he said to Mary Margaret. "My grandmother used to make an oatmeal cookie with currants, too."

"And where did your grandmother come from, dear?"

"Somewhere in Wales, I think."

Richard let his guard down for an instant. Quick as a lizard snapping a fly, Spike snatched the remaining cookie from him. Richard yanked his hand back and examined it to be sure he still had all his fingers. Spike swallowed the treat in one ravenous gulp.

"Look," I said, "maybe Michael could provide the kind of protection Orlando needs, but not if the whole world knows."

Richard shrugged. "My deadline is tonight, but the story won't be published until tomorrow. By that time, the kid will be halfway to New Zealand."

The oven timer began to peep, and Mary Margaret went to retrieve another batch of cookies.

I put my handbag on the floor, and Spike scrambled out. He looked up at Richard with an intense glare, daring him to pick up another cookie and not share.

"I suppose I could ask," I said.

"Admit it," Richard said. "You don't trust anybody to do a job as well as you can. You think you're the one who can best protect Orlando right now."

I glared at Richard. "I know who to keep him away from."

I used the kitchen phone to try Michael's cell number again.

This time he answered.

I was so glad to hear his voice that I had to sit down.

"Hey," he said. "A guy at the convenience store just asked if he should bring a date for New Year's Eve. What's that about?"

With Richard crunching cookies just a yard away, I couldn't do justice to the party subject anyway, so instead I told Michael about Orlando.

Michael figured out what I needed before I finished telling the tale.

He said, "We'll make sure the kid is safe. I'll make some calls and meet you at the farm."

Orlando was not as easy to convince. He came down to the kitchen sulking like any kid told he had to travel with strangers.

But Spike snarled at him, and Orlando perked up.

He said, "Can I ride with the dog?"

"Sure," Richard said amiably. "Why not?"

Mary Margaret packed up more cookies, then checked Orlando's backpack for his toothbrush and a change of clothing. She added a notebook and a fresh box of crayons. She fussed over him until he shoved out of her arms.

Subdued, Orlando followed Richard to the car. I picked up Spike so he couldn't dirty himself in the snow.

At the car, Richard said, "Which one of you wants shotgun?"

"What?" I said.

"What?" Orlando said.

Richard looked at us with pity. "Have the both of you always had chauffeurs? Shotgun is the front seat."

"I want the shotgun," Orlando said swiftly. "Gallagher lets me have the shotgun."

"It's not a real gun," Richard said. "It only means you get to sit up front like in the old stagecoaches." At our blank expressions, he sighed. "Never mind. Sit up front, kid."

Orlando was already grabbing the handle of the front passenger seat. "I want the dog in the front, too."

"No way," said Richard. "Either the dog is in her purse or he's in the backseat. I don't trust him."

"But I want to play with the computer."

"This car doesn't have a computer."

Orlando finally got a good look at the vehicle. "What a piece of junk."

"Yeah, but it's all we've got."

I turned Spike loose in the backseat. He immediately found a dribble of something edible on the upholstery. He licked it, then began to chew.

"Stop," I said.

Spike gave me a look that communicated my complete lack of understanding of canine desires and went back to chewing.

"Okay," said Orlando, sizing up the situation. "I'll sit in the back with the dog."

We got into the car and Richard told Orlando to buckle up.

"I can't find the seat belt."

"It's probably wedged down inside the seat. Feel around for it."

"I can't find it."

I got out of the car, opened the back door and helped Orlando find and fasten his seat belt. Spike panted while he watched me wrestle with the buckle; then he attacked Orlando's backpack. Orlando opened the backpack and found his package of cookies.

"Don't make crumbs back there," Richard warned. "And don't give the dog any cookies. He'll probably throw up."

I got back into the front seat and muttered, "You were the one feeding him cookies in the kitchen."

"Well, now we're in the car. The rules are different."

Orlando ate a cookie and fed another one to Spike. I could hear them both spreading crumbs all over the backseat.

Two minutes after we hit traffic, Orlando said, "May I have a Perrier, please?"

"I don't have any Perrier," said Richard, glancing at Orlando in the rearview mirror. "Is that all you drink? Fancy water?"

"Sometimes at school they let us have a Pepsi. But Uncle Hem says it's bad for me."

"I thought all kids drank Pepsi."

"I'd like a Pepsi," Orlando ventured. "I'd like one now."

I could hear Spike panting and looked back to see Orlando wrestling with the dog. They were feeding off each other's energy.

"Spike wants a Pepsi, too," Orlando said.

"He's out of luck," Richard replied.

"We need something to drink," Orlando insisted, still tussling with Spike. "Can we stop for a Pepsi? Please, please, can we stop? I'm dying of thirst. I need a Pepsi. I need a drink so bad I can hardly swallow. I want a Pepsi. My throat's going to crack open. You can die from dehydration. I want a Pepsi, I want a Pepsi, I want a Pepsi, I want—"

"You might as well stop," I said finally. "He's not going to give up."

Richard pulled into a fast-food drive-up.

Orlando said, "They only have Coke here. I want a Pepsi."

Richard drove to the next fast-food restaurant.

By the minute, Orlando seemed to transform from a perfectly mild-mannered child into a kid-shaped, Spike-like monster. "I want some French fries, too," he said when we arrived at the drive-up window. Feverishly, he read the outdoor menu. "If you buy me a whole meal I can have an action figure. I want the guy with the sword. Can you tell them I want the guy with the sword? This isn't the right guy. I want the guy with the sword."

"This kid is becoming a pain in my ass."

I said, "I'll go inside and ask for the guy with the sword."

"No," Richard said. "I'll go inside. If I stay in the car, I might kill him myself."

He went into the restaurant and came out with the action figure with a sword. He gave the toy to Orlando, who was already asking for another Pepsi.

"Spike drank all my Pepsi. I need another Pepsi. This one was too small. Spike is really thirsty. I want another Pepsi."

"You're not letting the dog drink out of your cup, are you?"

"He's thirsty."

Richard went back into the restaurant for another soft drink.

On the road again a few minutes later, a car zoomed past us. Richard said, "Hey! The driver of that car just gave me the finger."

Orlando giggled in the backseat.

Richard glared at him in the mirror. "Are you flipping off other drivers?"

Within ten miles, we were pulled over by a police officer.

"What's the problem, Officer?"

"Sir, may I see your license and registration?"

Richard complied.

"Sir, are you aware that your son has put a sign in the back window of the car?"

"He's not— What sign?"

I climbed halfway over the seat and dislodged the hand-lettered paper sign Orlando had made while waiting for his second soft drink. I could hear Orlando's strangled laughter. The sign said, HELP! KIDNAPPED!

I handed the sign to Richard. He crumpled it in his hands.

Several minutes later we were back on the road with the cop following us at a safe distance.

Orlando said, "Spike is puffing. I think the dog is going to throw up. He's making funny noises. Yep, Spike is definitely going to throw up. I think he must have the flu. I think he's—"

Richard pulled over. I got Spike out of the car in time for him to vomit his banquet of fast food onto the gravel. When he finished being sick, Spike looked dazed. I got back into the car and put him on my lap. For an instant, I thought I heard him whimper.

Five miles later, Orlando said, "I have to go to the bathroom. Can we stop the car? I bet that store has a bathroom. Can we ask that gas station if they have a bathroom? I need a bathroom."

I said, "Richard . . ."

His teeth were clenched. "I'm stopping, I'm stopping."

Richard accompanied Orlando into a convenience market, where they remained far longer than a simple bathroom stop. I had time to walk Spike in the grassy area beside the highway. The fresh air seemed to perk him up again.

By the time Richard and Orlando came out of the convenience store with several plastic bags of goodies, Spike was his nasty self again. He happily began to shred one of the bags.

Getting into the backseat, Orlando upended a bag of Skittles directly into his own open mouth. Richard said, "Go easy on the junk food, kid. If you're not used to that stuff, it can do some damage."

"Okay," Orlando said around a mouthful of candy. "Can I have my crossword puzzle book now? Does anybody have a pencil? Does anybody know another word for 'ghost'?"

"Demon," said Richard.

"I feel sick," said Orlando after five minutes. "I think the dog gave me the flu. I think I'm going to throw up. Maybe I have food poisoning. I'm going to throw up."

Richard pulled over.

Later, I said, "At least he didn't vomit on you."

"Do you mind rolling down your window?" he asked.

When we arrived at Blackbird Farm, two vehicles were parked on either side of my mailbox. One of Michael's acquaintances got out and without expression motioned Richard to stop his car.

It was Aldo, three hundred pounds of pasta-fed bulldog dressed in a maroon track suit with a black parka zipped over it. The parka was open at the neck just enough to see Aldo's gold chains. His face, as always, looked as if it had been run over by a beer truck.

"Hello, Aldo," I said when Richard had rolled down his window. "It's me."

Aldo gave Richard a once-over that was part inquisition, part intimidation. "Pop the trunk, buddy."

"What?"

"He wants to see if you're hiding Mr. Hoffa in the trunk," I said.

When Aldo waddled back to have a look, Richard said, "He's kidding, right?"

"I don't think so."

"Nobody really looks like that in the mob, do they?"

We heard Aldo rummaging in the trunk. After a minute, he slammed it shut, stepped away from the car and waved us on.

Michael met us on the back porch. He leaned one shoulder against the pillar, a relaxed posture that did not give away the leaps his nimble mind made as we all got out of Richard's car.

Orlando went up the sidewalk, dragging his backpack and looking suspicious. Michael returned his expression.

Richard said, "I hope you have a large supply of Pepsi."

When Michael raised his brows, I said, "Don't ask. It was an ugly situation."

Orlando looked as if he might burst into tears. Softly, he said, "I'll be good. I won't do anything wrong again."

"Damn," Michael said. "Spike and I were looking forward to raising a little hell with you tonight."

Orlando squinted up at him, trying to decide if Michael was serious.

"Go inside," Michael said to Orlando. "Take the dog with you."

The boy obediently went into the house. Spike followed, tail down.

Richard said, "How did you do that?"

Michael said, "You ever been in a prison yard?"

"Michael," I said.

He grinned. "I'll be inside protecting your furniture."

Michael left us alone, and Richard lingered on the steps.

Chapter Thirteen

*R*ichard said, "I can see why Gallagher went to Ireland. He had to get away from the kid."

"Thank you for bringing me home," I said.

Richard glanced up at the crumbling walls of my house and took note of the sagging porch roof and drooping eaves. "This place is a museum. When does Benjamin Franklin show up?"

"Actually," I said, feeling rejuvenated by the fresh air and the knowledge that Michael was back on the radar screen, "Ben Franklin paid a few calls on my great-great-something-grandmother. She was quite the beauty, judging by her portrait. Story goes, she gave him a hickey."

"Looks like you haven't done any home repairs since she lived here."

"I've got a few bills to pay before I can afford fix-up projects. Anyway, I've come to like the shabby-chic look."

He looked at me. "How come your boyfriend doesn't kick in a few dollars? I hear he's loaded."

"It's my house, not his."

"He doesn't live here?"

I didn't answer.

Richard shrugged. "I've always wondered. What does a guy like Abruzzo put on his tax return in the little box marked 'occupation'?"

To terminate that discussion before it went any further, I said, "Thanks for being so patient with Orlando. It was a long ride this afternoon."

"I wasn't patient." He allowed a rueful smile. "But you owe me big anyway."

"Okay," I said steadily. "How about if I give you some information?"

"Such as?"

"I think Gallagher was paid to leave town because he designed the Brinker Bra."

"The chauffeur?" Richard couldn't hide his surprise. "How do you figure?"

"He's an inventor. My bet is he sold his idea for a bra to Brinker Holt, and Brinker wants him to be quiet about it. If nothing else, Brinker knows how to intimidate people into doing what he wants."

"So who killed Kitty Keough?"

"Kitty knew Gallagher. She probably figured out he invented the bra."

"So Brinker had her killed? Or did he intend to get rid of Gallagher instead, and Kitty wandered into Pescara's sights at the wrong time?"

"I don't know."

"Does the boy know anything?"

"It's possible. When the time is right, I'll ask."

"If he does know something, he becomes a target, too." Richard glanced at the door through which Michael had vanished with Orlando.

"He'll be safe here. That is," I said, "until the newspapers are published tomorrow morning."

"About that." Richard put his hands into his coat pockets. "Believe me, I'm the first to write a story when it's something worth writing about. If this turns out to be a case of Brinker Holt killing

Kitty to keep his secret, I'll write it. But there's not enough evidence yet. Not today, anyway. Maybe by tomorrow I'll know more, but until I do—"

"Thank you, Richard."

He observed my smile for a long moment. Then he said, "I'll find a way to talk to Brinker tonight."

"How?"

"Let me worry about that. Look, I'll find out what he's doing. You stick around here and help Abruzzo protect the kid. Not that he needs any more help besides the teamsters." He jerked his head to indicate Aldo's makeshift checkpoint at the head of my driveway.

"I'll tell Michael he has your vote of confidence."

"Your safety, that's something else."

I started to turn away. "Good-bye, Richard. Thank you, but—"

He stopped me with a hand on my wrist. His touch dropped away immediately. "Nora, you haven't known this man very long. But I've studied guys like him for years now. He's a terrorist, you know."

"You're being melodramatic."

"Am I? You saw how he was with the kid just now. He was born into a life that's based on intimidation and violence. And it's a life he can't exactly resign from."

"You don't know him."

Michael was a man of honor and integrity. His own brand of honor, perhaps, but he had thought long and hard about the kind of code he should be living by. He did the right thing when he had a choice. But saying so out loud to Richard was going to sound as if I'd been brainwashed.

So instead I said, "He has a sense of humor."

Richard said, "I have a sense of humor."

"I wasn't questioning your—"

"I can be funny," he said with more insistence.

"Richard—" I said, and stopped.

We were standing close together on the porch. The wind stirred his fair hair, and I noticed his two-toned eyes again. One blue, one hazel. In them, I suddenly saw his impulse to kiss me.

Like a nervous prom date, he lingered, torn between desire and caution. Or maybe he suddenly envisioned Michael unpacking his tommy gun from its violin case behind the kitchen door. I took a step backward.

Richard did, too. "Call me if anything changes with Orlando," he said. "Let me concentrate on Brinker."

"Good luck tonight."

"Don't worry."

He departed. Inside, I found Michael and Orlando on the sofa with their shoes off and their sock feet on my coffee table. Spike sprawled manfully between them. Intently, the three watched a television program about a diminutive teenage girl who appeared to be kung-fu-ing vampires without messing up her pretty blond hairdo.

Orlando looked hopeful, his upset stomach forgotten. "Got any ice cream?"

Michael grinned. "Or beer?"

Orlando said, "We're just gonna hang for a while. Stay out of trouble."

"Don't make any promises you can't keep," I said, and Michael laughed. Orlando looked pleased.

I went upstairs and changed into jeans and a sweater. On my way back downstairs, the phone rang.

When I answered, Delilah Fairweather's exuberant shout resounded in my ear. "Girlfriend," she called, "I hear you're having a splash on New Year's, and I just wanted to warn you that I'm coming with friends!"

"Great," I said, trying to muster some enthusiasm. "It'll be wonderful to see you. Uh . . . how many friends?"

"Half a dozen, maybe a couple more. Everybody's thrilled you're having your party again. I told one of my assistants that you are the best, bar none, at mixing people, and she's dying to come, too."

"Well—"

"And she has a boyfriend who bartends in a thong, so I thought you'd definitely want him, too."

"Oh. Thanks."

Delilah had given up a computer programming job to live the dream of partying day and night. In a matter of a couple of years, she had become the city's busiest event planner. She usually called me from a dance floor or caterer's kitchen. Tonight, however, I could hear the bluesy blare of a saxophone in the background over noisy voices making conversation. A burst of laughter sounded in my ear.

Besides her talents with music, food, flowers and fun, Delilah knew everybody worth knowing in Philadelphia and half the cities east of the Mississippi.

So I carried the telephone into the library, where Michael had obviously built a fire earlier. The flames had died down to warm embers, creating a room that was actually cozy. I curled up on the leather sofa between the bookshelves. "Delilah, have you ever done any work for Brinker Holt?"

"Brinker, give a party? Get real! That guy's a colossal mooch."

"Do you know where he lives?"

"Those loft condos by the waterfront," she said promptly. "A couple of weeks ago when he came back to town he bought a place in the old warehouse Val McGinley rehabbed. I hear the units are a million four apiece, if you're in the market."

"Not unless I win the lottery. Those condos were all taken by artistic people, right?"

"Only the ones with money. The creative class—computer game guys, a few financial whizbangers, a woman who writes screenplays—oh, and the producer of a TV show that films here in the city."

"And Brinker."

"And Brinker. He paid Jerzy Coleman another quarter mil to improve the kitchen—just so he has a place to eat take-out pizza, I guess. Not exactly a classy guy, if you ask me. But I'd like to get my hands on one of those new gadgets of his. The Brinker Bra— people say it makes even a girl like me look like I've got tantalizing ta-tas."

"You're tantalizing just the way you are," I assured her. Delilah had once worn a dress made of bubble wrap to a gallery opening, and that night she managed to outshine the work of a nationally famous artist. "Know anything useful about Brinker's private life?"

"What are you asking for, girl? You aren't—"

"No, no. He's mixed up in something I'm concerned about."

She said, "I hope it involves arresting officers. He's slime, in my book. Which doesn't mean I'm against men who have shady pasts," she added hastily. "Just that I knew a girl who dated him back in his comedy period, and when they broke up she left town without saying see-you-later to any of us."

"What happened?"

"I don't know. Something that made her feel crappy about herself, I'm guessing. A pal-o'-mine has a place in his building—a few floors below the penthouse he bought. She told me . . . Well, I know I'm spreading rumors. . . ."

"I'll keep it to myself, Delilah."

"Okay, she told me a couple of nights ago there was a woman screaming in the elevator. It was stuck between floors and this girl was really hollering. Like she was being tortured. My friend called the cops, but everything was hunky-dory by the time they got to the scene."

"What happened?"

"Don't know. They couldn't find any screaming lady. She was gone."

"No clue what happened?"

"I can ask my friend again if you want. Hey, you knew Brinker back in the day, right? What do you think of the guy?"

"I think people should stay away from him."

"Take your own advice, then, girlfriend. He definitely has some bad mojo." Delilah's call waiting beeped, and she said, "I gotta run, Nora. See you New Year's. And if you hear of a way to get me a Brinker Bra, you'll let me know, right?"

"Right."

We disconnected.

When I looked up from the phone, Michael came to the library door and leaned against it. Even in his socks, jeans and untucked shirt, I realized he managed to look like a thug with a hangover. I smiled.

Outside, the wind had come up again, and I could hear it rattling the windows. Night was gathering. In the library fireplace the embers snapped and glowed. All I needed was someone on the sofa with me to make the evening complete.

Despite my inviting smile, Michael stayed in the doorway. "The kid tells me that your man Brinker had a deal with the chauffeur."

I sat up quickly. "What kind of deal?"

"Brinker bought something—some invention the chauffeur had lying around."

"Does Orlando know that for sure?"

"He says the chauffeur told him he'd been given a lot of cash and he was going to buy a house in Ireland where the kid could visit."

"The Brinker Bra. Gallagher designed it, and he sold it to Brinker." I smiled at him. "How did you learn all that so fast?"

"During the commercials." Michael came to the sofa and nudged my foot with his knee.

I moved over to make space for him. "Is Orlando okay?"

"He fell asleep. Spike, too."

Michael sat down on the other side of the sofa, a couple of feet away. I reached over and pulled him by the hand. I thought he resisted, but a moment later we met in the middle and toppled over until we were spooning in front of the fire.

"Is Orlando safe here?" I asked when I had my arms snugly around him and he had relaxed, the back of his head against my chest. He smelled like firewood.

"Sure. Aldo loves this stuff."

"I'll make some hot chocolate and take it out to them in a little while."

"You don't understand the whole siege mentality. They want to suffer, take turns walking the perimeter, scavenging for rations. It gives them a story to tell later. Like those World War Two movies where William Holden has a hard time."

"A little hot chocolate wouldn't hurt."

"If it makes you happy."

"Thank you, Michael," I murmured in his ear. "For everything."

He was quiet for a while.

Then he said, "I had things to do last night."

"I missed you."

"Nora," he said.

"I know. I know you're not cut out for domestic life. You shouldn't have to phone home, to check in with the little woman all the time."

"That's not . . ." He hesitated. Then more slowly, "I'm not the best thing that's ever happened to you."

"I don't care about that."

I put my nose into his hair and we listened to the fire for a little while.

He said, "Danny Pescara was hired to kill Kitty by somebody he met in a biker bar in New Hope last week. I don't know who yet. To cut a deal with the cops, he told them it was one of us—the Abruzzo family. He claims we ordered him to do it." In a mutter, Michael added, "Like murder isn't bad for business."

"Tell me you're kidding."

"I'm kidding. It jerks my chain, though. That's the dumbest criminal act I ever heard of, and somebody actually believes we're capable of it."

"You're not upset because the police suspect you, but because they might think you were stupid about it?"

"I've got my pride."

I poked him. "Can Danny explain why an Abruzzo would want to kill Kitty?"

"Somebody at the fashion show overheard your sister say it would be great for you if Kitty was dead. I think the cops planted that idea with Danny, and he went for it. Point is, he has implicated us."

"Us?"

"Me. Or my father," Michael corrected. "Or one of my brothers, maybe, but they're not exactly in the picture right now."

Michael's half brothers played revolving door at various prisons. I had stopped keeping track of which Abruzzo was currently incarcerated. "How are the police going to prove it was one of you?"

"They have Danny's testimony. It's his word against ours."

I hugged him harder, and he covered my two hands with one of his, over his heart. I could feel it beating against my palms. I asked, "How bad is this?"

"It's not good," he admitted.

"You need time, don't you? To finesse your way out of this?"

Michael didn't answer.

I sat up.

The fire must have consumed all the oxygen in the library,

because I suddenly couldn't draw a breath. Michael sat up, too, but kept his distance.

"No matter what happens," he said, "you'll always be taken care of."

"What does that mean?"

"If something happens to me—"

"You're thinking of going away, aren't you?" My heart lurched. "And there's some regulation in the Mafia rule book that kicks in? What, like Social Security for mob girlfriends?"

"Nora—"

"I can't believe this!"

"Don't."

"You, the criminal mastermind—this is the best strategy you can come up with? Making sure I'm taken care of?"

A door slammed somewhere in the house, but we didn't tear our gazes apart.

Michael said, "When you get some distance on this, some perspective, you're going to change your mind."

"About what?" I demanded.

"Us."

"Us?"

With a shutter coming down across his face, he said, "You're gonna decide I'm the guy who helped you get over your husband."

My mind suddenly became too full of details. The fire's crackle. Michael's stillness. My own erratic heartbeat. In a distant room I heard Libby's voice yell, "Yoo-hoo!" And Spike gave a yip of welcome.

To Michael, I said, "I thought you understood me. I thought you were with me in this relationship."

"Relationship?" He gave a harsh laugh. "Nora, wake up! Your friends can't wait to get a look at the freak show we've got going here. You belong with somebody else. Somebody like D'eath."

"What does Richard D'eath have to do with us?"

"He's better for you."

"So is a low-fat diet and regular exercise. Michael, I want to be with you!"

"Maybe I don't want to be with you."

I couldn't speak. Not without screaming.

"If we stay together, you're going to get pulled deeper into things you won't like," he said. "Already my father is trying to get his hooks in you. First it's gifts, and then it's something else. It'll be better for you if I go away now."

Libby burst into the room like a snowstorm and plunked a large cardboard carton on the coffee table. Oblivious to the electricity in the room, she unwound her long, festive scarf from her throat. She cried, "What a night! It's lovely outside—not a snowflake in sight. It's the kind of night that fills me with excitement! I feel completely energized!"

Michael got up and left the room.

Libby looked after him, blinking. "What's the matter? He doesn't want to see my inventory?"

"He's . . . not in the mood," I said.

"Well, that's a very bad sign. On the other hand, I know exactly how to help put the thrust back in his—"

"What have you got here?" I asked, mastering my self-control.

Orlando had followed Libby into the library and was already trying to open the carton.

Libby steered Orlando gently aside while using her other hand to fiddle surreptitiously with her bra. "That's nothing for little boys. Only big boys who are little, actually, and then these little trinkets can be a big help. It's my Potions and Passions shipment!"

I used every iota of strength to collect myself. "Orlando, this is my sister."

Libby formally shook his hand, smiling. "I have twin boys who are almost your age, but they're not nearly as handsome. How do you do? And what a wonderful job you're doing with Spike! He hasn't peed on the floor since I got here. You must be the dog trainer Nora keeps threatening to hire."

"I'm just visiting," he said.

Libby's eldest son, sixteen-year-old Rawlins, slipped through the door with his ragged backpack over his shoulder and a Pop-Tart in one hand. His face was a tackle shop of rings and metal studs. The three earrings in one ear had bits of Christmas tinsel inextricably twisted around them for a bit of holiday flair.

I gave Rawlins a hug and kiss. If I wasn't mistaken, he flinched.

His smile was uncharacteristically wan. "Hi, Aunt Nora."

To Orlando, Libby was saying, "Perhaps you'll visit my boys next. They're making an Internet Web site. Do you like the Internet? All teenagers seem to love tapping on their keyboards. Well, except Rawlins."

Rawlins actually blushed.

"I'm not a teenager yet," Orlando volunteered. "I'm only ten."

"Well, that's practically a teenager. This is Rawlins, and don't let him talk you into piercing any part of your body."

"Hey," grunted Rawlins.

"What's that?" Orlando pointed to the snack Rawlins munched.

"What are you—from Planet Nerd or something? It's a Pop-Tart."

Orlando scrutinized the food. "Is it a cookie?"

"No, it's . . . Man, you never had a Pop-Tart?"

"Got any more?"

Rawlins shrugged. "Sure."

"You boys run along while I discuss a boring subject with my sister."

Rawlins slouched into the living room, and Orlando followed with keen interest. Spike was right behind them.

"All right, tell me everything," Libby commanded. "Did you have a fight? Did he experience a nonperformance? So the Incredible Hulk isn't so incredible, after all?"

I sat down on the sofa unsteadily. "I don't want to talk about him right now. What's with Rawlins? He looks shell-shocked. What's going on?"

"It's Harcourt and Hilton," Libby said on a long-suffering sigh. She put her rump to the fire and rubbed her backside vigorously to warm up. "Honestly, Nora, I think I accidentally suckled wolves. They're picking on Rawlins."

Just as Rawlins was passing from his angry teen years into an almost appealing half-grown-up stage, Libby's twins Harcourt and Hilton were developing into cunning juvenile delinquents.

"Can't he stand up for himself?"

"He's lost his edge, I think."

"What are they doing to him?"

"They found an old journal Rawlins had hidden. They typed up some of his poetry and posted it on a Web site. Not very good poetry, I'm sorry to say. Perhaps a little too romantic for a young man, if you get my drift. And all his friends have seen it."

"I get the picture."

"So he's feeling very vulnerable. Not to mention homicidal. It's open warfare at my house. I thought I should get him away from the twins for a little while. Do you mind if he stays with you?"

"I love having him around."

"He brought his own supply of junk food. I think he's hoping to wait out Christmas vacation here. Or at least until his friends stop calling him Emily Dickinson."

"Poor Rawlins."

"He'll get over it. Now, what would you like to see first?" she asked with relish. "The contraptions for men? Or the sensual aids for women? I have more ErotaLotion, if you're feeling frisky."

"Libby—"

She opened the box and pulled out something large and rubbery with prongs and a coiled electrical cord. "Or how about this?"

"Good Lord."

"It's terrifying, isn't it?" She looked delighted. "And here's the massage lotion I was telling you about. Want to taste the flavors?"

She dug into her Pandora's box, and I recoiled from one item after another. Reeking candles, bewildering gadgets, lotions, gels—more revolting attractions than a German carnival sideshow.

"Libby." I gingerly picked up a set of large pearls on a long string and couldn't imagine what its purpose might be. "Isn't it more satisfying just to make it happen all by yourselves?"

"To everything there is a season," she said merrily. "I really think I can sell this stuff. I can't wait to get started! I was hoping you and the Incredible Hulk might help me practice my pitch. That's what my Potions and Passions supervisor suggests—a test couple."

"Libby—"

"And since Emma isn't around to help, you'll have to do. Oh, I nearly forgot! Here. The pictures I took at Christmas. I thought you'd like copies."

She dug a sheaf of photos out of her bag and handed them to me.

On top was a candid photo of Michael that Libby had snapped during the hubbub of our family Christmas gathering—the first Michael had ever attended with all of Libby's kids. As soon as we arrived, her baby had thrown up on him. Michael had taken off his shirt for me to rinse out in a sink, and while he was bare-chested, Libby must have given him the baby to hold and taken their photo. Man and child were in quarter profile with the rounded curve of Michael's bare shoulder creating a frame for their faces—one rough-hewn and dangerous, the other perfectly angelic.

An artist herself, Libby had managed to capture something both erotic and heart-stoppingly adorable. I stared at the photograph and felt my face get warm.

Libby kept talking, unaware of my reaction.

"What's going on around here, anyway?" she asked. "Why is Orlando here?"

Gently, I put the photo down. Feeling disconnected, I told her everything I knew about Brinker, the bra, Gallagher, Hemorrhoid and the Finehart twins. Libby stopped unwrapping unmentionable items while she listened. Toward the end of my tale, she sat down on the sofa with me.

At last, she said, "What are you going to do?"

If any information could absolve Michael or his family from Kitty's murder, it would have to come to light without his help. Tainted evidence would be worthless.

So I asked, "Do you know a biker bar in New Hope?"

"Of course I do." She looked affronted. "What do you think I am? Some kind of fuddy-duddy?"

"I think we should go."

She eyed her box of goodies. "Maybe I could find some customers there. Bikers like machinery, don't they?"

I headed for the kitchen and grabbed my coat. Orlando was safer with Michael's crew than he could possibly have been in anyone else's custody, and I wasn't prepared to speak to Michael again. Not until I could tamp down the hysteria that roiled inside me when I thought about him leaving.

I helped Libby load her box of Potions and Passions paraphernalia into the minivan and we set off for town.

My sister drove the winding road to New Hope, a few miles down the Delaware River from Blackbird Farm. The town was a picturesque village of country inns and quaint shops that teemed with tourists in the summer months and enjoyed the benefits of a thriving gay community, a few psychics and the occasional oddball writer. All was quiet now and beautifully decorated for the holidays.

Libby drove past the gift shops, galleries and at least one fortune-teller's storefront to a lively street illuminated by old-fashioned street lamps but parked full of motorcycles. Interspersed with the bikes were expensive sports cars.

"You'd have to really love motorcycles to ride one in the middle of winter," Libby said as we went around the block a second time in search of a parking space.

"Maybe I shouldn't carry my whole box of goodies inside." Libby judged the distance from her parking space to the door of the bar. No doubt she also decided she'd look more attractive without a huge cardboard box in her arms. "I'll just take a few items in my handbag."

She got out of the van and opened the sliding door. To gain access to her Potions and Passions box, she shoved aside the heap of family junk that had accumulated on the backseat.

I stood on the sidewalk and put her handbag over my arm with my own. "Need any help?"

"You're not afraid of snakes, are you?"

"Snakes? Libby, it's December."

"It's a fake. One of the pranks the twins played on Rawlins." She reached into the flotsam at her feet and hauled out a long rubber snake. Very lifelike.

So lifelike I couldn't help myself. I backed up a pace and felt my insides clench. "You really do have a problem with the twins. You're going to have a serious discussion with them soon, aren't you?"

"As soon as I figure out what to say. How do you stop kids from picking on each other?"

"By not ignoring it, for one thing."

"And by making everybody take responsibility for their actions, I know. But it's hard for me."

Libby wanted to be a friend to her kids. But sometimes they

needed a mom. Before they turned into Unabombers and began to wreak havoc on an unsuspecting world.

"You need some professional help," I said. "Why don't you go see that nice therapist you used to visit? Maybe he has some suggestions."

"If he can get over the little misunderstanding we had," Libby said.

"I'm sure there are other therapists. Ones you haven't tried to seduce."

She frowned. "Probably."

Libby dropped the snake, and she pulled a few more Potions and Passions unmentionables out and handed them to me. I stowed them in her bag. When it was full, she emerged from the minivan with her hair newly mussed and her cheeks flushed from the exertion. She looked ravishing, of course.

"Ready?" she asked.

"Lib, have you ever actually been inside a biker bar before?"

"Not exactly, no. But how different can it be?"

Chapter Fourteen

*I*t was different.

We charged through the door and found ourselves staring at a sea of men.

Men in leather.

"Hand me a lipstick," Libby said. "I think I'm in heaven."

The bar was low-ceilinged and packed wall-to-wall with every size and shape of the male persuasion. Tall or short, muscle-bound or lean, scowling or laughing—they were all there. Rough-talking, beer-drinking men.

Honky-tonk blues thundered around us, punctuated by a roar of laughter as a scantily clad barmaid turned her tail to a table of Hell's Angels and swivel-hipped away.

A blue haze of cigar smoke hung in the air like smog around a steel mill.

But I recognized that smoke. I hadn't been raised among gentlemen of refined and expensive tastes for nothing. This particular fog of smoldering tobacco didn't smell like cheap cigars bought at roadside gas stations. No, it was distinctly the finest fragrance of Cuba.

My bullshit detector switched on, geared to its highest frequency.

"Hi," said a giant who swung off the last seat at the bar. He had a full head of dark curls, untrimmed sideburns and gold-rimmed glasses. He looked like a bashful bear with spectacles. "Libby?"

My sister gave the large chap a disbelieving stare. "Perry? Perry Delbert? What are you doing here?"

Perry's large nose hovered over my sister's cleavage as if she kept a store of honey hidden there. He tried to play it cool, however. "Oh, just hanging out. I bought a Harley last year, so I thought I'd get to know the rest of the guys. I . . . uh . . . haven't seen you lately."

"I know," she said with a frosty edge.

"Right, last I saw, you were . . ." He pantomimed a pregnant belly by smoothing his hand over his own oversize tummy. "And," he added shyly, "you were beautiful."

She blinked. "Thank you. I . . . uh . . . Nora," Libby said, "this is Perry Delbert. He helped me get rid of some carpenter ants last fall."

"That was one heck of an infestation, too. I had to come back several times."

"Three times, that's all," Libby corrected, mustering some chill again. "Then you . . . I mean, the ants disappeared before we had a chance to . . ."

"I saw the birth notice in the newspaper. I figured you were busy with a new baby to look after. Hi." Perry shook my hand without quite meeting my eye. "I wanted to call myself the Exterminator, but the real Exterminator said he'd sue. I'm in pest elimination."

"I think of you," Libby said, "as the bug man."

"Oh." Perry looked crestfallen.

Tonight the Exterminator wore a T-shirt emblazoned with the phrase LOOKING FOR A HOT MAMA, and depicting the rear view of a short-skirted, pantyless woman on the back of a departing motorcycle. Perry also had a nervous nod combined with his slippery eyeglasses, so he kept one hand free to push them back into place every few seconds. His other hand was shoved into the front pockets of his pleated khakis.

"So, Perry," said Libby, "are you presently in the market for sensual aids?"

A new song cued up on the sound system just as loud as before, giving Perry time to think. He nodded while deciding whether he'd heard correctly.

I saw my chance and leaned closer to ask very originally, "Do you come here often?"

"Couple times a week," he said, still nodding, but relieved that he understood me. "I'm getting a feel for the crowd."

"Do you know a lot of the people here?"

"Most of the regulars. They don't know me, really, but I ask Ashley, the waitress, and she tells me about everybody. Eventually I'll introduce myself, but I don't want to push it yet. It takes a while to slide into a new crowd."

He made the hand motion of a surfboard cleaving across a wave.

Libby said, "You don't have a problem with erectile function, do you?"

Perry opened his mouth but couldn't come up with an answer.

"Because if you don't like the idea of polluting your body with a drug like Viagra," she continued, "I sell an herbal alternative that also gives you fresh breath."

Starting to look frightened, Perry turned to me. "Are you looking for somebody in particular?"

"Danny Pescara. Do you know him? Or what about a guy named Brinker Holt? Has he ever been in here?"

Relieved to know at least one answer to the questions we tossed at him, Perry nodded eagerly. "Brinker? Oh, yeah, he comes in here a lot. Brings his camera. Very funny guy. He's supposed to stop here tonight, in fact."

Libby and I exchanged glances. We hadn't planned on bumping into Brinker. I hoped Richard D'eath was with Brinker, as he'd promised.

Perry said, "Brinker's had some trouble with his bike ever since he took a slider on I-95 last summer. He's in the market for a new bike. At least, that's what I've heard. So he's been coming around here."

"This is a good place to buy a motorcycle?"

"Well, if you want something hot, sure."

"Hot? You mean stolen?"

Again with the hand gestures. He put one palm up to me as if to refuse a tray of canapés. "Whoa, I don't know anything about that. I only meant a quality bike. You know, a really good one."

I remembered Brinker's use of motorcycles in his fashion show. Richard had seen motorcycles as a way of getting closer to Brinker, so I hoped he'd find a way to follow Brinker here tonight.

To Libby, I said, "I'm going to talk to the waitress."

"Okay. I'll see if I can drum up some business." Libby leveraged herself onto a stool, which Perry thoughtfully held still in case it tipped beneath her weight. I thought I caught him admiring her soft behind during the process. But she played it cool and signaled for the bartender with one upraised forefinger. "Do you have something in a nice white zinfandel?"

I eased away from Libby and the Exterminator. Making my way along the bar, I tried not to draw attention to myself, but it was hard. The few women in the room were biker chicks, mostly dressed from the Frederick's of Hollywood catalog. I stood out like a weed in an exotic garden.

One man in biker leathers glanced up at me, then looked away quickly. I recognized him despite his costume—a young lawyer from Lexie's financial firm. Not exactly the kind of guy who kept a rusty knife in his wingtips in case a brawl broke out in a boardroom, but tonight he endeavored to look like an easy rider. A bottle of scotch sat on his table. No rotgut for him, I noted, but a fine Scottish single malt.

I saw the busy Ashley shimmy between some tables, so I followed. As she began to bus a table near the men's room, I cornered her.

"Hi," I said. "Ashley? A guy at the bar said you might be able to answer some questions for me."

She looked up from wiping spilled beer and blew her blond bangs off her damp forehead. In a short denim skirt and stretchy cotton shirt, her slim body moved as if she were hardly out of high school, but her face was older. "Oh, yeah? Who're you?"

"My name's Nora—"

"You a reporter?"

"Well, yes, as a matter of fact, but—"

"The festival is in June, and we invite everybody who rides a Harley. We rent out the campground, but some guys like to stay at the Comfort Inn. The races are on Saturday, and the street show is on Sunday."

"Thanks. That's very— Thanks. But I was wondering if you know a guy by the name of Danny Pescara."

She rolled her eyes. "He got himself arrested again, right?"

"Well, you know Danny. Always up to something with him."

No answering smile. "Does he owe you money?"

"No, I was wondering if you saw him in here last week."

She swiped her tip off the table, a dollar bill and a couple of quarters. Hefting the change in her hand, she snorted at it before sliding the money into the pocket of her short apron. "Yeah, Danny's in and out of here a lot. Thinks he's a player. Comes across as a guy who's connected, you know, but he's strictly small time. He's not worth the heartbreak, honey."

"Who does he talk to when he's here? Anybody in particular?"

She shrugged, picked up her tray and braced it on her outthrust hip. "Lots of guys. This place sees a lot of horse trading, you know? Bikes, that is. You want a good bike, you come here and ask around."

"I see."

"Danny's not into bikes, but he pretends, you know? But these guys?" She indicated the crowd with a snap of her head. "You want to spend some serious money on serious motorcycles, you come here. Which means things aren't always clean and pretty. You've got to look after yourself in this place, honey."

"Thanks. I wasn't planning to stay long."

She nodded. "Good. There are some guys you just don't want to tangle with, you know?"

Again, I hoped Richard had hooked up with Brinker already. I felt the need for some backup.

"I gotta get back to the bar, honey. Can we shoot the breeze later?"

"Of course. Thanks."

She was gone in a blink, whisking off to take more orders.

I lingered at the back of the room, trying to blend in but watching the crowd while I tried to decide if I should chicken out and go home.

I was still dithering when Brinker arrived. He came in carrying his trademark camera and followed by his entourage. They dodged among the other patrons to make sure Brinker had enough light to adequately photograph the surroundings.

The bikers in the bar roared his name rather like a parody of a television show. Suddenly the air was buzzing with excitement.

Ashley responded to Brinker's arrival by pointing him to the empty table right in front of me.

If I had planned to hang back to reconnoiter, I was out of luck. Brinker headed straight toward me. With dismay, I noticed Richard was nowhere to be seen.

Brinker strode through the bar, scanning the crowd with his camera. He lingered over a scene of two guys arm wrestling. But when nothing exciting happened, he gave up and sat down at the table, his back to the wall so he could watch the proceedings through the lens of his camera, just five feet from where I stood.

One of his muscle-bound compatriots came up to me. "Hey, you can't hang around here. We're waiting for somebody, and we need the space."

"Are you the owner?" I asked.

He was very handsome in the cut-cheek way of models, but gave me an unattractively slit-eyed look and didn't answer. "We're gonna do some business. You can't stay here."

Brinker heard us and turned. I saw the dark lens of his camera focus on me.

He gave me a head-to-toe once-over before realizing who I was. Then he lowered the camera and frowned. "Are you following me?"

"Are you following *me?*" I asked in return, mustering some indignation. "What do you want?"

"What d'you mean, what do I want? I come here all the time."

"I was here first."

"But— Oh, hell, just get away from me, will you?"

Instead, I sat down at his table.

"She can't stay here, Brink. The guy is on his way. You don't want to piss him off."

"Take it easy." He tracked me with the camera again. "Now what?" he asked from behind it. "Are you stalking me? Get in line. I've got women waiting all over the city."

"I just want to know how much you paid Gallagher. For the bra."

He took his thumb off the "record" button and put the camera on the table. Then he popped the tape out of the machine and removed a Sharpie pen from inside his leather jacket pocket. Carefully, he wrote my name on the tape. "So you think you know something," he said, capping the pen.

"I know you paid off an old man—"

He stopped me with a gesture. "Fellas," he said to his hangers-on, "why don't you get a round of drinks from the bar?"

"But what about—"

"This will only take a minute."

They melted away unwillingly, leaving us alone at the table.

I said, "You paid Gallagher a pittance to get your hands on a design that's worth a fortune."

"I call that good business."

He put the videotape with my name on it into his messenger bag and retrieved a new tape. He tore off the cellophane wrapping and dropped it on the floor before popping the fresh tape into the camera. He said, "I don't know what you're talking about. I invented the Brinker Bra, and I'll sue anybody who says otherwise."

"You did more than sue Kitty Keough."

"If you claim I had anything to do with her untimely death, you'd better have some good lawyers standing behind you." He fussed with the camera. "But you may be too busy with family problems to worry about Kitty Keough much longer."

"What are you talking about?"

He thumbed the "record" button on the camera and pointed the lens at me again. "I hear your sister drinks too much."

I stared at the eye of his camera. "Emma has a problem, but she's dealing with it."

"You know that for sure? You know, for instance, where she is tonight?"

I held still and let him record the expression of loathing on my face.

"She's with a friend of mine," Brinker continued. "Monte Bogatz works for me, you know. In a roundabout way. They're probably partying right this minute."

Partying. I nearly lost it. Instead, I asked, "What does Monte do for you?"

"A little bit of everything. He's expensive, though. It's not just the liquor I have to buy for him and his girlfriend, but he loves that hillbilly heroin, too. Maybe he's introducing your sister to its pleasures tonight."

"Emma wouldn't do that."

Brinker laughed. "Don't bet on it."

"She's not as weak as you think."

"It's not a matter of her being weak. It's the dope that's strong."

"You want me to back off," I said. "Or you'll hurt Emma. You're gifted, Brinker. You've only gotten better at torturing people."

He lifted his shoulders. "The ball's in your court now, isn't it? Thing is, I wish you'd hurry up and decide, because I've got business to do tonight."

"Is it Emma? Are you—"

"Don't flatter yourselves. I'm meeting someone who's got something I want, so you're gonna get out of here before he arrives, understand?"

"Where is Emma now?"

"You think I bother to keep track of people like her?"

"How can I reach Monte?"

He laughed. "Hit the road. I've got an important meeting."

"With whom? Another lowlife?"

The bar suddenly turned quiet. Within an eerie moment, all conversation stopped.

From behind me where he'd slipped in through the back like a ghost, Michael said, "Lowlife?"

"Don't listen to her." Brinker scrambled to his feet. "She didn't mean—"

Michael put his hand on top of the camera before Brinker had a chance to focus it on anything but the floor. Gently, he pushed the camera down to the tabletop.

"Give me the tape," he said quite reasonably.

Brinker obeyed, fumbling a little, but handing over what he'd just filmed.

Michael dropped the videotape on the floor and stepped on it. The crack of plastic sounded very final.

"Who's this?" Michael said, looking down at me with a complete lack of recognition in his face. "She with you?"

"No, no. She's nobody important," Brinker said. "You have the crotch rocket I asked about?"

"Don't rush it," Michael said, still looking at me with a poker face so good he could have cleaned out Atlantic City.

"No rushing. Okay, good."

Michael said to me, "You're a surprise."

I stood up from the table. "You must be the motorcycle salesman."

"I haven't decided if I'm going to sell anything yet. Especially to anyone who calls it a crotch rocket. And what's your story?"

"I'm here to ask Brinker a question."

Michael remained unfazed. "So go ahead. What's the question?"

Brinker said, "She just came up to me, man. Have a drink. Let me buy a round. Where's your crew? We'll get acquainted."

"Shut up," Michael said. "Let's hear her question."

I cleared my throat. "I want to know if Brinker met somebody here last week. A man named Danny Pescara."

"Who?"

"You heard her," Michael said.

Brinker heard something in his tone that I could not. "Pescara? Oh, yeah, I know the guy. A little, that is. We're not best buds or anything."

"Best buds." Michael almost smiled.

"Was Danny in here last week?" I asked. "Did you meet with him?"

Brinker glanced at Michael and realized he wasn't going to

complete any transactions until he answered my question. So Brinker said, "No, I didn't meet him last week. I've been tied up with the fashion show. Lots of details to take care of—you know what it's like," he added to Michael. "There are some things you just can't trust to anyone else. It's the price of being your own man. This is the first chance I had to get away."

I asked, "How do I know you're telling the truth?"

Michael said to me, "You don't believe him?"

"I don't . . . I'm not sure."

"He wouldn't lie to me," Michael said.

"How can you . . . Oh."

"Anything else?" he asked.

"Brinker," I said. "He has my sister."

"What do you mean, he has her?"

"He's . . . It's complicated. He's having her watched by some-one dangerous."

Michael shrugged as if he didn't care. "I think it's time for you to go home now. Say good-bye."

"Good-bye," I said.

Chapter Fifteen

What do you think?" Libby asked when we were speeding home and she was punching the buttons on the console to get some heat in the minivan. "Was Brinker telling the truth?"

"About Danny? I think he was scared witless of Michael and didn't dare lie. But I'm worried, Lib."

"About Brinker?"

"He likes nothing better than having the upper hand, humiliating people. And I just embarrassed him in front of his people. I made him show his fear. He's going to retaliate."

"How?"

I realized my teeth were chattering. "I'm most afraid for Emma."

I told Libby how Monte Bogatz had been hired to snoop for Clientec and keep an eye on Emma.

"We have to do something!" Libby grabbed her cell phone. She telephoned the hotel where Emma was staying.

After listening to several employees say they didn't divulge information about guests, Libby finally extracted the truth: Emma and Monte had checked out.

"Michael will look for her," I told Libby when the call was over. "He got the message that Em is in trouble. I'm sure he'll go find her."

"Even he can't force Emma to do something she doesn't want to do."

"No, but he can force Monte." After watching Michael in action in the bar, I had no doubt he could force anybody to do his bidding under the right circumstances. With Emma in danger, I was suddenly all in favor of brute force.

"Will he start looking tonight?" Libby asked.

"Probably." I shivered, hoping I was right. Michael would know how to find Emma. He had a lot of resources he could bring to bear.

For the first time, I had seen him in his milieu. He'd come alone, quietly. But Brinker and everyone in the bar had seen through that quiet and respected the potential danger Michael kept alertly coiled inside himself. The warm, funny man I'd welcomed into my bed could actually become the tough brute everyone warned me about. He didn't need to talk big or make idle threats the way Brinker had. Michael *was* big—powerful and unyielding and lethal. I'd seen it with my own eyes. And for the first time I could imagine him doing the things that lurid newspapers claimed he had done in the past.

"You okay?" Libby asked.

"I'm trying."

"You're not asking what happened to me in the bar," she said.

I swallowed hard. "Okay, what happened?"

"I talked to the waitress, Ashley. She said Danny Pescara was in the bar twice last week. And both times he spoke with a woman."

"The same woman?"

"Yes. I couldn't find out more. Ashley had to take a tray of cocktails to some customers, and I got busy, too."

"Busy how?" I had heard the delight in her voice.

"I sold my entire stock of Potions and Passions samples! Can you believe it? I'm definitely going back to that place, Nora. It's a gold mine! Half the men in that bar were gay. You have no idea how much gay men love their gadgets! Maybe gays should be my target customer."

"Lib, give me a minute to steam-clean a few mental images out of my mind, okay?"

"But then the bartender said he was calling the police. Can you imagine? He accused me of solicitation!"

I was doubly glad we'd left when we had. Libby dropped me at home. Aldo sent her a surly look as he allowed us into the driveway.

I found the boys snoring on the sofa in front of the television, surrounded by Pop-Tart wrappers. Somehow, Orlando had traded his tidy Oxford shirt for one of Rawlins's well-worn sweatshirts.

I woke them both and personally escorted Orlando up to a bed in the guest room next to mine. Barely conscious, he asked only that Spike be allowed to sleep with him. The dog was already snuffling in the bedclothes, and Orlando gathered him up and began to breathe deeply, the two of them looking suspiciously angelic.

In my own bedroom at last, I stopped dead in the middle of the floor and absorbed what had changed in the room.

Michael's clothes were gone. Even his toothbrush and razor.

I looked for a note and found nothing.

My teeth began to chatter again. I sat down on the bed, hugged myself, and tried to remember the last thing I'd said to him at the bar.

Good-bye.

During the night, my brain wouldn't let me sleep. Over and over I found myself reviewing what had happened and trying to figure a way to resolve things. I knew Brinker got the bra design from Gallagher. I knew Brinker and Hemorrhoid were cooking up something the SEC didn't like. I knew Kitty's murder had something to do with their plans. But why did Kitty have to die? And who hired Danny Pescara to do it?

In the morning I got out of bed and fired up my computer. Online, I checked the Web site of the city's foremost newspaper. Carefully, I scrolled through the pages looking for Richard's byline, but found nothing. As promised, he hadn't written his story.

Next I telephoned Lexie at her office. Even though it was barely seven in the morning, she was already at her desk.

"Sweetie," she said when I asked for assistance. "I'm happy to help."

"I need a diversion, Lex." And I told her what I required. "Can you make it happen this afternoon?"

"Sure." Her own creative juices began to flow. "How's this for an idea?"

After hanging up with Lexie, I telephoned Mary Margaret, who reported that Orlando's guardians would be in the city by late evening. Could I keep him safe until then? Of course.

Next I had a brainstorm and called the concierge at Emma's hotel. I should have thought of him before.

My friend Carlos Sanguilla picked up. "Nora, tell me the truth," he said sternly. "Am I the only one in town not invited to your party tonight?"

"Tonight?"

"It's New Year's Eve, honey-child."

I tossed caution to the wind. "Sure, why not? Bring the whole gang from the hotel, if you like. I'd love to see everyone again. Just . . . can you tell me when Emma checked out, Carlos? Was it last night?"

Carlos graciously consulted the hotel records and came back on the line an instant later. "She and her vaquero departed yesterday morning, Nora."

Yesterday morning. Which meant she had a lot of time to get into trouble.

Cross Your Heart and Hope to Die

I climbed back into bed with a cup of tea, half hoping Michael would show up with bagels to prove I didn't need to be afraid.

He had second thoughts? He didn't want to be with me? Those weren't the true sentiments of a man who sometimes made love to me as if he were drowning and I was his only rescue. He'd been desperate when I'd first met him—lost in a life he needed to change. Desperate for love and meaning and a place in the world.

With sudden clarity, I wondered if the person who hired Danny Pescara had been equally desperate for help.

I took a shower and tried to think two steps ahead of my opponent.

After dressing in jeans and a sweater suitable for housework and errands, I put on my coat and hiked the long driveway to speak to Aldo. After asking for his help, I invited him inside the house for breakfast. He accepted, but said first he'd make some phone calls.

When Rawlins, Orlando and Spike appeared downstairs, I whipped up a double batch of sour-cream pancakes and looked in the pantry for a bottle of blueberry syrup I had purchased at the farmer's market last summer. I listened to the boys talk.

"Can't we have Pop-Tarts?" Orlando asked Rawlins once they were sitting at the kitchen table. His hair stood up in tufts, and he seemed comfortable in the rumpled sweatshirt he had obviously permanently confiscated from Rawlins.

"You ate 'em all last night, nerd. Man, it's like you never saw junk food before."

"What other kinds of junk food do you have?"

Rawlins dug into his pancakes, hiding a secret smile that told me he enjoyed playing mentor. "You ever have Cheez Whiz?"

Orlando paused in the act of mopping blueberry syrup, enthralled by the melodious sound of the new words Rawlins spoke. "What's Cheez Whiz?"

"Cheesy stuff you spray out of an aerosol can. Sometimes I squirt it on my finger and—"

"Rawlins," I warned.

"No, I want to know more," Orlando insisted. "My mom wouldn't let me have junk food, and Uncle Hem says it will poison me. Except he keeps a candy stash in his desk drawer. I saw it. What else do you know about?"

"Well, if you like cheese, there's Cheese Doodles, Cheez-Its, cheese curls—"

"Chee•tos," Aldo offered.

"Yeah, I like to smash those on sandwiches made out of olive loaf."

"You like olive loaf?" Aldo asked, warming to the subject.

Rawlins and Aldo proceeded to regale their young audience with an encyclopedic knowledge of products I had never heard of. The list of unappetizing substances made me put aside the plate of pancakes I'd prepared for myself. But watching the boys, I was gladdened to see Orlando coming out of the cocoon his uncle had spun around him. His eyes sparkled in a way that reminded me of his fun-loving mother.

When the discussion came to an end, the boys put their dishes in the sink and dashed for the living room with Spike in hot pursuit.

Aldo put down his fork and patted his stomach. "You're not a bad cook when you set your mind to it."

I poured him a little more coffee. "Thanks."

He reached into an interior pocket on his tracksuit and withdrew a small, battered ring-bound notebook. "I got the information you wanted."

"So fast?"

He gave a modest shrug. "I called a guy. This is the address." He tore out a page and handed it to me.

I accepted the paper. "Thank you, Aldo. I appreciate your help."

"You know," he said, pulling his napkin from the neck of his tracksuit, "I wasn't crazy about you at first. But you turned out okay."

"Is that an endorsement of my cooking?"

He shook his head. "The boss's son, he's not usually impetuous. He had us a little worried when you came along. But you're all right."

I sat down at the table with him, hesitant to ask Aldo the questions I'd longed to understand. "So you work for Michael's father?"

"I help out, that's all." He looked at me from under his heavy eyebrows. "Just so you understand, we'll stick around."

"I'm sure that won't be necessary much longer. Orlando will probably leave this evening, and then—"

"After," Aldo clarified. "If there's a conviction. We'll be around."

"A conviction?"

"You know."

"No, I don't know."

"Sure you do."

"No, Aldo, I really don't."

He picked up his coffee cup again and shrugged. "Big Frankie's health isn't too good. So. You know."

I must have looked like a cartoon character struck by a falling anvil. "What are you talking about?"

"Big Frankie wouldn't survive a sentence. His constitution isn't up to it. So. The son takes the stretch." He sipped his coffee daintily.

"The son . . . ? Are you saying Michael would go to jail? To spare his father?"

Again the shrug. "You know. It's the way."

"The *way?*" I snapped. "Danny Pescara kills Kitty, and Michael goes to jail? So his father doesn't die in a prison cell? What way, exactly, is that?"

"I'm not saying it'll happen." Aldo put his beefy elbows on the table and supported the coffee cup under his chin so he could smell the steam. "There's a lot of slips between here and there. And the lawyers, they're the best money can buy. But these cops . . . they have a thing for Big Frankie. They're working hard to get him this time. It'll hurt him bad if the son has to go, but—"

"I don't believe this."

Michael had tried to tell me the same thing—that he might have to leave. Except I hadn't realized he meant going back to jail.

"No," I said. "This can't be happening."

I grabbed the phone and dialed Michael's cell again. No answer.

Aldo sat looking at me stolidly. "He has things to do."

"Where is he? What's he doing?"

Aldo put his coffee cup back on the table. "Not for me to know. Or you either. He'll be back if he can."

"If he can," I repeated. "What about Danny? Will he go to jail?"

Aldo smiled a little. "Doesn't matter."

"Why not?"

"Danny's not the surviving type no matter where he is."

"How . . . ? No, you don't mean the family will do something?"

Aldo got up from the table. "Nobody likes a cooperating witness."

"You're talking about killing a person!"

"I'll be outside," Aldo said. "Thank you for the breakfast. A little sausage would be good. I'll bring you some."

I locked the door after him.

I broke a plate as I washed the dishes. Shoving the pieces into the trash, I knew I had to start thinking straight or lose everything. I cleaned up the kitchen and went over things in my mind until I had a plan. I continued to clean the rest of the house as my scheme grew to trap the person who hired Danny Pescara. While I was vacuuming, everything became clear for me.

I called Libby. She showed up in the afternoon, when my home was immaculate.

"Wow," she said. "Next time you get upset, come over to my house. This place looks great."

I pulled her to sit down at the kitchen table, and I told her my plan.

"Are you sure about this?" Her frown was doubtful. "Nora, the police were just at my house."

"What did they . . . ?" I finally saw the serious expression on her face. "They were asking about Michael?"

"No," she said gently. "They were asking about you. They wanted to know how badly you wanted Kitty's job, and I tried to assure them . . . Well, that's not what's important right now. They said they found the gun."

"The gun Danny used? Where was it?"

She reached for my hand. "I'm sorry, honey. It was at his house."

"Danny's house?"

"No."

"Michael's."

Libby squeezed me hard. "They searched it this morning, with a warrant and everything—trust me, I asked. They're going to arrest him. They say he was part of the plot all along."

"Libby, you know that's not true. The gun had to be planted."

"I know you believe in him, but I— Just where is he, Nora? The police are looking for him for the police shooting, too. And he's disappeared."

"He's looking for Emma, that's why!"

"Are you sure?"

I sat still and tried to sort through the information, then picked up the phone and punched in Michael's number again. I listened to it ring and ring. I wanted to cry. I wanted to stop shaking.

Beside me, Libby said, "Why do we always pick the wrong men? It can't be so impossible. There must be something wrong with us. I just want somebody with no serious drawbacks, like mental illness or felony charges. Who's also good in bed, of course, and makes a decent living and doesn't get mixed up in drugs or murdering people or—"

I terminated the call.

"Are we still going out?" Libby asked.

I had to try. Michael was going to jail for sure unless I came up with some solid evidence that contradicted what the police had.

"Of course we are."

She respected my tone. "Okay, okay. Where do you want to go?"

"To Brinker Holt's condo."

"How is that going to help?"

"If he didn't hire Kitty's killer, I'm sure Brinker filmed himself coercing the right person into hiring the killer for him."

"He films everything," Libby agreed softly.

"With special attention paid to the moments when he humiliates people. So let's see where he stores his tapes. Lexie's lured him to a meeting this afternoon. She'll keep him busy while we check out his condo."

"Can we get inside?"

"I think so. One of Michael's people is helping me. First we have to find this address." I showed her Aldo's printed note.

"Aunt Nora?"

Startled, we both turned. Rawlins stood in the doorway, and it was clear he'd heard everything. Behind him lurked Orlando, looking scared and clutching Spike in his arms for comfort.

Rawlins said, "I want to help."

I tried to smile. "That's very kind of you, Rawlins, but the most helpful thing you can do today is stay here and look after Orlando."

It was the wrong thing to say.

"I don't need anybody to look after me!" Orlando pushed past Rawlins and rushed into the kitchen. "I want to help, too."

Spike jumped out of Orlando's embrace and ran to me. He bounded up and braced his front paws against my knee. His message was clear.

"No," I said to the dog. "You can't come either."

"But we can help," Orlando insisted.

"We can," Rawlins chimed in. "We can be lookouts."

"Or sneak through secret passageways," Orlando volunteered. "I'm the smallest. I can sneak."

"I want to help Mick," Rawlins said. "If he's in trouble, I want to help."

"Why you?" Libby demanded. "Have you been hanging around with That Man again?"

"Mom—"

"Rawlins, you are grounded. Absolutely grounded."

"I like Mick. He's been nice to me. He gave me a chance and taught me some good stuff. Like, like . . . well, some good stuff. Besides, if you want to be sure where I am all the time, let me come with you today."

Libby opened her mouth to refuse, but didn't have the motherly ammunition to combat his argument.

Orlando seized my arm, and his gaze implored me to do the right thing. "Please," he said. "Don't leave me alone here. I want to come with you."

"But you'll be perfectly safe with Rawlins."

"I want to be with you."

"Orlando—"

His grip slackened. "You don't think I can do anything," he said. "You think I'm a wimp. I'm a nerd and a wimp."

I tried to put my arms around him. "That's not true."

"I just need a chance," he said. "I want to learn stuff like Rawlins. I want a chance, too."

"But . . ."

Both boys stood stiff and braced for the worst.

I sighed. "All right. You can come. But this is potentially very, very dangerous. You have to do whatever I say, got that? If I say you have to stay in the car, that's what you'll do, understand?"

Orlando whooped with joy. "Thank you, thank you, thank you! We're going! We're going!"

Spike yipped gleefully and peed on the floor.

"Get your coats."

"I'll need my backpack," said Orlando. "I'll bring supplies."

Shaking her head, Libby led the way to her minivan.

Libby drove us to the city, and we found the backstreet location of Aldo's contact. It was a hardware store with dirty windows and one of those WE'LL RETURN cardboard clocks hanging on the door. The clock had no hands.

"Want me to go in?" Rawlins asked from the backseat as we all stared at the seemingly vacant store.

"Or me?" Orlando piped up.

"I'll take care of this," I said, stepping outside.

I went to the door and knocked. Inside, an elderly man shuffled over to unlock the door and let me in. Aware that Libby, Spike and Orlando watched me, their noses pressed to the windows of the minivan, I took a deep breath for courage and stepped into the store.

The hardware store smelled like old oil and coffee. Large shelves crowded with outdated merchandise loomed around me. Although the light was dim, I saw power tools, bins of nails, a collection of garden rakes and a row of wheelbarrows. A group of five elderly men in nearly identical cardigan sweaters sat on folding chairs at a rickety card table in a spot of the sales floor that had been cleared to make space for their table. They were playing dominoes and drinking espresso. The espresso machine, on the checkout counter beside an antique brass cash register, was the only inanimate object in the entire store that wasn't covered in a layer of dust. Underfoot, the floor crunched with pistachio shells.

I guessed the last time anybody bought hardware here had been during the Nixon administration.

With hesitating steps, I went over to the cash register.

Another gentleman got up from the table and hobbled to the counter. He had a grand total of twelve long wisps of white hair combed over a shining bald head. His eyebrows, however, were thick enough to hide a mouse in. With hunched shoulders, he stood about five feet tall, and his hands were gnarled with arthritis.

From under the cash register, he palmed a small envelope and slid it across the counter to me. Meekly, I accepted the envelope and peeked inside. It was the credit card–style passkey that Aldo had requested.

"How much do I owe you?" I asked, breaking the intense silence. He shook his head. No words.

"Okay," I said, trying to muster some cheer. "Thanks very much!"

I let myself out the front door, noting that everybody had been careful not to look at me during my two minutes in the store. Probably so they wouldn't be forced to identify me in a lineup.

I got back into the minivan.

"How was it?" Libby asked.

"Twilight Zone. Nobody said a word."

We drove along Front Street not far from Independence Mall, a normally busy neighborhood of restaurants, tourist-friendly parks, the Seaport Museum and high-priced condos near Penn's Landing and the piers. Despite the constant dull thunder of I-95 traffic, the neighborhood was unusually peaceful that afternoon. Few tourists wandered the sidewalks. A gang of teenagers slouched by, headed somewhere else. People were probably at home napping, preparing to expend the last of their holiday energies in one last night of revelry before the new year began. Libby made an illegal U-turn down near the Sheraton and went back until she found a parking space a block from the building where Brinker Holt lived.

"Now what?"

I checked my watch. Lexie's meeting with Brinker would be starting in a few minutes. "Let's watch for a while. To be sure Brinker's not around anywhere."

"This is like a stakeout," Rawlins said from the backseat.

"We need binoculars," Orlando added.

"And coffee," Libby suggested. "Even Charlie's Angels drank coffee on stakeouts."

"Doughnuts would be good, too," Rawlins said.

"I've never had a doughnut," Orlando said.

Libby turned around and gave him a shocked stare. "Never? You've been sadly deprived, young man."

Even Rawlins was taken aback. "That could be child abuse."

Orlando sensed an opportunity. "Where could we get some doughnuts?"

Firmly, I cut across their discussion. "We'll just watch, okay?"

Rawlins unbuckled his seat belt and climbed over the seat. He began to rummage in the flotsam of family junk that had accumulated in the back of the van.

"What are you doing?" Orlando asked.

"There might be something we can use." Rawlins's voice was

muffled, but determined. "My douche-bag brothers keep all kinds of—"

"Rawlins, please. We're a loving family, and we don't refer to—"

"Like what do they keep here?"

"I dunno, something. Here." Rawlins came up with a skateboard and handed it to Orlando.

"How can we use that?"

"See if you can do better, nerd."

Orlando unbuckled and began to dig through the junk on the van floor.

"Just stay out of my box," Libby said. "Hands off my stuff."

I could suddenly see why even fictional detectives went on stakeouts by themselves. All this togetherness could get on my nerves very soon. "Let's telephone Brinker's number," I said. "If he doesn't answer, we'll know the coast is clear."

Libby forgot about protecting her Potions and Passions inventory and pulled out her cell phone.

"You can't use that phone!" Rawlins cried. "What kind of Charlie's Angel are you? What if he's got caller ID? Your number will show up on his machine!"

"What do you suggest, young man?"

"Pay phone," Rawlins said promptly. "Mick always uses a pay phone, and never one with a surveillance camera nearby."

"Oh, dear heaven," said Libby. "You are grounded, grounded, grounded."

"Rawlins," I said, "why don't you take a walk? Look around for a pay phone. Libby, use your cell to call four-one-one and get Brinker's home number."

"Good idea," said Rawlins. "While I'm at it, I'll sweep the area."

"I don't want to know what that means," I said.

A few minutes later Rawlins slid out of the van and strolled away with the skateboard over his shoulder, blending into the landscape like any other aimless teenager.

"I hope he's careful," said Orlando.

The rest of us kept an eye on Brinker's condo for another fifteen minutes. Spike and Orlando were especially vigilant.

Meanwhile, Libby revealed she'd been contacted by Perry Delbert.

"Who?"

"Perry, the Exterminator. The bug man." She dropped her voice to keep our conversation private from Orlando. "You met him at the bar last night. He called me this morning."

I remembered the shy, bespectacled bear. "What did he want? No, wait, I know what he wanted. Did you give it to him? This morning? With all the kids in the house?"

Libby looked affronted. "We spoke on the phone, that's all. He'd like to see me. Outside the pest-control customer relationship."

"Are you going to see him?"

"I don't know. What do you think? Is he . . . Do you find him a little less attractive than other men I've dated?"

I felt sure I'd never laid eyes on at least half the men Libby had been with over the years. And Libby seemed to have a different concept of what an attractive man was. She tended to demand little more than a libido and a sense of erotic adventure. "He's a little . . . rugged."

"More Jeremiah Johnson than the Sundance Kid?"

"What?"

"He's not exactly Robert Redford at his best."

"Well, the sideburns are little much."

Frowning, Libby pulled the rearview mirror sideways so she could study her own appearance. She rearranged her hair and tugged at her bra. "I have never found sideburns alluring, although I recognize that they can be an outward manifestation of a very manly inner soul. Maybe it's a personal prejudice I need to overcome. Maybe Perry is exactly the man to help me overcome it."

I could sense where she was headed. "I'm sure he has other attractive attributes."

"Exactly. Exploring for good qualities can be a fulfilling personal quest." But she shook her head. "He abandoned me once before, though. A man who discards a woman in her time of need is bound to do it again."

"Libby, he came to your house to get rid of some ants. He wasn't ready to become the father of five children and fulfill your . . . um . . . manifestations."

She considered my opinion. "All right, at the time of our first encounters, maybe my situation was fraught with too many daunting responsibilities. To flourish, a relationship can't have too many initial obstacles, right? Maybe I should give him a second chance."

I was feeling charitable. After all, Libby had been very kind to me lately. So I gave her the opinion she wanted to hear. "Maybe you should."

She sighed. "We should have more of these sisterly discussions, Nora."

Rawlins saved me from further sisterly discussion by appearing at his mother's window. She rolled it down, and Rawlins leaned in. "Nobody's at home," he reported. "The coast is clear. We're ready for phase two."

"Phase two?" Libby asked.

"Get in the car, Rawlins," I said.

I gave Libby some simple instructions, then popped open the door.

"Be careful," she said. "I don't want to have to call the police, but if you're not out here soon—"

"Don't call the cops. No matter what. That will only make Michael look guiltier."

Before I could close the door, Spike jumped to the sidewalk.

"No," I said to the dog. "I'm not taking you."

Rawlins came around the minivan with his skateboard. "I'm coming, too."

"No, you're not. I'm going in alone and—"

The rear passenger door slid open and Orlando hopped out. "Me, too. I want to come."

"Forget it," I said. "No way."

"We'll look like a family," Orlando said.

"Yeah," said Rawlins, looking stubborn. "It'll be good cover. Besides, Mick will kill me if he hears I let you do this alone."

I eyed my nephew and saw a number of Blackbird qualities in his young face—qualities that told me an argument was going to be useless. And Orlando looked so hopeful that I knew I couldn't crush his heart by leaving him behind.

I sighed. "Somebody remind me not to have sons. Okay, you two, let's go. But I don't want either one of you to say a word or do one single thing without asking me first. I'm serious, Rawlins. Promise me, or I'm leaving you here."

When Rawlins mumbled his promise, I picked up Spike and put him into my bag. We left the minivan and set off for Brinker Holt's building, doing a very plausible impression of a real family. Rawlins slouched sullenly at my side, and Orlando trailed behind us, lugging his backpack and whining for us to slow down.

Chapter Sixteen

rinker's building was a former waterfront warehouse that had been gentrified by a developer who had visions of exposed bricks, working fireplaces and million-dollar price tags. Now a series of expensive loft apartments that faced the water, the place was a prime address for people who pooh-poohed material things, yet wanted to live in splendor and with a convenient commute to the symphony, ballet and theater district. Starbucks planned to open soon on the first floor, according to a posted sign. An automated teller machine gleamed nearby, money available twenty-four/seven.

We arrived at the front door, which was a huge plate-glass entrance located under a canopy an architect had designed to resemble the sail of a clipper ship. A tall canister ashtray sat beside the door, overflowing with plastic coffee cups, cigarette butts and ATM slips.

I pulled out the small envelope I'd picked up at the hardware store. From inside, I slid a credit card–shaped access key. I approached the magnetic security slot. Holding my breath, I zipped the card through the slot and hoped it worked.

A horrendous buzzer sounded, making us all jump, but I grabbed the door handle and pulled. Miraculously, the door opened. The card had worked.

"Cool," said Rawlins.

Conscious of the overhead cameras that recorded our arrival and perhaps broadcast it to a nearby security team, we crossed the lobby with manufactured confidence. The lobby was so sterile it might have been decorated by a scrub nurse. A single banana tree grew in a huge pot near the elevator.

We reached the elevator, and Orlando hit the "up" button. The elevator doors opened and we stepped into the car. Brinker lived on the top floor. Spike poked his head out of my bag and suggested we snap it up.

The elevator was large and had been designed to mimic a freight elevator in an industrial building. The walls were padded with heavy matting used to cushion cargo. Huge iron rings, also a design choice by a decorator going whole hog with a theme, had been bolted into the corners. I swiped the card again, punched a button. The elevator obeyed.

"Sometimes," I murmured, "it's nice to know criminals."

Once on the top floor, the elevator doors opened and I tucked the access card into my pocket for safekeeping. Then we stepped into Brinker Holt's loft.

"Wow," said Rawlins.

The huge empty space stretched before us, gleaming bare wooden floors leading to the exposed brick walls. Giant windows overlooked the seaport. A huge Brinker Bra poster leaned against the wall opposite the elevator, the only art in the place. Brinker's giant face glowered at us.

Tentatively, I called, "Hello? Anybody home?"

No answer. Orlando sighed heavily. My heartbeat slowed closer to normal.

Rawlins set down his skateboard and wandered into the apartment. Orlando and I followed uneasily.

Brinker had come into a lot of money recently, thanks to his fire insurance, of course, and he'd obviously spent it on electronic equipment, not interior comforts. The biggest television I had ever seen in a private home had been mounted on one wall with a spaghetti tangle of wires hanging down to the floor. Rawlins looked for an "on" switch.

The rest of the furniture amounted to a single black leather sofa and a single floor lamp—a long, arching metal arm with a dish-shaped lamp on the end. No rugs, no art on the walls, no throw pillows for color.

The windows were undraped. I found myself drawn to the magnificent views. To the north I could see the piers. To the west stood the tower of Independence Hall and the Liberty Bell Pavilion, and I even glimpsed of the trees at Washington Square.

But Brinker appeared to be more focused on the view provided by his enormous television. I walked across the wooden floor, my heels making sharp sounds in the empty space. Orlando followed me closely, his shoes scuffling.

In the kitchen—a space separated from the rest of the loft only by a long marble-topped counter—I made a grim discovery beside the Sub-Zero fridge—a pile of Styrofoam containers that came from a local gourmet diet food delivery service that promised, "Great taste and lose the weight!" The smell of spoiled salad dressing hung in the air.

On the kitchen counter beside the deep-bowled double sinks and heavy brass faucet someone had left a gift basket of flavored olive oils. I looked for a card, but it had been thrown away. Alongside the gift basket stood a cardboard carton emblazoned with the Brinker Bra logo. The box had been opened. It was full of Brinker Bras.

Around the corner from the kitchen lay an unmade bed with red satin sheets. A camera tripod stood beside the bed. I blanched at the sight of it, guessing what Brinker might have recorded there.

Orlando came in behind me and said nothing.

Across from the bed was a whole wall of small televisions. I caught my breath as I saw they were all turned on, no sound. I could see my own live image on two of the screens, two different camera angles.

The other screens showed various views of the apartment. I could see Rawlins on two more screens, and Orlando on another. I glanced around and spotted two cameras mounted high on the walls and constantly recording. Under the window on the floor stood a line of enough VCR machines to keep CNN in business.

I went over to the machines. Turn them off? Take the tapes?

Then I noticed the mountainous stacks of videotapes that leaned against the wall. Hundreds of tapes. Maybe thousands. I bent closer to look.

Here, Brinker had been more meticulous. Two large stacks of action-adventure movies were organized alphabetically. Several more stacks of Brinker's own work were stacked alongside. Each tape had been marked with names, carefully printed in the same hand.

"What did you find?" Orlando asked.

"The jackpot, thank heaven. You can help, Orlando. Do you see these labels?"

"Yeah."

"They're marked with names. Look for 'Danny' or 'Emma,' okay?"

"Okay."

We knelt down to sort through the stacks. Spike hopped out of my bag, and I got to work. On the top of the third pile Orlando read *Danny,* and pulled it out with excitement. There was no time to view it, so I jammed the tape into my bag. Orlando went back to searching, and I returned to my stack. The next tape was marked *Sabria.*

Sabria Chatterjee?

And three more "Sabria" tapes lay beneath that one. I pulled them out and put them on the floor.

Rawlins came around the bed. "We'd better hurry up," he said, sounding spooked by the empty apartment.

"Look for the fire stairs," I said to him. "They're probably behind the kitchen."

Rawlins nodded and left.

As fast as I could manage, I sorted through all six stacks of tapes looking for names I recognized. Buried in one of the last piles was *Fawn*.

The tape surely featured Fawn Finehart, budding supermodel.

Suddenly the telephone jangled in the silent space, punching a yelp from Orlando. Spike barked.

On the second ring, I said, "Calm down, guys. We'll just let it ring. Let's get moving."

The phone continued to jangle. I got to my feet and so did Orlando. The pile of tapes had grown too large to fit into my handbag. The three of us gathered up all the tapes I had collected.

"Hey," Rawlins called. "You'd better get the tapes out of these machines. They'll give us away."

"You're right."

As we hunkered down to figure out how to stop the recording, Brinker's answering machine clicked on. It was eerie to hear his voice say curtly, "You got me. Leave a message."

The answering machine beeped, and another louder, more urgent voice suddenly burst into the apartment.

"Hey," Libby shouted. "It's me! Get out of there! He's coming! He's coming right now!"

Orlando swung around to me, his mouth popping open. Rawlins turned paper white. No time to steal the tapes presently humming in the VCRs. Libby's hysterical voice continued to shriek at us from the answering machine.

"What do we do?" Orlando cried.

"Come on!"

I ran to the elevator and punched the call button. Too late, I realized it was already on its way. With Brinker in it.

"We gotta hide," Rawlins said, already backpedaling toward the bedroom area. "We gotta hide now!"

"Find the stairs, Rawlins! There have to be fire stairs!"

Rawlins ran out of the room.

Orlando turned and ran in the opposite direction. He dove into a narrow space beside the refrigerator among the discarded food boxes. Spike scrabbled after him.

With my arms full of videotapes, I glanced around for the stairs. While the boys found an escape route, I needed a place to hide. But in that big, empty loft, there was nowhere to go.

The elevator opened.

From inside, Sabria Chatterjee stared at me without moving. Beside her stood Hemorrhoid.

Behind me, Libby's voice cried, "Oh, God, I hope I called the right number!"

Finally, Hemorrhoid said, "What's she doing here?"

Sabria just looked stunned.

"Hi," I said.

Hemorrhoid held a sleek leather briefcase in one hand, and he fastidiously balanced a cake box on the upturned palm of his other. He wore a slick suit, a festive tie and a cashmere scarf thrown with careful precision around his neck. Sabria was weighed down with plastic bags that bulged with groceries.

"She has Brinker's tapes," Sabria said.

Incredibly slow on the uptake, Hemorrhoid said, "I don't get it."

"I'm so sorry," I said as pleasantly as I could manage. "But I don't have time to explain. I'm having guests tonight, so I've got to run. It looks as though you're having a party, too. I'm sure you understand if I dash."

Sabria reacted first. She dropped her bags in the elevator and stepped off, the soft flutter of her sari disguising her purposeful stride. She stopped me with one hand flat against my chest. With her other hand, she grabbed the top tape in my pile. She read her own name on the label. Her dark gaze rose to meet mine and narrowed.

"What are you doing?" she demanded, low-voiced.

"Sabria, I know what they did to you."

She dropped her hand as if my body had burned her. "What are you talking about?"

Hemorrhoid finally caught on and came out of the elevator, balancing the cake box and looking as ridiculous as a singing waiter at a Mexican restaurant. "Did you break in here? Are you stealing stuff?"

"She has videotapes," Sabria said. "We have to stop her."

"Why?" asked Hemorrhoid, eyeing my jeans and leather jacket with the air of a man offended by my unsuitable wardrobe. "Why are you stealing Brinker's videotapes?"

"She can't leave," Sabria said. "We have to do something."

"Like what?"

"She's going to the police."

That newsflash galvanized Hemorrhoid. "Oh, my God."

"We have to tie her up. Go get Brinker's cord." When Hemorrhoid didn't react, Sabria pushed his shoulder and yelled, "Go get some cord!"

Hemorrhoid flinched and turned toward the kitchen. But his right foot came down on the skateboard Rawlins had left on the floor. The skateboard shot out from under him, and Hemorrhoid went down like a stone, cake box and all. The box hit his lap and burst open. The frosting flew upward and splattered all over Hemorrhoid's suit. He looked down at himself and shrieked.

At that instant, Spike came tearing out from behind the kitchen counter and made a furious beeline for Hemorrhoid. Maybe it was the smell of fresh cake. Or maybe it was the smell of fear that launched Spike directly at Hemorrhoid's throat. Hemorrhoid threw up his arm to save himself, and Spike sank his teeth deeply into his sleeve—penetrating clothing to soft flesh. Hemorrhoid screamed even louder than before.

Sabria cursed. As Hemorrhoid scuttled crablike in our direction, she stepped forward and kicked Spike in the head, stunning him. I cried out and bent to grab Spike with one hand, spilling half the videotapes onto the floor. I slipped in the smeared frosting and nearly fell.

Sabria grabbed Hemorrhoid by his lapels and jerked him to his feet.

"Oh, my God," he cried. "My suit is ruined!"

"Shut up," Sabria snapped. "Shut up and give me your tie!"

"Why my tie?"

"I need to tie her up. Get it off!"

"This is Hermès!"

"I don't care. Get it off!"

Sabria wrestled the tie off Hemorrhoid's neck.

While they grappled, I made a dash for the open elevator. With Spike in one arm and half the videotapes in the other, I jumped in and punched the button. I had to give the boys enough time to escape. Snatching the tie free at last, Sabria jumped on the elevator behind me. With a field-hockey body slam, she pinned me against the rear wall. The rest of the videotapes exploded from my grip and scattered on the floor at my feet. Sabria was shorter than me, and used her lower center of gravity to hold me fast. I fought her, and if I hadn't been worried about Spike, I could have shoved her off. But the puppy was limp against my chest.

To Hemorrhoid, Sabria shouted, "Get in here! I need your help! Tie her wrists to the rings."

"I can't! There's a rat in there! It bit me!"

"It's a dog, you idiot. Hurry up. I need you."

I struggled against her hold, and Hemorrhoid finally saw that Sabria couldn't overpower me alone. With whining curses, he got onto the elevator with us.

As the two of them closed in on me, the elevator doors began to close. Backed against the rear wall of the elevator, I saw Orlando's head pop up from behind the kitchen counter. He looked terrified. As the doors came together, I shouted, "Find the stairs! Get out of there!"

The elevator started down.

"Shut up," Sabria hissed. "Hold still."

"Don't," I said, trying to push out of her capture. "You don't need to tie me."

The three of us struggled, panting and pushing as the elevator dropped floor by floor. Despite the slime of cake frosting, Hemorrhoid managed to pin my wrist against the padding of the elevator wall. Gasping from exertion, Sabria wrapped the tie once around my arm. While they concentrated, I finally worked one leg loose, and with all my strength I slammed my knee upward. Hemorrhoid gasped, and his eyes rolled up in his head. He dropped to my feet.

"Get up, get up," Sabria shouted at him. "Quit being such a priss!"

"Sabria." I gasped. "I'm not the enemy here. They're using you, don't you see?"

"You don't know anything," she said, breathing hard in my face. "I got the Brinker account, and I'm going to keep it. Clientec's going to make me a vice president. I'll do whatever it takes."

"Even let them hurt you? It was you screaming in this very elevator a few nights ago, wasn't it?"

"I can stand it," she snapped.

"They're just using you to entertain themselves."

"I get what I want in the end. You're a silly woman," she said. "Your clothes, your sisters—you know nothing about what's important. All that social shit. It ruins careers."

Everything made sense at once. "It was you, wasn't it? You wanted Kitty dead!"

"She was going to spoil everything," Sabria panted.

The elevator bottomed out at last and I braced to make my last stand. All I needed to do was keep her fighting until Orlando and Rawlins got out safely.

The doors opened.

And Brinker stood there, waiting to get on.

In one hand he carried a bottle of vodka decorated with Christmas ribbon. In the other hand was his camera.

"Well," he said, startled but not stunned by the tableau we made. "Who invited you to my party?"

I couldn't wipe the terror off my face in time. And Brinker saw it.

He smiled and raised the camera to his eye. He flicked the "record" button, then stepped over Hemorrhoid and onto the elevator.

"What's the matter?" he asked. "Don't you want us to tie you?"

"Let me go," I said, summoning a stern voice.

Brinker dropped the vodka into Hemorrhoid's lap. He whimpered as it landed. To Sabria, Brinker said, "Hold her."

I dropped Spike's boneless body to the floor and fought them with all my strength. I struggled and kicked, trying to claw Brinker's face behind the camera. But Sabria was faster than I expected, and Brinker stronger. Locked together, we plunged against the back wall of the elevator, slamming into the padding. I tried to stomp Brinker's foot with my heel, but he evaded that and slapped me.

The elevator door closed as we struggled. While Hemorrhoid moaned beneath us, Sabria wrapped three loops of Hermès around my wrist and yanked. I cried out as the pain shot up my arm. Brinker laughed, watching the action through his lens as Sabria slammed me again. She threaded the tie through one of the rings set into the elevator wall, then, breath coming hard, crushed me tight with her shoulder.

The elevator began to rise. It was headed back to the boys upstairs.

"Don't," I heard myself say, though I tried to bite off the word. "Please."

Sabria hauled on the tie until my right arm slapped high on the elevator wall. For an instant, I thought she'd dislocated my shoulder. Immediately she began to knot the restraint. Brinker crushed the whole left side of my body against the elevator wall. With my right arm tied, I was trapped.

"Take it easy," Brinker said, still filming. "You're going to like this."

On the floor, Hemorrhoid was still curled in a fetal position. I heard Spike start to pant.

I gasped. "Let me go before you get yourselves into worse trouble."

"Fat chance." Brinker reached out with his free hand and pinched my nipple so hard I cried out. "See? Aren't we going to have a good time?"

I tried to choke down a second cry of pain.

"You like it rough." He rested his thumb against the bruise on my face. "Don't you?"

I twisted my face away from his fingers. "You're sick."

"Tell me how sick," he coaxed. "How sick do you want me to be?"

"You pushed her to do it, Brinker. Maybe you didn't hire Kitty's killer yourself, but you did everything to make Sabria your puppet. You coerced her."

"And she loved every minute. Same as you. I'm just sorry we didn't get to see the bitch die. That would have been the film to watch."

Suddenly Hemorrhoid screamed. Spike had come back to life and latched his jaws around Hemorrhoid's nose, snarling wildly. Hemorrhoid curled into a tighter ball, batting at my dog.

At that moment the elevator doors parted on Brinker's floor. Hemorrhoid tried to escape Spike by crawling halfway out of the elevator. But he made it only partway and lay there, fighting off the dog and blocking the elevator doors open.

Brinker cursed and tried to kick Hemorrhoid out of the way. Then he stepped over Hem's body and onto the hardwood floor.

Instantly, a horrific explosion of gunfire ripped through the loft, accompanied by high-spirited orchestral music and Mel Gibson's voice yelling, "Get down, get down!"

"What the hell?"

Brinker's foot hit a lake of olive oil on the floor, and he executed a desperate pirouette before crashing flat-out on his stomach. His camera skittered on the floor. In the next instant, Rawlins popped up from behind the kitchen counter and began throwing the remains of Hemorrhoid's cake directly into Brinker's face. Handful after handful, he pelted Brinker, keeping him pinned to the floor like a soldier without a foxhole. The terrifying sound of gunfire erupted from the television again, volume on the highest, earsplitting setting.

A heartbeat later, Orlando leaped into the elevator, headed

straight for Sabria. Screaming at the top of his lungs, he held aloft the wriggling body of a life-sized snake.

Sabria shrieked. I elbowed her stomach, and she lifted her weight off of me.

She made a break for the apartment, hit the oiled floor and skated only briefly before belly flopping onto the hardwood. Orlando threw the fake snake on top of her. She screamed as it writhed over her.

"Come on!" Orlando shouted at Rawlins, already pressing the down button. "Make a break for it!"

Grabbing a Brinker Bra, Rawlins slid his way through the oil and reached Brinker. He seized the man's hand and—quick as a calf roper—whipped the bra around Brinker's wrist. Brinker spat out a mouthful of cake, but not before Rawlins grabbed his other hand and snapped the bra around it, too. As if captured by handcuffs, Brinker tried to yank his way out of the bra, but couldn't. Rawlins dashed for the elevator. He avoided the oil on the floor and leaped over Hemorrhoid's thrashing body.

"Orlando," I said. "Grab the camera."

Orlando dashed out and scooped up Brinker's camera with the confession tape inside.

"Spike!" Orlando called, scrambling back to me.

Spike broke off his attack and leaped onto the elevator at precisely the moment Rawlins did. The elevator door began to close. Mel Gibson sprayed the room with covering gunfire, and we made our escape.

As the elevator descended one more time, Rawlins and Orlando struggled to untie me. They were encrusted with cake and fragrant oil, and both talking at once.

"The oil on the floor was my idea," Orlando said.

"And I put the video on," Rawlins said. "I knew we'd need to scare 'em."

"We couldn't find the stairs."

"We had to use what we could find."

"I brought the snake from the car."

"Aunt Nora, are you okay?"

At last Rawlins managed to unfasten the tie that bound me to the elevator wall. "Yes," I said, finding my voice at last. "I'm okay. Thanks to you. Thank you, Rawlins. Oh, thank you, Orlando."

Orlando touched my elbow. "Are you crying?"

Rawlins put his arm around me. "Are you going to faint?"

The elevator arrived in the lobby. The doors opened.

The three of us screamed and grabbed each other.

A platoon of police officers stood outside the elevator, all pointing guns at us. Behind them stood my sister Libby, spraddle-legged and gasping for breath.

"Wait!" she shouted. "That's my sister!"

"They're upstairs," I said. "Three of them, on the top floor. They've got evidence on videotapes, and they're going to destroy them. You've got to hurry—"

The police officers broke formation and scattered, leaving the boys to help me off the elevator and over to Libby.

She said, "I know I wasn't supposed to call the police, but when I saw Sabria and Hemorrhoid arrive, I knew Brinker wasn't far behind. Are you okay?"

Outside, the street was flashing with police cars. As Libby helped me to the end of the sidewalk, two more city police cruisers roared up to the building entrance. The first one rocked to a stop, and officers jumped out. Two ran into the building. A third rushed over to help us. Spike barked at him.

But Libby flashed her most inviting smile and said, "Hi, there."

Chapter Seventeen

*T*wo torturously long hours later, when the police were fin-ished with us, Libby took the boys home. She dropped me on a city corner. I dashed into the Pendergast building and flapped my ID at the security guard. He waved me in with a called, "Happy New Year!"

If the trip to the *Intelligencer* offices hadn't been twelve floors, I'd have taken the stairs. I never wanted to see the inside of an ele-vator again. But I braved it out of necessity and rode upward.

I found Kitty's desk topsy-turvy—a mess of invitations, notes and old clippings of her own columns, all left in a jumble by police searches and who knew what else. I pushed it all aside and sat down.

I let out a long, tense sigh, closed my eyes and gathered my wits. My hands no longer trembled, perhaps thanks to the doughnut Libby had bought—one of the dozen she purchased at a coffee shop. I felt considerably better. But I opened my eyes cautiously. I almost expected Kitty herself to come storming around a corner to order me out of her chair.

"How does it feel?"

I jumped, still a nervous wreck. "Stan! I didn't hear you."

"Sorry." The lanky editor came over and perched on the edge of the desk. "I hear you broke Kitty's murder case."

"You heard already?"

He smiled. "News indeed travels fast. The guys downstairs are frantic for details. You want to give them an exclusive interview?"

"To tell the truth? No. Not tonight."

He nodded. "Your prerogative. They can get what they need from the cops. All three were arrested?"

"Sabria for hiring the hit man. Charges against Brinker and Hemmings Lamb will be sorted out. I'm here to write Kitty's column."

"Ah." He checked his watch. "I was starting to think you were going to blow your first big deadline."

"Not a chance."

Stan smiled and folded his long arms across his chest. "You ready to write about Kitty? Warts and all?"

"She was a bitch," I admitted. "But in her own way, she changed the social climate of the city, Stan. Pedigree was the only thing that used to matter. Kitty made it acceptable for rich people to get their pictures in the paper for charitable giving, and the giving only got bigger."

Stan said, "Sounds as if you're softening your opinion of Kitty."

"I learned from her. I didn't always enjoy it, but she taught me a lot."

"If you write that, it'll be a great first column, Nora." He stood up from my desk. "I hope there will be a lot more. Do your best work, and I'll do my part to see that you get this desk on a permanent basis."

"Thanks, Stan."

"But hurry up," he said cheerfully, checking his watch. "Aren't you throwing a party tonight?"

"You heard that, too?" I laughed.

"Who hasn't? Half the city's driving out to Bucks County tonight."

"Are you coming?"

"I might." He winked. "Get to work, kid. Make me proud."

As he strolled way, I fired up Kitty's computer and looked at the time. My guests were just now arriving at Blackbird Farm. With luck, Libby had gotten there in time to play hostess.

I wrote about the last time I'd seen Kitty—dressed to the nines and waving her invitation overhead like a triumphant flag to gain entrance to a celebrity bachelor auction where over a million dollars would be raised for a cultural institution. And half of that million would be raked in because she promoted the auction in her column and would picture the handsome winners when it was all over. In her long career, Kitty had helped raise perhaps hundreds of millions of dollars, and along the way she'd taught important life lessons to a lot of us. Like how to spot a real class act. And how to spot a phony. To separate the givers from the takers. I thought I knew the people in my social circle, but Kitty had forced me to see them in a new light.

And although she wrote with a pen dipped in poison, she'd been trying to do the right thing by exposing Brinker's appropriation of the bra that Gallagher designed. She'd been championing the little guy, who didn't realize he'd been taken to the cleaners by a swindler.

Not a bad legacy for a girl from the rough side of the tracks.

I polished up my phrases, double-checked to make sure the paragraphs expressed what I truly felt, then pressed "send." My first column whisked its way to Stan's office. I hoped it passed muster. If it didn't, the *Philadelphia Intelligencer* could hire somebody more deserving to take Kitty's place.

But me, I had a party to throw.

I washed my face in the bathroom and was glad to see my bruise was nearly gone. A little more makeup, and I'd be presentable. I rode the elevator to the lobby. Reed was waiting for me outside the

Pendergast building. As he opened the back door of the town car, he handed me a bag.

"Your sister sent this," he reported.

"Reed!" I was so touched by the extra time he'd taken to bring me a change of clothing that I stretched up on tiptoe to kiss his cheek. "Thank you so much. And happy New Year."

"Yeah," he said. "Same to you. Hurry up and get in. If I don't get you home soon, somebody's going to bust my ass."

With hope leaping inside me, I asked, "Have you spoken with Michael?"

Reed shook his head.

I put on my makeup with the interior lights on, then turned off the light and changed my clothing in the dark backseat as we sped through the night to Bucks County. The roads were clear and dry, and Reed might have driven at a slightly higher speed than his usual conservative crawl.

Parked cars lined the road for a quarter of a mile before we reached Blackbird Farm. My driveway was barely passable. Reed threaded the town car past the other vehicles to reach the back of the house.

"Reed," I said as he pulled the car around to the back porch, "please come inside with me."

"I got places to go for myself, you know. I don't need to go to your old party."

"I need someone to lean on," I said, "in case it's a disaster."

"You going to faint?"

"I might," I said ominously.

He sighed and gave me his arm.

"How do I look?"

He glanced down at the clothes Libby had sent for me to wear—a midnight-blue cashmere sweater and satin lounging pajama trousers. They were both more to her taste than mine, but definitely party clothes. The sweater revealed my bare shoulders. The Brinker Bra performed astonishingly well.

"You look . . . pretty," Reed said.

Libby met us at the back door. She was decked out in a sheer blouse that completely revealed her Brinker Bra in all its glory. Her smile was wide and delighted. "Happy New Year!" she crowed. "Don't you look fabulous! Have a glass of champagne!"

"I have champagne?" I asked.

"Lexie sent some cases this afternoon."

I accepted the flute she extended, but didn't have the strength to lift it to my lips. I handed it off to Reed. The house rocked with live music I could hear all the way from the living room along with the raised voices of at least a hundred people. Some were actually singing.

"How about some caviar?" Libby asked.

"Lexie sent caviar, too?"

"No, Jill Mascione brought leftovers from a shindig she catered this afternoon. It's delish, strictly the Russian stuff. It mixes wonderfully well with all the food the boys concocted for you."

"The boys?"

"You won't believe it. Rawlins made me stop at the grocery on the way home. We splurged, and look what they've done!"

Libby stepped back to reveal my kitchen. My rustic table had been transformed by a bountiful display of holiday excess. Trays of hors d'oeuvres stood waiting to be whisked to the guests.

But I looked more closely.

"See?" Libby said. "Jell-O squares and marshmallow treats, crackers with Cheez Whiz. It's brilliant! Men never admit it, but they'd rather eat Doritos than have sex. The boys made everything. Well, almost."

In addition to the junk food, I noticed Libby had added a few other items. Big Frankie Abruzzo's prosciutto—prettily sliced—glistened in readiness with small bites of melon and surrounded by pillowy rolls, aromatic mustards and an avalanche of crisp vegetables.

"Where are Orlando and Rawlins?"

"Around here somewhere. Orlando is playing butler, and he's having the time of his life. Spike follows him everywhere."

"Libby," I said. "Thank you for everything you've done for me these last few days. You are the kindest sister in the world."

She hugged me. "You can pay me back by having a Potions and Passions party on Tuesday. I've already made up a tentative guest list."

I laughed unsteadily and decided not to think about that yet.

"We all pitched in," Libby continued to explain as I walked around the feast. "Delilah brought some kind of gumbo thing that you eat with pita chips—it's in the living room, I think. You will positively die when you taste it. And there's a sweet boy tending bar in the dining room with hardly a stitch of clothing on. And you, young man," she said to Reed, who'd been hanging back, "I know just the girl you'll want to meet, so come with me. Nora, I suppose you'll want to say hello to Emma."

Before kidnapping Reed, Libby steered me into the butler's pantry where we surprised Emma and Monte Bogatz, canoodling over a cutting board covered with chili peppers and two sharp kitchen knives.

Emma wore Monte's Stetson along with her tightest jeans and a Brinker Bra under a snug T-shirt that advertised the Grand Ole Opry.

Monte was saying, "Peppers can get a man hotter'n just about anything except maybe you, sugar, so be careful where you put your pretty fingertips tonight. You never know where some poor cowpoke's tongue is going to find itself later."

"Hey, Sis!" Emma grinned at me while unlooping her arms

from around Monte. "You can even throw a party when you're not here. That's talent!"

"Em," I said, hugging her. "Where have you been for two days?"

She shrugged. "Showing Monte some horses I know. Spring will be here soon. I've got to get back in training, and Monte thought he might like to invest in some show jumpers. Seems he's had enough of corporate America. And horses will keep us both sober."

"Give me a trusty horse any day," Monte said. "You always know which end bites and which end shits on your boots."

Emma looked remarkably sober and even sported a hint of pink in her cheeks. She sent me a wry look that snapped my self-control back into place, but then her expression softened. "Hey," she said, affectionately, knocking my shoulder with hers, which was as demonstrative as my little sister could get. "Thanks," she said. "You know, for not giving up on me."

"I won't. I can't." I smiled.

Monte said, "Hell's bells, girls, I think I'm gonna cry."

Behind Monte suddenly loomed the large figure of a grizzly bear with glasses.

"Perry," I said, recognizing the large, furry man. "Happy New Year."

"Hi, yeah, same to you. Say, have you seen Libby?"

"She's over there." I pointed.

Perry nodded. "Is there a place I could be alone with her for a few minutes? I think I know how to solve her problem."

"Which problem is that, big fella?" Emma asked.

"Getting that item of underclothing off. You see, I've studied some chemistry—that's a big part of my business, y'know—and I think I know a way to remove the thing she's having so much trouble with. The silicone makes a chemical reaction, see, with that lotion she's been using."

"I knew there was something dangerous about that ErotaLotion. Emma, this is Perry Delbert, Libby's new . . . friend. Perry, the powder room is through there," I said, pointing. With a wave, I caught Libby's attention. She waved back and made her rendezvous with Perry outside the powder room. We watched them put their heads together.

"Nothing good will come of that," Emma said darkly. Then she jerked her head toward the music. "You better greet your guests, sis. Everybody's having a great time without you, but—"

"Sweetie!" Lexie shouted from the doorway. "There you are at last! Happy New Year!"

For tonight, my dear friend had laid on the glamour with winter-white trousers, a simple white shirt and enough diamonds to pop the eyeballs of the whole Harry Winston company.

"Lex," I said with complete sincerity, "you're a godsend. If it weren't for you, I'd be feeding these people stale Puppy Chow."

"Nonsense, I'm just a friend who wants you to have the best damn New Year possible. Are you okay? I'm sorry my meeting with Brinker was so short. He smelled a rat, I think. I couldn't keep him long. Did everything turn out the way you hoped?"

"Almost."

"Where's Michael?"

"I'm not sure."

Lexie put her arm around my shoulder and squeezed some courage into me. "There's somebody else who stopped by. He didn't realize you were throwing a party, but I took the liberty of inviting him in. He's quite charming, sweetie. Lots of potential. He's in the library, I think."

I wasn't sure I wanted to see Richard yet. And I needed to greet my other guests first anyway, so I headed for the living room.

Orlando bumped past me, holding a silver tray aloft and looking happier than a kid possibly could. "Coming through!"

He barreled into the kitchen to refill his tray with more treats. Behind him scampered Spike, panting with excitement. The puppy never noticed me.

As I passed the powder room, I heard Libby's voice petulantly through the door.

"I can't hold still! What are you doing? That's sticky!"

"Just hang on, honey. I'll be done in a minute."

"What are you doing?" she cried. "Oooh! It's hot!"

"Just a little more—"

"Oh!" she screamed. "Oh, oh!"

Hastily, I hurried away.

In the living room alcove I found Delilah's friend, who effortlessly mixed drinks in his astonishingly small thong. His suntan indicated he spent a lot of hours on nude beaches, and his wide smile showed he was delighted with the crowd's reaction to his antics. A bevy of giggly young women I'd never met hung around him.

In the living room, Kenny Andersen played Cole Porter on my out-of-tune baby grand, while Jake Jacobson, in his full Patty Lupone regalia, leaned provocatively against the piano and led the crowd in a sing-along. A few couples danced to the romantic music. I saw Rawlins, front and center, gaping at Patty's sparkly dress.

All voices rose louder as I stepped into the room. I waved to everyone and took a bow in the middle of the song, but they didn't stop singing. There was laughter, and a few guests bounded forward to give me hugs.

I air-kissed my way through the crowd, happier to see everyone than I imagined I could be.

I met Delilah Fairweather in the foyer where she was—of course—shouting over the music into her cell phone while plugging her other ear with a long, enameled forefinger. Her braids danced from the topknot on her head.

"Gotta go," she said to her caller when she laid eyes on me. She snapped the phone shut. "Girlfriend! You know the most exciting people! Did you know there's a country singer here and a former governor and that doctor who does all the transplants, and just a minute ago I met the girl who's going to Broadway next month, and I think she's gonna sing racy songs later. All we need is the Mafia Prince to finish spicing things up, and you're got everything covered! Give me a kiss!"

I did and wrapped my arms around her, too. "Delilah, thanks so very much. If it weren't for the information you gave me—"

"You caught Kitty's killer? I mean, the person who hired the hit man?"

"Yes," I said. "The police are working out charges now."

"Will Brinker go to jail?"

"Probably on the arson charge. Sabria says he hired Danny to torch the comedy club, which is how Brinker hooked her up with Danny to kill Kitty. She's the one who officially hired Kitty's killer. And it's all on videotape that Brinker filmed himself."

"Kinky. But, damn," said Delilah. "I want one of those Brinker Bras real bad. I wonder if the company will implode before anybody gets to buy the bras in stores?"

"It's very possible."

Delilah's expression softened. "You deserve a vacation, Nora. How about going to my condo in Puerto Rico for a few days? Take a friend. Enjoy some fresh sea air and some hot nights."

"You're too generous. I'd take you up on that offer, but I've got a shot at a job and I need to focus on that for a while."

"You do what needs doing," she said. "Who's Mr. Good-looking in the library? Honey, the Mafia Prince had better be more delicious than Denzel if you're choosing him over this guy." She hooked her thumb in the direction of Richard D'eath.

Her phone rang and I left her to talk with her caller.

In the doorway, I hesitated. The party music was behind me. The library seemed very quiet.

Richard turned from studying the books on my shelves. He had a glass of something in one hand, but he'd left his cane leaning against the leather sofa. Even from across the room, I saw the wash of relief cross his face.

He said, "You're safe."

"Yes."

"And you got the story."

I smiled wryly and went into the room. "Not exactly."

"Let me guess. You didn't write it up?"

"It wasn't my beat," I said. "That's the right word, right? My 'beat'?"

He didn't venture across the floor without his cane, but waited for me to arrive in front of him. He wore a worn button-down shirt that looked soft to the touch. But I kept my hands to myself. He didn't answer me.

I said, "Did you get your story written, too?"

"Not yet," he allowed. He put down his drink. "I need time to untangle the information. I'm sorry I couldn't find Brinker last night. I heard you did."

"Yes."

"You do good work when you put your mind to it."

"Thanks."

"But if you need some help improving your journalism skills," he said, "I could be available."

We smiled at each other, not like colleagues, but something closer. He smelled delicious, but the music that wafted into the library wasn't potent enough to change how I felt. Nature just didn't tug me in Richard's direction. And no amount of Cole Porter was going to change that.

I felt my smile turn regretful and mustered some good humor. "What are you reading?"

We looked at the book he held in his hand.

"You are the strangest woman I've ever met," he said. He opened the book to reveal a crisp one-hundred-dollar bill between the front cover and the first page. "You keep all your folding money in books?"

"Where did that come from?"

He pulled down another volume to demonstrate. "Haven't you heard of banks?"

I opened a copy of Robert Penn Warren's poems. Another hundred-dollar bill lay within the pages. "What in the world?"

"You didn't put the cash here?"

"No, I . . . It must be Lexie!"

"There's money in just about all these books—maybe thousands of dollars. Who did this?"

"My friend. She kept pushing me to have this party, and I didn't . . ." My voice trembled. "I should have known she had a plan up her sleeve. She organized this whole thing."

"What are you talking about?"

I closed the book of poetry and kept my head down so that Richard couldn't see my expression. "I did it once for a friend, too. It's a foolproof way of helping out someone who needs money. Lexie knows I could never take cash as a gift. So she planned all this to help me."

"Nice friend."

"All my friends."

"Hey," Richard said. He put the book back on the shelf, then came close and pulled me gently against his body. He said, "Don't cry. They're good friends who obviously care about you."

"I can never repay them."

"So don't. You've obviously given them something equally valuable. Use it in good conscience."

Richard's shirt was very soft after all. But beneath it, his chest was solid and warm.

He said, "Listen, I don't know what's happening."

"Nothing. Nothing's happening."

He laughed softly. "You have to feel it, Nora. You've been mixed up with this other guy for a while because you're hooked on the danger. I know all about that adrenaline rush. But maybe now you're ready to move on, to be with somebody who's a better fit."

I released a shaky sigh. "How did my life get so messy?"

I felt his hand in my hair. "It doesn't have to be messy."

"I can't help it. It's already . . ." I took a deep breath. "I could be in some trouble right now."

"What kind of trouble?"

"The old-fashioned kind," I said miserably.

He pulled back and looked down at me with concern. "You're carrying his child?"

I wasn't sure. There was no physical evidence yet, but my life was a roller coaster with more loops and plunges than the Coney Island Cyclone. And I definitely felt I was poised at the top of a very long, bumpy ride. The sensation of teetering high above an abyss was suddenly so real that I closed my eyes.

I didn't have a chance to answer Richard.

We were interrupted by Orlando, who came into the room with a silver tray of crackers sprayed with an aerosol, cheese-colored substance festively sprinkled with parsley. But Orlando's face didn't look very festive anymore.

Low-voiced, he said, "My guardians are here."

I left Richard and went to the boy.

"Oh, Orlando."

He allowed me to take away the tray and hug him. He said, "I'm going back to New Zealand. They're waiting for me outside."

"Would you like me to come outside with you?"

He nodded, unable to say more. We left the library through the servants' hall and ended up in the kitchen without seeing many of the other guests. Rawlins was waiting with Orlando's backpack. "Hey, nerd," he said. "Keep in touch, okay?"

Orlando gave Rawlins a closed-fisted double bump that passed for a handshake. As they said their good-byes, Spike appeared at our feet. When I accompanied Orlando onto the back porch, Spike bounded anxiously at our ankles.

Orlando kept his head down. "Thanks," he said to me.

"Thank *you*, Orlando," I said. "You were so brave. You saved the day. You saved the party. You saved me. I'm so glad I got to know you better."

I wanted to be the one to break the news to Orlando about his uncle Hemmings, but at that moment I saw a familiar figure come out of the darkness. She had a pretty smile and red hair.

"Minky," I said with a wave of relief as I recognized Orlando's former nanny. "Oh, I'm so happy to see you!"

Minky gave the boy a fierce hug, and he buried his face against her jacket. She held him fast. "It's going to be okay, Orlando," she said. "I've got a house for us in New Zealand. It has trees to climb and places to go fishing. We're going to have a good time. Gallagher's going to visit. It's going to be great."

"Can you stay, Minky?" I asked. "We're having a party."

"We have a plane to catch," she said, communicating to me with her steady gaze that she wanted to whisk Orlando away as quickly as possible. "Or I'd stay for hours and get caught up. But we must hurry. Orlando, are you ready to go?"

Spike jumped up against Orlando's knee and barked.

Determinedly, Orlando ignored the dog. He shook my hand instead and said, "Good-bye."

Spike barked again and whined.

Minky took Orlando's hand and they started down the steps.

Spike sat down and looked up at me.

"Well?" I asked, meeting his inquiring gaze. "It's your choice."

Spike gave a bodily quiver and whined again.

"I love you."

He said he loved me, too. But life was too quiet with me, and he was needed elsewhere. He had a mission.

"I know," I said.

With one last snarl, Spike said good-bye. Then he bounded down the steps and dashed after Orlando. The boy turned and scooped him up, looking at me.

"Keep him out of trouble," I called.

Orlando grinned and waved. Minky blew me a kiss. Spike attacked Orlando's scarf and didn't look back.

I watched them pull away in a long black town car, hugging myself against the cold air. I wasn't ready to go back inside to the party yet, so I stood alone and listened to the music. I thought about the little boy I'd met just a few days before and how he'd changed, grown, blossomed. My throat ached, and I put my head back to look upward. The night sky was dark, but a few pinpricks of starlight glowed.

It was enough light to see a tall figure as he came crunching through the snow, carrying a cardboard box under one arm. Michael.

He said, "Did our baby just run off to join the circus?"

Shaken, I said, "What?"

He paused at the bottom of the steps and put the box down. "Spike. He went with Orlando?"

"Michael," I said, hardly able to catch my breath. I went down two steps and hugged him around the shoulders. My heart expanded until it hurt.

He held me for a long time and felt anything but dangerous. He felt like home—warm and difficult and full of trouble, but my home nonetheless. Against my ear, he said, "I think you just declared war on New Zealand."

"I was so afraid," I whispered. "Don't go away again. I need you here with me."

He smoothed my hair away from my face and looked solemnly into my eyes. "I heard what happened. I wish you'd told me more about what was going on. If anyone understands sadists who operate at the highest level, it's me."

"Don't," I said. "Let's not talk about Brinker. I don't want to talk about the past anymore. I just want a future."

"I could have helped you."

I smoothed my hand down his cheek and felt the rough prickle of an unshaven face. "All I care about now is that you're not going to take the blame for Kitty's death. You're safe now. We both are."

"Nora," he said. Then he changed his mind. He glanced down at what I was wearing. "You look . . . even more beautiful than ever. What's different?"

I laughed unsteadily and posed for inspection. "It's the Brinker Bra. What do you think?"

His grin flashed in the starlight. "It makes me want to take it off you, as a matter of fact."

"I don't think it will ever reach stores, though. I might have one of the few Brinker Bras ever made."

He grinned and gave the box a kick. "Good thing I picked up a few more."

"You did? How in the world . . . ? Wait, did these fall off a truck somewhere?"

"Something like that. I thought you might want to give them out as party favors."

I laughed. "So you'll come inside? You'll meet my friends?"

"Sure. But . . ."

I smiled at him, then saw something new in his expression. Inside me, a light flickered and died. "What is it?"

"Nora." He glanced away from me into the night. "The Keough woman's murder is solved. But the car theft bust the other night. When the cop was shot . . ."

"Yes?"

"He died this afternoon."

I felt my head lighten. "Oh, God."

Michael came up a step and took my arms in his hands. He held me firmly. "So the cops want to nail the guy who did it."

"Of course they do."

"I love you," he said, holding tight. His voice changed. "I love you more than anything. But I've got to disappear for a while."

The world lurched around us. "Why you? You had nothing to do with the shooting. You were here that night. I'll tell them. I'll—"

"This is something I have to do."

"Michael, let the legal system work."

"Sometimes you have to go outside the system to make things right." His touch changed, turning gentler. "While I'm gone, I want you to think about this thing we've started."

"I don't have to think about it. I want to be with you. And you want to be with me, too."

"It's not right, though. We both know that. We don't belong together."

I tried kissing him. But he resisted and I backed away. We stood in silence, until I felt the roller coaster give a frightening little wobble at the summit—the warning before the plunge.

Then the kitchen door banged open behind me, and Libby flew

outside, flinging her coat around her shoulders and moving with surprising speed. "You won't believe it!" she cried.

"What's wrong?" Michael asked.

"The police are here! They're at the front door! They want to arrest me!"

"For what?"

My sister buttoned her coat and looked furious. "It was that bartender! He sent the police to arrest me for selling my Potions and Passions merchandise in his stupid bar! Can you believe it? They say I'm a public indecency!"

"They're here right now?"

"Yes, at the front door! Lexie is stalling them. I just managed to get that horrible Brinker Bra off—with Perry's expert help—and the next thing I know someone's pounding on the bathroom door telling me that—"

"Come on," Michael said, smiling. "I'll take you somewhere."

"Oh, you're so kind. I'll never live it down if I'm arrested!" My sister hurtled down the stairs, headed for the sidewalk in full flight. "Nora, take care of my children!"

Michael lingered on the porch for a moment. "Here." He handed me his handkerchief. "Dry your eyes. Take the box inside. See if you can bribe the cops with some Brinker Bras. Keep them inside so Bonnie and Clyde can make a clean getaway."

I balled up the handkerchief and caught Michael's hand as he turned away. "You'll come back?"

He kissed me on the mouth, making a promise.

Libby's voice floated back to us. "Shouldn't the police be looking for real criminals?" she demanded. "Honestly! Why are they picking on entrepreneurial women like myself? Are they chasing Donald Trump around for following his passion? Of course not! But put a few amusing sex toys on display and everything goes haywire. Are you coming?"

"Yes," said Michael.

He turned away and went after my sister as Libby plunged into the snow.

"My goodness, we're going on the run, aren't we?" Libby gushed, taking Michael's arm. "We'll be fugitives together! Oh, my God. Well, it will be a good chance to get to know each other better. Do you think I should have a disguise to avoid detection? It might be a good time for a makeover. I've been thinking of going blond anyway. What do you think? Maybe a few highlights at least?"

I could hear Libby chattering long after the darkness closed around them. "I just don't think law enforcement officers have confidence in their own sexual authority. Why else would they need guns? And those powerful cars? Now, aren't those phallic substitutes?"

Michael made a reply, but I couldn't hear him.

"Exactly!" Libby cried. "Would you like to see one of my catalogs? I'd love to hear your opinion."

A minute later, the kitchen door opened again and Richard stepped outside. "You okay?"

He hesitated when I didn't answer, then came slowly to the edge of the porch and leaned on his cane. At our feet lay the cardboard carton Michael had brought. "What's in the box?"

When I didn't answer, he knelt down and opened it. "Oh-ho," he said, bringing out a Brinker Bra. "Stolen goods?"

I tried to dry my face with Michael's handkerchief, but something scratched my cheek. I realized the fabric was tied up around something hard. I unfastened the corners with shaking fingers.

A ring fell out into my palm. A diamond ring with a stone the size of Newark, New Jersey.

"Whoa," said Richard. "That's got to be a fake, right?"

Inside the house, I could hear my guests. They were chanting, counting down the last ten seconds before the New Year began. I slipped the ring on my finger.

261

Richard stood up just as the piano began to bang out "Auld Lang Syne." We could hear singing, and people blew silly horns.

Beside me, Richard said, "Nora? Can I wish you a happy New Year?"

I let him kiss me. I slipped my arms around his neck and allowed Richard to pull me snug against his body. But I felt nothing when his mouth touched mine. My hand lay along his shoulder. The diamond on my finger sparkled with starlight.